CURSED BY NIGHT

A REVERSE HAREM URBAN FANTASY

JADA STORM
EMILY GOODWIN

Copyright © 2018, Jada Storm, writing as Jasmine Walt, and Emily Goodwin. All rights reserved. Published by Dynamo Press.

This novel is a work of fiction. All characters, places, and incidents described in this publication are used fictitiously, or are entirely fictional. No part of this publication may be reproduced or transmitted, in any form or by any means, except by an authorized retailer, or with written permission of the publisher. Inquiries may be addressed via email to jada@authorjadastorm.com

If you want to be notified when Jada's next novel is released and get access to exclusive contests, giveaways, and freebies, sign up for her mailing list at www.jasminewalt.com Your email address will never be shared and you can unsubscribe at any time.

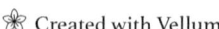 Created with Vellum

1

R*ise and shine, bitches.*

I don't need to look at my phone to know who's calling. There's only one person—and one reason—my phone is ringing at five-thirty AM. Only a mile into my run, I stop, breath clouding around me, and pull my phone from my armband. A bead of sweat rolls down between my breasts.

"Bisset," I answer, and start walking to keep my muscles warm.

"Sorry to wake you, Detective," the officer on the line says, and I recognize the voice as Mike Anderson, a rookie cop working the graveyard shift.

"I was already up. Have a body for me?"

"We do. Joggers found it about twenty minutes ago on a run. Just another reason not to be a runner, eh?"

"I'm literally on a run right now."

"Well, too bad you didn't find it. These girls are pretty shaken up."

"I can imagine." I stop at a crosswalk and take a minute to stretch my calves. "So why are you calling me?"

"Once you see it, you'll know why."

Desperate to work my way up the ranks, I took on the cases no one else wanted. The ones deemed "spooky" or "weird" that got me the nickname of Mulder amongst the other detectives. What started as a joke quickly became a compliment. The occult and magic don't exist. There was always a logical explanation, well, as logical as any murder can be. Taking on—and solving—some of the Philadelphia Police Department's most obscure cases was no easy feat, but I've never been one to back down from a challenge.

"Text me the address."

"Sending now."

"Thanks, Anderson." I stretch my legs and wait for the text to come through with the location of the body. Then I'm off, turning around and running home to change and take off again, though this time by car.

The body was found along a road on the outskirts of town. Three college students stumbled upon it on their run this morning, noticing a bloody shoe sticking up from the weeds.

I park behind a marked police car and get out, looking at the small gathering of people. Most are official law enforcement, and a few others are gawkers. There aren't too many houses on this road, which is both good and bad. The road has been blocked off on either side, stopping any traffic from coming through and tampering with my crime scene. The area around the body has been taped off, and the girls who found it are sitting inside a squad car to keep warm.

"Morning, Detective Bisset."

"Morning," I say, ducking under the yellow police tape Officer Nick Beasley is holding up for me. I gather my hair at the nape of my neck, securing it in a messy bun to keep it out of the way. Nick casts me a sideways glance, one I purposely ignore, and walks in stride with me to the crime scene. "So what are we looking at here?"

"I'm not really sure. We can't make sense of it. Just wait and see."

I pull latex gloves from my pocket and put them on. The body is in a ditch on the side of a rural road, and I can smell it before I can see it, letting me know right away it was dumped here days after the murder took place. I move down the ditch, careful not to get my feet tangled in the tall dead grass that's been buried under snow until recently.

Flies swarm around the body, landing on the man's face. His lips are dry and cracked, parted slightly. One fly lands on the side of his mouth and crawls inside. His eyes, once brown, are slit halfway open and sunken into his skull. I start with the head like I always do, well, when my victims have heads, that is, and scan my eyes down.

There are multiple puncture wounds on his neck. At first glance they look like they're from barbecue skewers, but the bruising around them looks more like a hickey. I run my eyes down his arms and—fuck.

Now I know what everyone was talking about.

Both of the victim's arms have been sliced open from the elbow to the wrist and his bones removed. That is definitely something I haven't seen before.

"Do we have an ID on the vic?" I ask, crouching down to further inspect the body. I turn my head and inhale. Even after years on the force, the smell of a rotting human body doesn't get any easier to take in.

"Yes," Officer Beasley tells me. "Eric Brownell, thirty-two. He lives alone in an apartment downtown, and wasn't reported missing. We did call the gaming store where he worked and he was a no-show for his shift on Wednesday."

"When was the last time he was at work."

"Tuesday. He closed the store along with one other person. She said she saw him get in his car and drive away."

I nod, looking at the victim. He wasn't murdered on Wednesday, I can tell from the state of the body. Today is Monday, and I'm guessing he wasn't killed until Friday, left to decay over the weekend. Once he started to smell, the murderer dumped him.

I inspect the site around him, looking for any evidence left behind. We canvass the area and I have two officers go door to door on the few houses on the street, asking if anyone saw anything.

No one did.

Going back to the body, I look for defensive wounds, careful not to touch him until the crime scene photos have been taken. It's hard to tell, since the poor guy's flesh has been ripped open and pulled back, but I think there are bruises consistent with being tied up around his wrists.

"Hey, Ace," Tiffany Woo says, standing at the top of the ditch. She's one of the crime scene photographers I frequently work with, and the closest thing I have to a friend. She pulls her camera from her bag and attaches the lens. "How was your weekend?"

"It was pretty low-key. Better than his." I motion to the body. "How about yours?"

"Good. We took Mavis to the zoo for the first time. She loved the monkeys."

"Aw, I bet that was fun." I look away from the body to smile at Tiffany. We've gone out for drinks a few times after work, but she has a family to keep her busy and I, well, don't.

"Jesus," she mutters, holding up her camera. "What the hell happened?"

I shake my head and lean in, covering my nose. Flies buzz around me, and I swat them away with my free hand. "It looks like the bones were broken first, then the skin was ripped open and the bones pulled out."

"What the fuck?" Tiffany comes around me and takes more photos.

"My thoughts exactly."

"Don't get me wrong, all murders are grisly. But this...this looks like something straight from a horror movie. With demons or aliens."

"I'm gonna catch the bastard who did this."

"I know you will." She takes more photos. "You always do. Sorry, don't mean to jinx you or anything."

"You know I don't believe in that shit."

"Well, I do. So knock on wood, or whatever you're supposed to say to counteract it."

"If that makes you feel better." I stand, turning my head to take in a breath of fresh air. I do more investigating and question the joggers who found the body before it's bagged and taken in for an autopsy.

"This whole thing is weird, right?" Tiffany asks quietly as we walk back to our cars.

"All murders are weird, in a sense."

"Yeah, but this is different, which is why you're here, I suppose."

I give her a wry smile. "Different and weird are my areas of expertise."

She zips her camera bag and pulls her blonde braid over her shoulder. "I smell like death, don't I?"

"We all do. That scent clings to you."

"I'm going to have to shower before I can even pick Mavis up." She sighs. "And I was in the shower when my phone rang this morning. My hair is still wet." She pulls her keys from her pocket. "You're closing on that house today, right?"

Shit. I almost forgot about it. "More or less. I have an appointment with the bank this afternoon." I take a look back at the body.

"No. Don't even think about canceling," Tiffany scolds. "You did that last week."

"I know." I take my work seriously and put it first. Always. I might not have any family, but this guy does. Or did. And they deserve to know what happened. "I don't think I can put it off any longer, anyway. The government wants their taxes on the place and the bank certainly isn't going to pay it."

"I think it's cool. Or at least it looks cool from the pictures you showed me. I'd love to inherit a huge house like that. Hell, I'd love to inherit a small house." She laughs. "When is your appointment?"

"Two."

"I'll remind you at one-thirty."

"Thanks, Tiff."

"See ya in a bit." She unlocks her car and gets in.

I go to my own, pausing when I get to the driver's side door. As a cop, I know to always trust my intuition. But right now, I'm questioning it. Because it's telling me the world I've worked so hard to prove doesn't exist might very well be real.

2

I do not have time for this.

I double-checked the address I'd entered in the GPS. There's only half a mile left until I reach my destination, and there's nothing in sight. I'm already driving slow, cringing when I hear the gravel fly up under the tires of my Charger. I continue down the road, looking through the thick, overgrown trees for any signs of a house.

"You have reached your destination."

"Really?" I give an incredulous look to my GPS. "Are you sure about that?" I take my foot off the gas and let the car idle along the road. It took longer than I expected to sign all the papers at the bank, and then at the title company. The house is officially mine now, and officially a thorn in my side. And I haven't even seen it yet.

Through the trees, I spy what I think might be the mailbox, well, what's left of it. The numbers have peeled off, leaving the faint outline of the number three. I put the car in park and get out. The woods on both sides of the road are alive with chirping birds, almost deafening, yet a welcome distraction from the noise of the city I'm used to. My small apartment in downtown Philly is surrounded by the freeway and trains.

Loose stone crunches under my boots as I walk around the car, going to what I guess is the driveway. Once gravel like the road, most of the stone has washed away from years of neglect, leaving behind only two shallow tire ruts in the earth.

Zipping up my leather jacket, I step into the brambles to drag a fallen tree branch off the driveway. I toss it to the side and it disappears into a tangle of overgrown weeds. I take in a deep breath, getting a lungful of thick spring air. A storm is coming, and I hope to be in and out of this place before it hits. I'm not sure my sports car could make it out if the driveway became muddy.

The feeling of being watched falls over me, causing the nerves to prickle along my back. My hand inches toward the gun that's almost always on my hip. I take a final look around, unable to see past the row of pine trees lining the driveway, then rush back into the running car.

I make it a few yards before having to get out and move another large tree branch. An old, leafless oak tree stretches to the red sky, looking like it's one good windstorm away from coming down completely.

The driveway takes a sharp turn, and once the pine trees clear, the house comes into sight.

"Wow," I whisper out loud. I knew the house was large, since I saw the square footage on the many official papers I signed at the bank, but I had no idea it was this ostentatious. The photos don't do it justice. I let off the gas, allowing the Charger to roll to a stop before putting it in park.

I kill the engine and get out, grabbing my bag on the way. My eyes are on the house as I exit the car, unable to look away. The feeling of being watched intensifies, and a small voice in the back of my head tells me to get my ass back in my car and get the fuck out of here.

As a cop, I knew the importance of listening to that little voice. But something else—something stronger—is pulling me forward. My heart speeds up, and I blindly reach inside my bag for the keys, which seem to have disappeared into the black hole my bag magically becomes every time I'm trying to find something. Unable to take my eyes off the brick mansion before me, I stand rooted to the spot as I feel around for the damn keys.

Suddenly, I know where the feeling of being watched is coming from. It's the house, and I know that makes zero sense. But as I stand there looking at the red brick estate in front of me, it feels alive. The freaky gargoyles aren't helping either.

Two are positioned on either side of the steps leading to the large, covered front porch. Their wings are out, mouths open in a hiss, showing off large, fanged teeth. They are similar, yet different in ways I can't describe, and their eyes are more detailed and lifelike than carvings in stone should be.

The cobblestone path leading from the house to the gravel drive is overgrown and patchy with moss. Still staring at the gargoyles, I walk along it, swatting mosquitoes away from my face. My fingers wrap around the cool metal of the key needed to get into the damn place, and I look away from the gargoyles for a moment to pull the key from my purse.

When I turn my face back, I swear one of them moved. Too curious to be afraid, I keep moving forward, not stopping until I'm right in front of the large stone statues. Up close, I can see the incredible detail carefully carved into each one. Ridges of muscle. The wrinkles of skin around their knuckles. Tiny little hairs on their feet. Veins running along either arm, up their necks, and throughout their wings.

And the eyes.

The sunlight is fading fast, making it hard to tell if their eyes are made from obsidian or if the stone darkened over time. Whatever it is, it was unnerving, though not necessarily in a bad way.

There is something familiar about the pair of gargoyles, and I cannot for the life of me place it. I didn't know this house existed, let alone belonged to my estranged Aunt Mary, until last week, when I was told it had been passed down to me. I step back, taking a good look at the house before going up the stone steps.

Another gargoyle perches on the top pitch of the house, looking down at me. Like the others, his wings are spread and his mouth is open, but there is something off about him, almost as if he is pained.

The setting sun is directly behind the house, blinding me as I look. I hold my hand up, shielding what I can, and see an outline of more wings. Four gargoyles seem a little excessive, but who was I to judge? From what I was told, my great aunt was a little on the eccentric side, and I'm hoping the strong Gothic vibe coming from the place will attract buyers willing to pay for the authenticity.

I go back to the porch, compelled to reach out and touch the cool stone of the closest gargoyle. Only he isn't cool. The stone is as warm as human flesh. I jerk my hand back. It's from the sun. It has to be from the sun. There is no other reason for the stone to feel so warm.

I knock down dust-covered cobwebs from in front of the door, then stick the key in the lock. The deadbolt shoots back, and the second my fingers graze the metal doorknob, I get an electrical shock. I pull my hand back, shaking it, and then open the door.

Dim light from behind me spills in, illuminating the large foyer. My breath catches, and I'm yet again stunned by the house. The foyer stretches two stories up, and a sweeping, curved staircase is before me. Dark hardwood is underfoot, and a large, twelve-light chandelier hangs above me.

The lady at the bank told me the electricity had been turned on. I turn around, looking for a switch. The house was built over a hundred years ago but hasn't sat empty for long. Crazy Mary rented the place out to someone even crazier than her, who kept the house in decent enough condition until leaving a few years ago.

The light above me flickers a few times before turning on, bringing a soft yellow glow around me. I look around, taking in the vastness of the house, before turning to shut the front door.

The birds aren't chirping anymore.

I am going to get in and get out as fast as I can, but only because I have work in the morning and it's a forty-five-minute drive from my house, not because it feels like the house has a heartbeat.

The house isn't in terrible condition, cosmetically at least. Who knows what the plumbing and the wiring situations are like behind the walls. I move through the foyer, going under the stairs and into a two-story living room. A great stone fireplace stretches to the ceiling, flanked by windows on each side. Furniture has been left, and while it is beautiful, the dark colors and Victorian-era style aren't to my taste. It's fitting to the house, though, and I can probably bump the price of the house up to include the furnishings.

The daylight is fading fast, and the lights inside are fitted with low-wattage bulbs. The living room connects to a library, and when I pull open the double French doors, the romantic smell of paper and ink hits me hard. I should have known better than to expect the surprises to be over.

The room is huge, with floor-to-ceiling shelves filled with books. I'm a bookworm at heart, even though work doesn't often permit me to spend hours reading like I wish I could, seeking what I long for on the pages of books. I'm the kind of girl who flips to the last page before diving in, needing to know if the book ends happily or not.

Real life sucks ass enough. I need a little happily-ever-after in my fiction.

There's no hanging light in the library, only the original candelabra, fitted with six of the ten candles it could hold. I go to a side table next to one of the large windows and turn on a lamp. It offers just enough light to look around. I walk down the aisle of bookshelves, running my finger along the spines of tomes long forgotten. Most are educational, and probably dated by now.

Only one book is out of place, lying on the stone hearth in front of the fireplace. It was left open, creating a permanent kink in the spine. I go to it, bending down to see what was left behind, and am hit with a rare wave of emotion when I read the title.

I'm not an emotional person. I don't see the point in crying or moping around feeling sorry for yourself. Tears never solve problems, and pity gets you nowhere. Holding it together even though I'm dying inside was more my style.

But staring down at Jane Austen's *Emma* causes feelings I've worked hard to repress to come to the surface. It was my mother's favorite book, and her face flashes through my mind. I'm almost the age she was when she died, and I look more and more like her every day.

My grip tightens on the book, and I go to stuff it on the first shelf I can reach. Then I stop and bring the book to my chest. I never met Aunt Mary, and the stories I was told were starting to fade from my memory. But she was related to Mom, and Mom had come to this house in her youth. Is it crazy to think maybe she held this exact copy of *Emma*?

"Yes, Ace, it's fucking nuts," I say out loud to myself. I put the book on a shelf and leave the library, needing to check out the rest of the house so I can be on my way.

I check out the rest of the downstairs, then head to the second floor, going up the servant staircase located off the kitchen. The light is fading fast, so I pull my phone from my bag to use as a flashlight. There are five bedrooms upstairs, and all are furnished. I stop in the threshold of the largest, guessing this room to be the remodeled master bedroom.

A large canopy bed with a multicolored quilt is centered against the wall, opposite large windows that open above the covered front porch. I take pictures as I move through the house, with the intention of sending them to a realtor in the near future. I have no need for this house, and my salary as a detective would make living in this place tight, if not impossible. Utilities alone have to cost an arm and a leg.

By the time I get back downstairs, it's pouring outside. I look out the living room window at my car and decide to wait. Downpours like this don't typically last long, and I'd rather not get soaking wet right now. It's cold in here, so I try turning on the heat. The furnace makes a terrible noise. I shut it off, go down into the basement, realize I have no idea how to even begin getting it back into working order, and go back up.

I yank a cover off a velvet settee and drag it to the center of the living room, putting it under a light. I sit back, propping my legs up on the coffee table, and pull a file folder from my bag. The moment I joined the force, I was faced with the struggle of proving I was more than a glorified meter maid. Doing so meant taking on some of the city's more obscure cases, and I've made it my specialty to investigate—and debunk—crimes reminiscent of the occult. Driven by logic, I don't believe in magic, or even luck for that matter. If you want to be lucky, then you get your ass out there and work hard.

Though right now, I'm coming up empty-handed as I look down at the photos taken at this morning's crime scene. Not only were the bones removed from the victim's forearms, but the marrow had also been sucked out of seven of his finger bones. Along with the puncture wounds on his neck, he had several on his inner thighs. The medical examiner couldn't make sense of it. The state police couldn't make sense of it.

Yet I was sure there was a logical explanation for it.

I read through the file again, then check the timeline I'd previously made. Leaning back on the settee, I feel a wave of tiredness come over me. I move the files from my lap to the coffee table and close my eyes.

I didn't realize I'd dozed off until something crashes above me. I shoot up, hand on my gun and heart in my throat. It was thunder, that was all. Thunder paired with sleep deprivation and a creepy house.

I gather up the papers, neatly putting them back in the file folder on the coffee table, and grab my phone to check the time. I'd been asleep for nearly twenty minutes. Clearly, it's time for me to go home and get some decent sleep before going into work and doing it all over again tomorrow.

I take one last look around the house, feeling almost sad that I decided to put the place up for sale.

"I have no use for you," I whisper. "Someone else could move in and fix you up like you deserve." I shake my head. "Shit, I need sleep. I'm talking to the house. I still am."

I stretch my arms over my head to wake myself up, and something boomed overhead again.

It wasn't thunder.

I freeze, waiting. Listening. Ready.

And...nothing. I swallow hard, blink a few times, and turn off the living room light. I'm so tired it's not out of the question to be hearing things. Thank God there's a Starbucks on the way home.

I turn to leave and I hear it again. This time there is no mistaking it. There is someone on the roof. Gun drawn, I silently move up the back staircase, holding my breath as I listen.

Whoever is on the roof is dragging something heavy. I pull my phone from my pocket, thinking it might be a good idea to call for backup.

"You've got to be fucking kidding me," I grumble, seeing I have no service. I shove the phone back in my pocket and follow the noise to the master bedroom. A dark shape moves across the window.

The fucker is on the roof of the covered porch. I push down my nerves and rush forward, going to the window. Finger hovering over the trigger, I pull back the latch and open the window.

"Police!" I shout. "Put your hands up!"

Rain falls in sheets, and thunder rumbles in the distance, low and steady like a freight train.

No one responds. No one moves. Taking a breath, I lean out the window. No one is out there.

And then I hear it again, right above me. I climb through the window, testing my footing. The roof is solid, but slick.

"Police," I shout again. "Come out now—" I cut off when I realize the gargoyle sitting above the front door is gone. "What the hell?" My heart hammers and the little voice inside of me is raging for me to go back inside, leave, and never come back.

And that is exactly what I plan to do. Except something swoops down from the roof above me, landing with a heavy thud at my feet. I aim my gun at it. "Put your hands where I can see them! Now!"

I'm not sure what I'm looking at, and all I can do is watch in horror as the black shadow stands, stretching into the shape of a man. A man with wings. And claws. And fangs.

Lightning flashes, reflecting off his dark eyes. No. No fucking way. He tips his head, eyes drilling into mine. Dark, wet hair falls into his face, and I recognize him as the big gargoyle from on top of the porch.

But that's not possible. This man before me is just that—a man. But not. Not completely. Shaking my head, I step back, desperate to get away. I don't look where I'm stepping, and my boot slips on wet leaves on the roof. My gun clatters to the slick shingles below. My feet go out from under me, and I throw out my arms in a desperate attempt to keep myself from plummeting off the roof. Only, there's nothing to grab onto, and I fall backwards into the night.

3

Another bolt of lightning lights up the sky. Everything happened so fast, and I know I only have seconds until I hit the cobblestone path beneath me. I close my eyes, bracing for the pain.

It never comes.

Instead, someone catches me, strong arms stopping the fall with ease before I hit the ground. So many thoughts rush through my head, with the first being how grateful I am not to be lying on the stones right now. The second is wondering who the fuck caught me, though deep down, I already know the answer.

I twist, pushing against his chest. It's bare. Hard with muscle. Cold from the rain. He lets me go, setting me down on my feet. I don't have my gun, but I'm far from defenseless. Though one look at the man before me leaves me doubtful my years of martial arts training will do a damn thing.

In the dark, he's a monstrous shadow, a looming shape inching toward me. I curl my fists and inhale, ignoring my pounding heart. The man steps forward, and another bolt of lightning flashes overhead. His eyes, dark brown, deep, and holding back emotion, meet mine. Suddenly, the air turns electric and everything around me stops.

The wind.

The rain.

Everything fades, and it's just my heart beating along with his. He's familiar in a way that doesn't make the smallest bit of sense, and I find myself craving to move closer, almost as much as I want to run away. For a fleeting moment, as I look at him as he looks at me, something passes between us.

The rain pelts down harder, and thunder rumbles in the distance. I can feel the others closing in on me, and I whirl around to see three more dark shadows drawing near. They're surrounding me, yet for some insane reason, I don't feel threatened.

Then the power flickers back on, and light from the porch lamps spills into the yard. I've seen a lot of fucked up shit throughout the years as a cop, and I've never once come close to screaming. But what I see before me right now makes a scream rise in my throat. I inhale sharply, mouth falling open, and step back, only to stop and whirl around.

The three men behind me aren't any different. I rapidly blink raindrops from my eyes, brain going crazy trying to discern what the hell I'm seeing. Because it makes no sense. I risk a half-second glance behind the advancing men, needing to be sure.

"What the fuck?" I mumble out loud. The gargoyles from the porch are gone. I look back at the men before me. It can't be, but it is.

They're not men, not exactly. But they're not the stone creatures that guarded the house mere hours ago. It's too much. I blink and shake my head, positive I really did slip and fall and am suffering a concussion that's causing me to hallucinate.

The one who caught me is close. I can feel his heat against my cold skin. I whirl around, arms out slightly to my sides, ready to fight. But what I see leaves me breathless, and I unfurl my fists.

His mouth is slightly open, the tips of his fangs visible behind his full lips. Large wings are folded at his back. His flesh is the color of stone, but his eyes are all human, and right now he's looking at me as if I'm his long-lost puppy.

He takes a tentative step forward, staring at me with such intensity it makes a chill run down my spine.

"Braeya?" he asks, voice rough and gravelly. His face softens, eyes filling with longing. He raises his hand and I jerk away.

"No," I say, shaking my head. The others are closing in, and I shake away the shock, going back into cop mode. "Stop where you are," I order.

And they do.

"Take a step back."

The one in front of me moves backwards, looking confused. I exhale and push my brunette hair out of my face. Nothing has prepared me for this. For the first time, I have no clue what to do. My phone has no service, but even if I could call the station, what the hell would I say?

They'd think I'd lost my shit.

"I'm Detective Bisset," I start, gathering my composure. "From the Philadelphia PD. You better do what you're told or I'll arrest you all." I eyeball them all and point at the man who'd caught me. "Over there, with the others."

His eyes go from me to the others, and the same look of confusion takes over their faces as well. He moves gracefully for a man of his size. I take a minute to look them over.

They're all tall and muscular, and handsome in a strange way. They're more human than monster, save for the wings, fangs, and claws where fingernails should be. I push my shoulders back, take a deep breath, and try to come up with something intelligent to say to them to show my place of authority.

But all I can come up with is another, "What the fuck?"

The largest of the four steps forward. "Who are you?" he asks. His voice is deep, and his words rumble through me, causing tingles to rush between my legs.

"How about I ask the questions," I counter, not liking how damn attractive I'm finding these strangers right now. "*What* are you?"

"We are brothers Templar."

Rain starts to soak through my jacket. I suppress a shiver. "You're Templar Knights?"

"We were."

I blink, lips parting as I'm once again at a loss for words. "But now you're…"

One of the men who was perched on the side of the porch cracks a smile. He's youthful, looking the youngest of the bunch, and very good looking, even with the fangs.

"Now we're gargoyles." He laughs, and the odd sense of security I felt earlier vanishes. Gargoyles. No. Fucking. Way. I pull my arms around myself, trying to stay warm.

"How?"

"You're shivering," the one who caught me says.

"Yeah. It's forty degrees and raining."

"You should take shelter."

My fingers are starting to feel numb, and the colder I get, the harder it will be to take part in a fight if one was to break out. But the thought of having those things inside the house with me is unnerving.

"Please, my lady," he urges, looking at me as if he knows me…as if he *misses* me.

The cold is starting to seep into my bones, and the temperature is low enough for me to become hypothermic. Seeing that my options are either to stand here in a stare-off and slowly freeze to death or go inside, I choose the latter.

I move onto the covered porch, feeling better just to be out of the rain, and go to the door. Then I stop, whirling around. The door is locked. I came outside from the open window upstairs.

"Is something wrong?" one of the younger ones asks. He has sandy blond hair, a chiseled jaw, and rough stubble covering his face. Like the others, his flesh is more gray than tan. The discoloration webs across his broad chest, moving along with the veins under his skin, mottled and blotchy.

"It's locked. I didn't intend on being thrown off the roof when I went out there." I'm impressed with the strength of my voice. I'm standing here shivering like mad, looking down the porch steps at four half-man, half-gargoyle creatures. I'm teetering on the edge of losing my shit for real.

"You slipped." The dark-haired one moves in front of the others. "And I caught you."

"I wouldn't have slipped if you hadn't startled me."

He diverts his eyes. "I didn't mean to frighten you. With your permission, my lady, I can take you back to the roof."

My mouth falls open and I slowly shake my head. He extends his hand and waits on my response. Things are already crazy. Why not take it one step further?

"Sure."

Heart in my throat, I go down the porch steps. Thunder cracks and he lunges forward, arms going around my waist. It's been so long since any man has touched me, I'd forgotten how good it feels to be in someone's embrace.

Even his.

He's strong, his hold on me unfaltering. My heart jumps and the strange urge to throw my arms around him takes over. Before I have a chance to process anything, he spreads his great wings and takes flight.

Landing on the top of the porch with grace, he keeps his hands around my middle to make sure I'm able to get my footing. He slowly looks me over, hands still on my waist, and inhales deeply. His lips part and the air fills with static tension again. For a brief moment, I think he's going to kiss me.

And for a brief moment, I want him to.

"Gargoyles aren't supposed to be able to fly," I say to myself, and shake off his embrace. Hell, gargoyles aren't supposed to *be* at all. They're just creepy statues. Nothing more. Nothing less.

Until now.

My gun is lying near the window. I make a dash for it, feeling a shade better when it's back in my hands. I turn, expecting him to take a swing or something. My heart is racing and every nerve in my body is on fire from adrenaline.

Yet he just stands there, watching me.

I back away to the open window, mind racing with what the hell to do once I get inside. Slam it shut? Run downstairs and call for backup? Grab my keys and make a run for it? These things can fly. I don't think I'd be able to get away.

"I'll open the front door," I tell him, and slip inside. Water drips onto the hardwood floor as I pull the sash down and twist the locks back into place. I don't have any spare clothes, and stripping down and wrapping up in a blanket until my clothes dry isn't an option.

The dresser near the door catches my attention as I leave the room. I pause, turn on the light, and then take a step back to open the top drawer. I rifle through the old clothes and pull out a long black dress. Moving into the bathroom—just in case my new winged friends were watching—I quickly strip out of my wet clothes and slip the dress over my head.

It's the last thing I'd choose to wear, but at this point, I'm so cold I'd welcome a potato sack if it was dry. I take the back stairs down, hanging my wet clothes on a kitchen chair to dry, and go to the front door.

As much as those things scare me, talking to them is the only way I'll find out what is happening. With my gun in my right hand, I twist back the deadbolt and open the front door, hoping I'd imagined the whole thing.

I didn't.

"May we come in?" the biggest of the four asks.

"Why the hell not?" I step aside, watching the large men lumber into the house. What could possibly go wrong? I shut the door and our awkward stare-off resumes. At least we're out of the rain this time.

"Okay," I start. "Someone needs to explain what the hell is going on." The men look at each other in question. "You don't know?"

"It's been years." The big one closes his eyes, thinking. "Centuries."

"Since you've been, uh, alive?" I ask.

"Yes."

I blink, and look them up and down in the light. They're dripping wet from the rain but don't seem to be bothered by the cold. Each is bare-chested, wearing only ragged brown pants that have dirtied over the years from the elements. The pants are wet, clinging to their muscular bodies, and outline every feature. It takes effort to keep my eyes from wandering below the belt.

"How...how did this happen? And who's Braeya?" I have so many questions, and part of me knows I won't like all the answers. I shiver again. "Wait, no...who are you?"

"My name is Jacques Clairvaux," the one who caught me says, pushing his dark, wavy hair out of his face. "These are my brothers Templar. Hasan." He motions to the biggest one. "Thomas and Gilbert."

In the light, I see Thomas's and Gilbert's sky-blue eyes, contrasting harshly with the dead appearance of their skin.

They look at me with curiosity and amusement mixed with something else...hunger, perhaps? But not for food.

Jacques narrows his dark eyes. "Who are you? What did you do to us?"

"I'm Acelina, but everyone calls me Ace. And I didn't do a damn thing."

Thomas and Gilbert turn, looking at each other. I'm guessing they are actual blood brothers as well. They look too much alike not to be.

"Then how did we break free from the stone?" Thomas asks, running his eyes over me. He doesn't even try to stop himself from checking me out. Or hiding the obvious lust the sight of my pert nipples through this thin dress causes him to feel.

I can't stop shivering. I pull my arms around my body, keeping my finger near the trigger on my gun just in case. Hasan moves through the foyer, going into the two-story living room and right to the fireplace.

"Where is the wood?" he asks, accented voice echoing through the large house.

"I don't know." I turn in his direction.

"How can you not know where the wood is?"

"This isn't my house," I explain. "Well, I guess it is now. I don't live here. I've never even been here until today." As soon as the words leave my lips, something clicks into place.

I've never set foot inside the house until today.

The gargoyles awoke for the first time in centuries.

You don't have to be a detective to make the connection, only I don't know what two things I'm connecting. How could I have anything to do with this? I've spent my entire career proving magic and the occult doesn't exist. I've never taken on a case where I failed to provide logic and reason behind the crimes.

Until ten minutes ago, I would have bet my life on the fact that magic wasn't real. I swallow hard and get hit with a wave of dizziness.

Magic still isn't real. It can't be. I turn back around and look at the three men in the foyer. Water drips from their wings.

Wings.

Hasan picks up what's probably a valuable antique chair and snaps it like a twig, tossing the pieces into the fireplace.

"I've gone crazy." I squeeze my eyes shut, telling myself the gargoyles will be gone when I open them. They're not. "I've cracked. They warned me this could happen. Said I compartmentalized too well, didn't process the full extent of how fucked up people can be."

"Acelina," Jacques starts.

"Ace," I interrupt. "Call me Ace."

He gives me a curt nod, not trying at all to hide the indignation he's feeling. I get the feeling he's not interrupted often, and definitely not by a woman. "It can be a lot to take in. I myself remember the shock of being cursed."

"Cursed? So now curses are real, too?" I let out a breath. "I need a drink. And I don't drink."

Gilbert comes forward, smirking. "We didn't believe it either. But the sooner you accept this, the sooner we can figure this out."

I hold up my hand. "Wait...Templar Knights are from a thousand years ago. How are you even speaking English?"

The smirk vanishes from Gilbert's face. "A thousand years?"

"Give or take a few hundred."

He turns to his brother, looking more human than ever. "We've been asleep for a thousand years," he says quietly in disbelief.

Thomas's blue eyes glisten for a moment, then he grins. "I knew there was a reason you looked like shit, brother."

"You don't look much better. You have moss in your hair and you reek like rat piss, though I can't say that's much different than before," Gilbert counters.

Thomas brings a clawed hand to his head, brushing out moss and a few wet leaves. "Don't be jealous. You know how—"

"Enough," Jacques says, silencing the two immediately. He rounds on me, eyes narrowing. "Who are you?" he practically hisses. The venom in his voice sends a chill down my spine. Behind the anger, I can see his fear. He's just as clueless as I am, which freaks me out even more.

Someone is supposed to have answers, and it sure isn't me.

"I already told you. My name is Acelina Bisset. I'm a detective on the city police force. This house belonged to my Great Aunt Mary and I've never been inside until today."

"Detective?"

"I solve crimes. Hunt bad guys. And I always win." I push my shoulders back, trying to look as dignified as I can in this crushed velvet '90s slip dress.

"But you're a woman."

"No shit, Sherlock," I retort, defenses automatically going up. I fought tooth and nail to get to where I am today in a male-dominated field. "Times have changed. Women are equal to men." I let out a breath, bringing my defenses down. "A lot has changed over the years."

"Has fucking changed?" Thomas asks, giving me that same crooked grin. "It's been so long since I lay with a woman, even before the curse."

"A thousand years and you're still thinking with your cock," Gilbert mutters under his breath, shaking his head.

"That'll never change."

"I don't think fucking has changed. The concept is still the same, right? Though people are more open about their sexuality now," I start, then shake my head. "So not the point, either."

A glow comes from the living room, and I turn to see Hasan standing back from a fire. His eyes meet mine in the dark.

"Come," he beckons. "Warm yourself."

"Follow me," I tell the others, and walk to the fire. I sit near the hearth, holding out my ice-cold hands. I give myself a minute to get the heat back into my fingers before drilling the gargoyles again. I rake my long brunette hair over my shoulder, hoping it will dry quickly. Wet hair on my back always makes me cold.

Jacques pulls a blanket off the couch, shaking off the dust. His eyes meet mine again for a fleeting moment as he hands it to me. There's no denying the longing in his eyes as he again looks upon me as if he knows me.

"Thanks." I take the blanket and drape it around my shoulders. My eyes go over the four men in front of me. "So you're gargoyles."

"Yes," Jacques answers.

I stand, pulling the blanket tighter around my shoulders. "Okay, then. I'm going to go home and never come back. Because this cannot be happening."

"It is happening." Jacques steps in front of me, blocking me in against the fireplace. "It's happening because of you."

"Back off," I order, and his body moves back on its own accord. "I already told you, I have no idea what's going on, and right now... right now I want to go home."

"Wait," Jacques calls. "If you woke us, maybe you're the one."

"The one?"

"The one to break the curse."

4

The fire cracks and pops behind me, casting long shadows throughout the grand living room. Wind blows against the floor-to-ceiling windows, and the rain continues to come down in sheets.

"I don't know a thing about curses," I say slowly. "Not how to cast one and not how to break one." There is hope in Thomas's and Gilbert's eyes as they gaze upon me. Hasan remains stoic, staring into the fire behind me.

"Are you sure about that?" Jacques's lips pull back as he speaks, showing off his fangs. He doesn't believe me, and to be honest, I wouldn't either if I were him. All evidence points to me being the one to awaken them.

"Yes. I told you, I didn't do anything to wake you."

Jacques holds out his hand, eyes falling shut. "I can feel it inside you."

"Feel what?"

"Magic."

I shake my head. "Magic isn't real."

Thomas gives me a cocky grin. "Neither are gargoyles, right?"

"This is so fucked up," I mutter, and run my finger along the barrel of my gun, needing to remind myself who I am. Stick to the facts. I'm not crazy.

I'm a detective. A damn good one. I've taken on case after case and proved magic is never the culprit because magic is not real.

"What are you holding?" Gilbert asks, eyes going to the M9 in my hand.

"It's a gun."

"Gun," he repeats, saying the word like it's the first time he's heard it. "What does it do?"

"Right. You wouldn't know. It shoots bullets and can kill people."

"That thing can kill?" he asks incredulously. "It's so small."

History has never been my strong suit, but I know the Templars lived their days battling it out with swords, daggers, and bows and arrows. I flick the safety on.

"Don't underestimate it."

My phone rings, and the *Wonder Woman* theme song echoes from the living room. All four gargoyles react as if there were a monster lurking.

"Calm down. It's just my phone," I say. "A phone is harmless."

I stride into the living room for some privacy and pull my phone out of my pocket. There's only one reason I'd get a call at this hour. I've never declined a call from work before. My finger hovers over the red icon on my screen. At the last second, I answer.

"Bisset," I say into the phone.

"I hope I didn't wake you," the officer responds. "But we've got another body. The ME isn't here yet, but I think it's safe to say the cause of death is from loss of blood. And bone."

"Shit. How many bones this time?"

"All ten fingers and one femur. Body was still warm when it was called in. A couple of storm chasers found it in the bushes."

"Text me the address. I'm on my way." I end the call and wait for the address to come through.

"Is everything all right?" Jacques asks, walking into the living room. I wish he'd stop looking at me like he knew me. It's unnerving, but mostly because I have a weird feeling like I know him too.

Like I know all of the men.

"Actually, no. Things aren't all right. There was a murder and I need to go investigate."

"Dressed like that?"

I look down at the stupid dress. "Shit." I don't wear dresses. Or skirts. In fact, the only dress I own is a knee-length black wrap, which I purchased solely for funerals. Fortunately, I've only worn it a handful of times. "I guess."

My phone buzzes with a text, and I get directions to the crime scene. It's only four miles from here.

"You're leaving?" Thomas's wings catch on the arched doorframe leading into the living room. He pulls them in closer to his body, making me even more curious. I want to touch them, ask them to spread their wings and let me get a good look. But I can't. I won't. Because I'm still not entirely sure this is actually happening.

"Yes. I'll, uh, I'll be back. So don't go plunder a village and eat the local children, okay?"

Jacques's eyes narrow. "Why would we do that?"

Thomas holds up his hands, wiggling his claws and motioning to his fangs. "She thinks we're monsters."

"I'm stereotyping, I know." I give him a guilty look. "Sorry."

"What is stereotyping?" Jacques asks.

"You have got to be kidding me," I mumble. "Look, I have to go."

"You'll be back." Jacques's dark eyes pierce into mine. He grabs my hand, causing goosebumps to break out along my flesh. "I have your word?"

I swallow my pounding heart. "Yes."

He nods and lets go of my hand. I miss his touch the moment he lets go. Turning, I grab my bag and my shoes and get the hell out of there, not slowing down until I get into my car. The tires slip in the muddy driveway, making my heart race all over again. I rev the engine, not breathing until the car lurches forward and makes it onto the gravel road. I speed away, and once a mile has been put between us, I slow, gripping the steering wheel tightly.

A hundred years ago, when the house was built, there was nothing around it. Over the years, the city has stretched its limits, and I'm not too far from civilization. I pull over in a Walmart parking lot and enter the crime scene address in my GPS.

My hands are shaking and my heart is beating too fast. I can't show up like this. My mental state is all over the place, and this dress is terrible. Everyone will wonder, and more importantly, I won't be able to concentrate if I'm freezing cold.

I put the car in park and lean back, closing my eyes. Images of the gargoyles flash before me and I sit up, still trying to make sense of it.

"They're men in costumes," I say to myself. "Movie-quality costumes. I'll go back and arrest them for…for…uh…freaking me out." I turn off the car and grab my bag.

"Which doesn't explain how they flew."

Rushing through the rain, I enter the store, well aware how fitting I am for a *People of Walmart* feature. Keeping my head down, I delve deeper inside, grabbing new socks, black leggings, an oversized sweatshirt, and a raincoat. I change in the restroom and toss the ugly black dress in the trash. I rake my fingers through my hair, then pull it into a messy braid over my shoulder.

I'm not one to put much effort into my appearance. If I had someone in my life to dress up for, it'd be a different story. But since my days are spent investigating grisly murders, I don't see the point. Satisfied I look put together enough not to raise questions, I flip the hood up on the raincoat and go back to my car.

"And you didn't see or hear anything out of the ordinary before you found the body?" I ask the clearly shaken twenty-one-year-old boy who found the body.

"The storm was pretty intense then," he says, arms wrapped around himself. "All we heard was wind and rain."

I motion to his camera. "Were you recording the whole time?"

"Yeah." He brings the camera strap over his head and hands it to me. We're standing under a gazebo in the park, just yards from the body. I rewind the last video he took, going back a few minutes before they stumbled upon the body. I watch first, and don't see anything out of the ordinary. The screen is small and the filming is jumpy. I rewind again and bring the camera to my ear, listening to the background noise.

"I need to take your memory card for evidence," I tell him.

"I, uh, have some personal photos of my girlfriend on there." He meets my eyes then looks away.

"Is she over eighteen?"

"Yeah."

"Then you're fine. I'm not interested in them, just the clip of you finding the body." I pop out the memory card and bag it. "You already gave your statement, so you're free to go. I'll make a copy of the clip and you can get this back in the morning."

He gets off the bench, face still pale. "There's one more thing," he starts.

"What is it?"

"It's probably nothing, but you asked if I saw anything out of the ordinary."

"Did you?"

"No." His brow furrows. "I smelled something. Like rotten eggs. We thought it was a backed-up sewer, you know, from all the rain. But I don't smell it anymore. And it got stronger the closer we got to the...to...to *him*."

I go back to the body, which appears to have been dragged from the parking lot into the tall grass.

"Stupid rain washed away all my blood," Tiffany says, coming up next to me.

"There might not have been much from the start," I tell her, crouching down. I pull on latex gloves and carefully move the victim's head to the side to look at his neck. "Puncture wounds, just like the others."

"What could have done this?"

"Who, Tiff, who." I stand, feeling a little dizzy. For the first time, I feel unnerved. I've always been confident it was a *who* not a *what* when it comes to murderers. But after what happened tonight…

Nope. Not going there right now.

I move to the other side of the body, imagining myself as the killer. I'm in the middle of pulling out this poor guy's bones, sucking up his blood with something in the process. It's dark and stormy, and I'm not expecting anyone to interrupt me. Then two idiots trying to record a viral video stumble upon me.

Why don't I attack them?

The man before me is tall, six foot two, and weighs one-seventy-five. According to his license, that is.

Maybe I'm startled…wounded from taking down this guy? So I run. Where do I go? I look around and my eyes land on a creek bed that's been dry until tonight. It goes under a bridge and into a wooded walking area.

I'd go there. Hang back, and watch them discover the body, get enjoyment out of the shock and horror, maybe. Then I notice several pieces of bent grass and I know the perp went this way. Chances are he's long gone by now, unless he's one of those really fucked up psychos who gets off watching law enforcement inspect his handiwork. Though if he was jerking off as he watched us work, at least he'd leave evidence behind.

The rain has slowed to a fine mist, and the clouds are thinning. I carefully pick my way through the grass, moving next to what I think could be a trail and trying not to disturb potential evidence. I get to the bridge and notice footprints.

I click on my flashlight and bend down. The prints look fresh in the mud.

"Motherfucker," I mutter, and stand, ready to call to Tiffany to come over and get photos. Before I open my mouth to get the words out, something moves through the trees just feet from me.

My hand goes to my gun and I swiftly move off the bridge, emerging into the forest. The light doesn't reach beyond the trees, and mud squishes beneath my feet. I exhale, breath clouding around me, and wait.

The woods are riddled with deer. There's a good chance that's all it was. But there's an even better chance it wasn't. Adrenaline surges through me and I look around, scanning every inch of visible forest. I like the chase and find thrill in hunting down the bad guys.

Because I always win.

Twigs snap yards from me, and a dark shape jumps from the shadows.

"Police," I order, raising my gun. "Freeze!"

The fucker takes off, and so do I, chasing him deeper into the woods, boots splashing in muddy puddles. I leave the path, holding out a hand in front of me to keep low-hanging branches from scratching my face.

I come to a sudden stop at the top of a ravine. It goes down sharply at least twenty feet, only to rise up again in an even steeper incline. The bottom is filled with a few inches of rainwater.

Holding my flashlight and gun out, I whirl around. The forest is silent, save for my beating heart. I take a deep breath, fill my lungs with air, and exhale slowly. Everything is silent.

Too silent.

I spin around, looking at my surroundings. Where did he go? Keeping the gun in my right hand, I lower my left and reach for the walkie I always wear on my belt when investigating crime scenes. I know he came out here, and I need to call for backup.

My fingers close around the walkie, but I never pull it from my belt. Something jumps down from the tree above me, red eyes glowing like embers in the night. It opens its mouth, letting out a low growl. Thick, yellow saliva drips from a row of sharp, jagged teeth.

My heart leaps in my chest, and I stand there, stunned, like a deer in headlights. And then another comes down behind me, hitting me square in the back. I pitch forward, and my gun and flashlight fall from my hands, sliding down into the ravine.

The thing in front of me growls again and then lunges forward. I duck and avoid being hit. Instead, I tumble down the incline and into darkness.

5

My body tumbles down, gaining speed and then coming to a harsh stop at the bottom of the ravine. Cold water seeps through my clothes, but I don't have time to stop and think about it. I scramble up, looking at the top of the ravine.

What the fuck?

My heart is racing and I reach for my walkie on my belt, yanking it free. Water drips from the thing, and nothing happens when I push the button to talk. What a piece of shit.

I exhale and step back, water sloshing around my feet. I don't have my gun, but I'll be damned before I give up. I blink, trying to get my eyes to adjust to the dark, and pick up a rock, ready to bash whatever attacked me over the head.

Clouds move over the moon, offering just enough light for me to get a glimpse of my surroundings. The ravine is steep on either side. I could scramble up, but if those things are at the top, I'll be walking into a trap.

Shivering, I run through the water and jump onto land the first chance I get. I shake my walkie, trying to get the water out of it, and press the communication button again. This time I hear static.

"This is Detective Bisset requesting backup immediately," I say. Someone answers, but I can't make out what they say in return. Chances are, they couldn't make out what I said either.

"Just fucking help me," I mutter through gritted teeth. "Get your ass here and help me." A strange sensation runs through me, leaving me a tad disoriented. It's a wonder I'm still standing after the night I've had, actually.

I clip the walkie back on my belt and pick my way up the side of the ravine. Teeth chattering, I look around. Whatever jumped from the trees is still out here. And it's not one psychotic killer, it's two.

And all I have is a fucking rock.

I push my shoulders back and hold my hand to the side, ready. It won't be that long before someone notices I'm missing. Backup will be here soon, and more than anything, I'd love to have the fuckers subdued on the ground by the time it gets here.

I move to the clearing, and clouds roll over the moon. My vision darkens, and the forest turns to tangles of black before my eyes can adjust. Blinking feverishly, I smell him before I see him.

Sulfur.

There's no mistaking the scent. It's strong and sickening, filling my nostrils and making my stomach hurt. Brandishing the rock like a weapon, I whirl around and bash him over the head. The thing stumbles back, dropping a blood-covered knife from his hands. He falls to the ground, scrambling away.

It looks like a man, but with glowing red eyes and a mouth full of sharp teeth. Blood stains his face, crusted around his mouth.

"You're under arrest," I say, trading the rock for the knife. "Don't fucking move."

He jumps forward, teeth bared, and grabs me by the shoulders. His nails dig into my skin and he brings his mouth to my neck, trying to bite me. I fight against him and realize he has inhuman strength. He shoves me back against a tree and I have no choice but to use the knife.

I bring my hand up, intending to stab him in the shoulder. It would cause enough pain to distract him but not seriously harm him. And then his teeth make contact with my flesh. I jerk back, and the knife plunges into his heart.

He steps back and looks down at the knife. What the hell? How is he...no...there's no way. The knife is *in* his heart. He should be dead. Or at the very least, panicking because there is *a fucking knife in his chest*.

I watch with wide eyes, trying to wrap my head around the fact this thing isn't human. The one behind me takes advantage of my shock and grabs me by my shoulders, throwing me back against the tree. My head hits the trunk, and pain radiates through my body, causing white stars to flash before my eyes.

"You're assaulting a police officer," I force out, trying to push through the pain. Nausea twists deep inside my stomach, both from the sudden splitting headache and the stench of these murderers in front of me. "Stop before you—"

The man who shoved me moves forward with freaky speed. His face is youthful and almost handsome, save for the glowing red eyes. He inhales deeply, smelling me. He tips his head, confused, then parts his lips. Fangs move down from inside his gums, covering his front teeth.

Fuck, I need that drink.

I bend my knees up and kick him hard in the chest. He goes back on his ass, and it's all I need to get up and make a run for it. I make it fifty yards before he catches up to me. He tackles me, and we both go to the ground. I twist, bringing my wrist up in a swift movement. Using the palm of my hand, I shove his nose up into his head. He snorts and backs off, licking the blood that drips from his nostrils.

"Sick," I say out loud, and clamor up and away. I race through the woods, stopping only when I've put a good distance between us. I duck behind a tree, trying to catch my breath.

I've either gone crazy or everything I've believed in has been a big fat motherfucking lie.

Gargoyles.

Whatever the hell those things are.

"What is happening?" I whisper, still panting.

I've gone deeper into the nature park than I intended, and I need to double back in order to make it out alive. If those things ran when the wannabe storm chasers walked up on them, chances are they don't want to be seen by a bunch of people. I pull my radio from my belt again, giving it another try. I get nothing but static this time, and flick it off, not wanting the noise to give away my location.

I peer around the tree, scanning my surroundings. The forest is silent. It's too cold for crickets, and too late for birds. A slight wind blows, causing little droplets of water to fall from the remaining dead leaves clinging to the trees. I hold my breath and wait for it to stop. I need to know where these things are.

A minute or two passes before I move, going just a few feet before stopping again. I stay close to a large tree trunk, watching and waiting. Something moves to my right. I crouch down, blindly feeling around the forest floor for a weapon. All I can come up with are soggy branches, slimy from being under wet leaves all winter long.

Another minute passes. And then another. And another.

Holding my breath, I dodge out a few feet and move to another tree. It'll take forever to get back to the park this way, but it beats having those things sink their teeth into me.

The ravine is in sight, and I know I'm close. I pause, listening again while trying to decide if I should move painstakingly through the woods or make a run for it. Before I can decide, the creatures surround me.

And this time, there are three.

I'm fucked. Three human men...yeah, I'd take my chances. But whatever these things are...they're not human. Not anymore. They're too fast, and too strong. The one I hit over the head *and* stabbed is encroaching on me, seemingly unbothered by the blood dripping down his head or the gushing hole in his chest.

For the first time in the history of my career, I feel hopeless. These things are going to kill me, drink my blood, and pull my bones from my body. Tiffany will take photos of my corpse, and then what? I have no family to press the case. No one to mourn me. A handful of coworkers will show up to my funeral, say some kind words about how dedicated I was, and that'll be it. I'll be shelved as a cold case for the rest of eternity.

But that doesn't mean I'll go out easy. I'll make every moment count until my final one, swinging, kicking, fighting.

"Bring it, douchebags," I say, and ball my fists.

The closest one comes at me, and I greet him with a punch to the side of his face. He staggers back, giving me just enough time to bring my knee up and hit him hard in the dick. I shove him to the ground and spin, kicking another in the chest. He falls back into the third, who pushes him over and lunges for me.

I try to move out of the way but can't. He grabs me by my hair and yanks me back. I reach up and dig my nails into the flesh on his hands, madly trying to break his hold. He drags me back through the mud. I kick and thrash, doing everything in my power to get away.

The smell of sulfur gets stronger, and I know more of these things are coming for me. I throw my legs to the side, twisting my body over. My face presses into the damp ground as I'm dragged forward, and we go a few more feet before I'm able to yank one arm free. I grab his ankle and he trips. Several strands of my hair break and snap in his hand as he falls.

I scramble up, kick him hard in the ribs once, twice, three times before taking off. I sprint through the woods with no sense of direction. If I stopped and looked up, gave myself a minute to get a feel for the land, I'd be able to tell where I was going. But stopping to get my bearings would mean certain death.

I'll come to a road or a clearing eventually. This nature park isn't that big. And these things...these hillbilly psychos on bath salts...they won't follow. I'll come back prepared and I'll—

Something hard collides with the back of my head. Pain radiates through me and I pitch forward, ears ringing. My vision is spotty and I desperately move forward, holding my hands out in front of me.

I smell him before I see him. The guy I bashed over the head with a rock stands before me, grinning and holding a rock in his hand. Nausea twists inside of me and I try to push through the pain. Something warm drips down my temple and I cannot get my vision to focus.

He raises his hand, drool running down his chin, and I flinch, bracing for the pain. Before he can bring his hand down, he's yanked backwards into darkness. The rock falls to the forest floor with a dull thud. The bare branches above me shudder as if a thousand birds took flight.

Two of the creatures look at each other, confused. Then they run at me, but *he* gets there first.

Hasan comes from the sky, landing right in front of me. His large wings are open, acting as a shield. I can't see what's going on, but I can hear the carnage. Reaching up to my head, I carefully feel the wound. It's bleeding like crazy but doesn't feel deep. It'll sting for a good while, that's for sure, and I'm already pissed about the little bald spot this is going to create. I don't think I need stitches, but there's a chance I have a concussion.

"Acelina." Jacques's voice rings out in the dark. His feet hit the earth and he folds his wings in, coming for me, holding out a hand. I shouldn't trust him. I don't know him. I don't understand what he is. For all I know, he could have sent these creatures after me.

Out of the corner of my eye, I see Hasan lift one of them off the ground and snap its neck, twisting until he rips the head clean off. He tosses it down and lurches forward, half running, half flying. Thomas and Gilbert aren't far, and I see flashes of their wings and claws through the trees. They're fighting the creatures.

Killing them with ease.

They can do the same to me.

"Ace," Jacques repeats, and I snap my attention back to him. I only have half a second to make a decision to trust him or not. I'm soaking wet—again—and bleeding from my head. I can't keep sitting here on the forest ground if I want to live. Especially not when those things keep coming.

I take his hand. He pulls me to my feet, then wraps his arms around me, bringing me to his chest. His flesh is warm like mine but rough, almost calloused. I guess that's what happens when you spend a thousand years sitting out in the elements. Gently, he presses his hand to the wound on my head, trying to stop the bleeding.

"You're shivering again."

"Yeah," I say through chattering teeth. "It's still cold and I fell in a creek."

"Why did you do that?"

I narrow my eyes, not liking being patronized. If I wasn't so fucking cold, I'd push him away. "I didn't do it on purpose. I was trying to get away from those...those things."

"Vampires."

"Excuse me?"

"Those things. They're vampires." He looks down at me. "I'm guessing you're not familiar with vampires, either."

"Not in this sense."

Jacques brings his hand back, wiping the blood on his pants. I push away, looking around him, and see Hasan grab the remaining vampire, lifting him one-handed by the neck. He looks more like a Greek god than a monster right now, with flexing muscles and powerful wings. Blood's spattered across his face, and his dark eyes are set.

He says something to the vampire, speaking an ancient language I don't understand. The vampire responds with hisses, madly swinging his arms at Hasan. With a frown, Hasan grabs his head and twists.

Thomas and Gilbert appear from the trees, both smiling.

"That was fun," Gilbert says.

"Too easy, though." Thomas pushes his golden locks behind his ear. "I thought there'd be more."

"There usually are."

I step away from Jacques, glad to stand on my own but missing his body heat. I'm so incredibly tired of being wet and cold tonight. Bodies lie on the forest floor. What am I going to say to the crime scene investigators?

"Those things are vampires?" I ask in disbelief. "If you tell me they sparkle in the sun, I'm going to puke."

"They die in sunlight," Jacques says seriously. I don't think he'd know sarcasm if it came up and bit him in the ass. He turns his attention back to me. "Are you ill?"

"No," I say, though there's a good chance I've gone insane. Gargoyles. Vampires. What's next, fairies?

"Are they still eating bone?" Gilbert nudges a body with his foot.

"Yeah...how did you know?"

He looks at his fellow brothers. "When they're first turned, blood isn't enough. They eat the bone as well for the first few years. Once the transformation is complete, blood is all that's needed to sustain them."

The implications of his words hit me hard, and I'm dizzy all over again. "Something is out there turning people into vampires?"

"Yes."

"Lovely." I pull my hood up over my head, but all it does is dump wet leaves down my back.

"You need to warm yourself," Hasan says. His voice is gruff, but he looks concerned. His eyes meet mine, and my heart flutters. It's been a while since anyone has looked at me like that. And even longer since someone cared like that. It makes me feel warm inside. I want him to look at me like that again. "Before you fall ill."

Should I tell him it's been proven cold doesn't actually make you sick? The entire concept of medicine and disease will be foreign to them.

"I plan on taking a long, hot shower when I get—fuck. I need to get back to work." I put my head in my hands. *Don't lose your shit, Ace.* I rub my eyes and look back at the gargoyles. "How did you find me?"

Jacques looks at me as if it's obvious. "You summoned us."

6

"I didn't summon anything," I insist. "I don't know how to."

"We heard you," Thomas says, and taps the side of his head. "In here."

Being able to telepathically communicate with the gargoyles is crazier than the dead vampires feet from me. "You heard me summon you?" I repeat, needing to hear it again.

"Not quite like that," Gilbert explains. "It's more like we could sense you were in danger."

"How?"

Jacques's brow furrows, and he considers his words before speaking. But as soon as he opens his mouth to talk, static comes through the radio.

"Shit," I say, and pull the walkie from my belt. "How the hell am I going to explain this?"

"You don't," Hasan says, and his gaze meets mine once more. His face is set, brows pushed together, but I see it again. There's something tender under his hard exterior, and I long to see more of it.

"I have to say something about the bodies out here. You said they were turned. So that means they're people. Missing and murdered people who could have families and friends and pets waiting to be fed at home. I can't just leave them."

"The people from our time were unaccepting of dark forces," Thomas starts. "From your reaction earlier, I think it's safe to say they still are."

"Yeah, they're not at all and are probably a lot less accepting now. We don't blame demons for half the problems people did back then." I bring the walkie to my face and tell whoever is contacting me I followed a dead lead and am on my way back.

I've never lied like this at work before.

"We will handle the vampires," Jacques says, putting his hand on my shoulder. His touch is warm and sends a pulse of heat through me, right to my core. "We've sworn an oath to do God's will. It is our duty."

"Right," I say, remembering the little history I know about Templar Knights. They fought in the name of Christianity, which is something I've struggled to get behind my entire life. If there really was a higher power, why does so much bad shit happen? I see the worst of humanity on a daily basis.

"Detective," Gilbert says slowly, looking into my eyes like he's trying to remember something. "You use clues to solve crimes, and you work for law enforcement."

"Yeah, that's right. How do you know?"

"I'm not sure." He closes his eyes for a few seconds. "It's almost like a memory. The red thing you got into. It's familiar."

"The red thing is a car." I rub my ice-cold hands together. Jacques steps behind me, sharing his warmth. "Some neurologists think we pick up on things around us while we sleep. People used to live in the house. They drove cars, talked, and probably watched a lot of TV. You would have heard life go on around you."

"TV?" Thomas questions.

"You still have a lot to learn."

"Go before they come," Hasan says, and his deep voice sends a jolt through me. "We'll handle this."

"You've done this before."

"Many times." His dark eyes meet mine. "Go."

"Meet me back at the house," I tell them. "And don't get seen."

Once again, I shove the shock aside and take off, wiping away as much blood as I can as I backtrack to the ravine. I carefully pick my way down it and then up again, finding my flashlight glowing on the ground where I dropped it. My gun is a few feet from it.

I pick off the wet leaves and shove it back in the holster on my waist. Composing myself the best I can for the second time tonight, I walk back to the active crime scene and bullshit a story about falling down the steep drop-off thanks to slippery footing.

I start to finish up everything I have to do before I can go home, feeling a ball of guilt start to form in my stomach. The CSI team is working hard. Tiffany left her young baby and new husband to get out here and take photos of the body.

Everyone is working tirelessly on the case, desperate to catch a killer that doesn't exist. I can't keep quiet forever, can I? What would I say?

Vampires are responsible for the killings and they attacked me, too, but don't worry, my gargoyle friends showed up and saved the day. Want evidence? Sorry, there is none, because the thousand-year-old friends I just mentioned are apparently experts on hiding bodies.

I'd be checked into a psych hospital faster than you can say *vampires actually fucking exist.*

"Ace!" Tiffany's voice rings out across the field. "Where have you been?"

"Sorry." I smooth out my hair, finding more wet leaves around the base of my neck. Regardless, I flip up my hood to try and hide the blood. "I went off following a lead. It was nothing."

"Take somebody with you next time." She shakes her head. "I do not want to photograph your dead body, you know."

I walk into the light and her eyebrows go up.

"What the fuck happened to you?"

"I slipped in wet leaves."

"You slipped and fell?"

"Yeah. Down a ravine with water at the bottom. Even I get clumsy every now and then." I know the subconscious indications people do when they are lying, and I make sure to not do a single one. "I'm freezing."

"I bet. I'm cold and I'm not wet and muddy. Go home before you get chilled."

I've been chilled for a while now. "I'm almost done. What about you?"

"I think I got all I can. The coroner is bagging up the body."

We walk back to the crime scene together, wrap up our work, and go to our cars. I'm parked near Tiffany.

"See you in the morning," she says with a small wave. "Unless there's another murder."

"Yeah, see you." I wave back. There won't be any murders. Now that I know who's behind this, I'm going to stop them.

I switch over my music from the '90s XM station I usually listen to and turn on a local radio station. Just in case anyone calls in to say they saw something large flying through the sky.

I've never been more thankful for my heated seats than I am right now, and I peel off the soaked raincoat and toss it in the back before I head to my apartment. It's a good thirty minutes from here and I know as soon as I walk through the doors I'm not going to want to leave.

Ever.

Because leaving means dealing, and dealing means accepting that everything I've fought for my whole life has been a lie. It's more than just that, and I'm working hard to keep the thoughts from rising to the surface. Though no matter how hard I try, I can't keep their faces from flashing before me.

Mom.

Dad.

Blood. Screaming. The horrible smell that until today I described as rotten eggs.

Sulfur.

The same way the vampires smelled. My parents weren't killed in a way that would make me think vampire—not even now—but I can't help but wonder, if vampires smell like sulfur, do other monsters?

EXHAUSTION HITS me when I step out of the shower. Finally warm, I twist my wet hair into a bun on top of my head and sit on the foot of my bed, resting my sore body for just a moment. It's nearing two AM and I got up yesterday at five-thirty for a run.

I pull on black leggings, tall socks, my favorite gray sweater, and then shove a blanket and clothes for tomorrow in a duffle bag. I zip it up, then decide I'd better bring extras just in case I get soaked again.

I fill another bag with snacks and bottles of water and wonder what the hell gargoyles eat. I myself am starving, and you can't go wrong with pizza, right? I phone in an order and head out.

I'm not sure what to expect when I pull up at the estate. The gargoyles showed up to help me, but does that make them trustworthy? I spend the entire drive thinking about it, as well as fighting a battle to steal a piece of pizza while driving. It smells so good and I haven't eaten since lunch.

My heart speeds up when I turn onto the gravel road and continues to beat rapidly the closer I get to the house. My hands threaten to tremble as I pull into the driveway and park near the house. I don't know what to expect, and I can't decide what I want.

The gargoyles back in their places, cast in stone once again?

The four of them sitting around the house, waiting for me?

I want one almost as much as I want the other, though I can't ignore the nagging inside of me, the part wanting the gargoyles to be there. I kill the engine, toss my keys in my bag, and get out. My gun is on my hip, and I've left my right hand free—just in case.

Smoke rises from the chimney and a soft glow from the fireplace emanates through the house. An odd sense of welcoming spreads through my chest, and suddenly it's like I can't get in the house fast enough.

I strap my bags over my shoulder and pick up the pizzas. Unsure of how many pizzas to get to feed four regular men, let alone four I-just-woke-up-from-a-thousand-year-curse types, I got four larges, figuring one for each. I'll steal two or three slices from someone.

The front door opens before I'm up the steps of the porch, and Gilbert's blue eyes glisten under the moonlight.

"What is that?" he asks, sniffing the air.

"Pizza."

"Can I eat it?"

"Yes," I laugh. "You can."

He steps aside, letting me through, then shuts and locks the door behind me. The same unexplainable sense of familiarity washes over me. I set down my bags in the foyer and carry the pizza into the large living room, then sit on the floor by the fire and set the boxes of pizza on the coffee table. This old house is drafty, and the small fire does little to warm it.

Hasan is standing across from me, looking out the window. A vision of him picking up the vampire like it was nothing flashes before me, and I can't help the wave of heat it brings pulsing through my body.

Thomas is standing near the fire, holding his hands out to the flames. He turns, looking at the boxes of pizza curiously.

"It's pizza," I explain, and scoot the coffee table closer to me. I don't want to move too far from the fire. "I assume you're hungry, right?"

"It's been so long since I felt hunger," Jacques says, crouching down next to me. I try not to stare at his ornate wings.

"It's been so long since I've felt a lot of other things," Thomas mutters to Gilbert, who snickers in response.

"You do eat, right?"

"Yes," Jacques tells me. "Of course we do."

"Well, I took a gamble on the pizza. The only thing I was going on was the fact you don't eat children. Pizza is a safe bet, most times. So are tacos, but the only decent Mexican restaurant is on the other side of town. And yes," I add before they can interject, "I know you have no idea what that is. I'll explain it all tomorrow. So come on, dig in." I open a box of pepperoni pizza and take a slice. "That means eat."

The four large gargoyles crowd around the small coffee table, curiously looking at the pizza.

"Sorry I didn't think to bring plates," I say. I've been single for so long it's easy to forget things like this. When I'd order a pizza at home, I'd keep it in the box and eat it while binging Netflix. Classy, I know. "You can just pick it up."

I pull apart four slices of pizza and hand one to each gargoyle. Feeling a little envious of tasting pizza for the first time ever, I watch them hesitantly take bites. It doesn't take long before they go back for seconds. And thirds. And fourths.

I eat two slices before I feel full, and I'm sure part of it is due to being so tired. I'm a three to four slices kinda girl.

"This is good," Thomas says. "Really fucking good."

I laugh. "Pizza is a favorite for a lot of people. Eat as much as you like. I assume you're hungry after not eating for years and years."

"Now that I'm eating, I feel the hunger again," Gilbert tells me. "It was there before, but dull. Now it's back."

"Uh, sorry?"

"No," Jacques says definitively. "Do not be sorry."

I wipe my hands on a napkin and lean back against the hearth, careful not to get my hair too close to the flames. "What does it feel like to be awake again?" I ask carefully, not knowing if I need to follow social norms before I bombard them with questions.

Jacques meets my eyes. "I have no sense of time when I'm asleep." He looks at the others. "Neither do they."

I just nod in response, studying the gargoyles. Compartmentalizing emotional or traumatic situations is a must in my line of work. I have to consciously turn it off and allow myself to feel sometimes. And right now, I'm struggling with whether I want to or not. Because on top of learning that magic and demons exist, I know in the back of my mind this has to be hard for the four men in front of me.

They were cursed to be monsters and just found out they missed a thousand years.

"Tired?" Hasan asks gruffly when he sees me yawn.

"Physically, yes. But I have so many questions."

He stiffens, assuming my questions are going to be directed at him and his brothers. Tough luck, buddy. If I'm the one who woke them, I deserve a sit-down round of Twenty Questions. Each. But I'll get to them later. As far as I know, they're not going to kill me or murder other innocent people. Priorities, right?

"Vampires," I start. "They don't look like they do in movies."

"Movies?" Hasan questions.

"I'll explain that another time. The vampires responsible for the murder in the park were taken care of, but that doesn't solve my problem, does it? You said they were young, meaning another, older vamp is out there turning humans, right?"

"Yes," Jacques answers.

"How do I kill them? Is decapitation the only way? What about a wooden stake through the heart? Silver bullets are for werewolves, right? And any idea where the, uh, sire would be hiding out?"

Thomas tips his head to Gilbert, trying hard not to smile. "You want to hunt down the sire and kill him. Yourself?" he asks.

"I'll do what I have to do." I sit up and rake my fingers through my damp hair again. I'm used to working alone, but I can't rip anyone apart—literally rip them apart—the way Hasan did. "I took an oath to protect the people in this town, and that's exactly what I'm going to do."

7

"You? On your own?" Gilbert's eyes narrow with concern, and for some crazy reason, I know it's genuine. "You could get hurt. You *did* get hurt."

"I know, and I'll be better prepared this time. Nothing throws you off your game like shoving a knife through someone's heart and having them not die. Trust me, I can handle myself."

"I'd like to see you handling yourself." Gilbert smiles, sky-blue eyes dancing in the firelight. Maybe I'm becoming delirious from sleep deprivation, but I swear his eyes are more vivid than before and his skin is more olive than gray.

"I'm a detective. That means I look for bad guys. So far, I've been good at my job. I catch the bad guys. I've spent the last few years taking on cases no one else would touch, cases some of the law's most respected cops swore to be cursed, and solved them, proving a human was behind the crime." I pull my shoulders in, suddenly cold again. "And now I can't help but think this...you guys...the vampires...it's all happening at the same time for a reason, and I'm not one to believe in fate or any of that shit."

"I understand," Jacques agrees quietly. "I too doubted fate until..." He trails off, looking away. I notice a long scar running down the back of his neck, disappearing behind his wings. "You should rest, my lady. The sun will be rising soon."

"Yeah," I agree, and roll my neck.

"Sore?" Thomas asks.

"You could say so."

He flashes a cocky grin. "I can help you with that."

I swallow hard, fanning the rising heat inside of me. "I'm sure you could." The image of his hands on me flashes before my mind's eye, and the smoldering heat threatens to turn into flames.

"I have to work in the morning," I mumble. "I don't think I'll be able to sleep with...with..." *With you here.* "With knowing there are more vampires out there."

"We'll keep you safe."

I look into his deep, dark eyes. "I know," I say, and despite everything inside me telling me not to trust him, I do.

"The bedroom upstairs," he starts, and a shiver goes down my spine at the thought of us going into the bedroom together. "Will that suffice? It has a fireplace."

"The couch is fine." I eyeball the small sofa. "And the fire is already going down here. I'd rather not use any more furniture for kindling. I'll, uh, get some firewood in the morning. I brought a blanket for myself." I have no idea how clean the bedsheets are upstairs. I'm by no means a neat freak, but the thought of sleeping in God-knows-whose bed skeeves me out. "Are you guys tired? I'd think a thousand-year nap would tide you over for a while, right?"

"We'll rest in the morning," Jacques says.

"Okay," I tell him, and get up to use the bathroom and get my bags. By the time I'm back in the living room, only Jacques remains. The couch has been scooted closer to the fire, with the dust cover pulled off and messily folded on the floor beside it. I wrap my blanket around my shoulders and sit on the couch, adjusting my alarm for the morning. There's no way I'm working out, but I'm farther from the station.

"It's a phone," I tell Jacques, who's looking over my shoulder at the glowing screen.

"What does it do?"

"A lot of stuff. Want to see it?"

His dark eyes narrow ever so slightly. "Yes." He strides over, folding his wings at his back, and sits on the couch. I turn my head, taking him all in and wondering if it's uncomfortable to have his wings scrunched up like that.

"So this is a phone. Technically, a phone is something you can call someone on, but now phones do so much more than that.

Your voice goes through and gets converted, then transmitted as radio waves to the nearest tower."

Jacques's blank stare lets me know I made the right career choice by becoming a cop instead of a teacher. He moves his head closer and my heart speeds up. He might be part monster, but he's also a man. A very attractive, half-naked man who's sitting very close to me. I blink and turn back to my phone, hoping he can't see the blood rushing to my cheeks.

"We call it technology," I start again.

"Like the lights in the house instead of lanterns."

"Right. And just wait until you take a shower. Indoor plumbing will blow your mind."

"Blowing is a good thing?"

I fight the urge to snicker. "In this sense, yes. It means shock you in a good way."

His eyes go to the phone. "You can contact anyone with that?"

"As long as they have a phone and you have their number, yes. I'm guessing your form of communication was handwritten letters, right?"

Jacques nods.

"Now we call it texting, and you send it right away. It's instant."

"Instant?"

"Sometimes there might be a few seconds' delay, but yeah. You write your message, hit send, and the recipient gets it."

He gets a weird look in his eyes, like he's reliving a painful memory. I put the phone down, deciding that was enough of a reverse history lesson for one night anyway. I lean back and yawn.

"Where are the others?" I ask.

"Guarding the house."

"Why aren't you?"

"I'm guarding you."

I want to tell him I don't need to be guarded, that I'm not some damsel that needs to be protected or rescued. But my voice dies in my throat and I want to squirm away from his intensity.

Because I find it so damn attractive.

"I can hold my own," I say when I can finally muster up my voice.

"I believe you can. Not many humans can stand up to vampires and live to tell the tale."

"If you hadn't shown up, I don't think I would have. Speaking of...you said I summoned you. But I didn't."

"There is powerful magic tied into this curse. Somehow you've tapped into that power. Maybe it's like those radio waves you were talking about." A smile pulls up his full lips, making him look all the more human.

"Maybe." I pull the blanket tighter around my shoulders.

"Are you still cold?"

"A bit. It's like the cold seeped into my bones. Ugh, bones. That just reminded me of the vampires." I shake my head. "It's all so weird."

"It was weird when I first learned of it, too." He slowly opens his wings behind him and moves over. "Here. It will keep you warm."

I sit up, eyeing the wing with curiosity. "It won't hurt if I lean on it?"

"No."

I carefully lean in closer and move against him, almost tucking myself in between his body and his wing.

"Thank you." I look up at him.

"You're welcome." He turns his head and moment our eyes meet, he looks away. A slight flush comes to his cheeks. "You should try to get some sleep. You'll need your strength again soon, I'm sure."

"Because I'll fight more vampires." I shake my head at how weird that sounds. "You said it was hard when you realized you weren't human anymore," I say quietly. It's hard imagining myself in his situation, waking up and not being me anymore. "I'm...I'm sorry."

He looks at me, surprised. "Why are you sorry?"

I shrug. "It's not fair that happened to you. It had to be scary."

He swallows hard and drops the walls around he keeps up. "No, it's not fair. And yes, I was scared when I realized what happened." He lets out a sigh of relief, as if it's the first time he admitted it to anyone and the confession is freeing. Carefully, I reach over and take his hand.

It's weird—and probably wrong—to let myself have feelings for this strange man, but I can't help it. Jacques curls his fingers through mine, and for the first time since I woke him up, he relaxes. Resting my head on his shoulder, I'm certain there's no way I'll be able to fall asleep tonight.

My alarm sounds, and I jolt awake. The last thing I remember was Jacques taking me under his wing—literally—and closing my eyes for just a second. Well, that *just a second* turned into a few hours, and unfortunately, a few hours was all the sleep I'm getting before going into work.

Rubbing my eyes, I sit up. My body hurts and my head throbs, reminding me that a vampire threw a rock at me.

A vampire.

Right. Everything really happened...didn't it?

"Guys?" I call out, and my voice echoes through the large house. The clouds left overnight, and bright morning sun fills the room. The fire has gone out, and the air around me is cold. Holding the blanket at my shoulders, I move from the couch.

"Jacques?" I call as I go straight to the front door. I have a feeling I know where the gargoyles are. I unlock the door and step onto the frost-covered porch, looking at the backs of Thomas's and Gilbert's large frames.

Ignoring my cold feet, I pad my way out to look at them. From the little gargoyle lore I know, the sun turns them to stone. But I thought I awakened them and lifted part of the curse? Reaching up, I gently touch the wound on my head.

Everything did happen. I'm sure of it. I'm not crazy. I remember it all too vividly. The fear I felt when the vampires chased me. The way the knife pierced the vamp's heart.

Jacques's wing curled around me, keeping me warm.

I flick my eyes up, and it's all I need to ease my mind. Jacques and Hasan are back on the roof, but the pained expression is gone from Jacques's face.

"I don't know if you can hear me," I say, looking from one gargoyle to the other. "But I have to go to work. I'll be back tonight." I put my hand on Thomas's wrist, looking into his eyes for a moment before going back in.

I rush to get ready for work, knowing I'm going to need to stop for coffee on the way. Today is going to drag since I'm running on just a few hours of sleep. I remote-start my car before I get in, feeling the chill come back already. Needing to make a note in my phone so I don't forget, I remind myself to find someone to come out and make sure the fifty-year-old furnace is in working order before I fire it up and burn the whole house down.

My car bumps down the gravel driveway, and a weird sense of disappointment builds inside me. I don't want to leave the house. Well, technically what's *on* the house. I'm curious about the gargoyles, but it's more than that and there's no way I can deny it to myself forever.

Jacques has the sexy, broody thing going on strong, Hasan is all muscle and oh-so easy on the eyes, and Thomas and Gilbert have that cocky charm and old-world swagger down to a science. It's like everything I could want in a man divided up and put into four very different bodies.

But they aren't men. Not anymore.

8

"Good morning, Ace," the police captain says as I walk through the office.

"Morning." I look up and smile, sipping my second coffee of the day already.

"Come into my office when you have a minute."

"Sure," I tell him, and, for the first time, I feel nervous. I'm not exactly a rule follower by nature; I don't believe all laws are to our benefit, but I've never come close to doing anything at work that would require being reprimanded. But last night I did several.

Regretting chugging so much coffee, I set my mug down at my desk and take off my coat, hanging it on the back of my chair. I pull the case files from my bag and toss them on my desk, then make a quick trip to the bathroom before going to see what Captain Harris wants to talk about.

"Hey, Ace." Tiffany comes out of the lab, passing me in the hall. "One hell of a night, right?"

"Tell me about it." I rarely wear my hair down. It gets in the way, especially when I'm leaning over dead bodies. But this morning I'd left it hanging loose around my face for a reason, though I'm stressed and tired and temporarily forget the reason.

Out of habit, I push my hair back behind my ear, gathering it all in one hand and bringing it over one shoulder.

"Jesus, Ace, what happened?" Tiffany's blue eyes widen.

"Is it that bad?" I ask, wrinkling my nose. The tear in my skin is hidden behind my hair, but the bruising is clearly visible along my temple.

She steps in and parts my hair, looking at the wound. "What happened?"

Usually a good liar, I struggle in that moment. I don't want to lie to my friend. "I fell."

"Again?"

Again? When did I—oh, right. I told her I slipped and fell down the ravine. "Yes. I went back to that house I inherited last night because I left something there. The stone steps on the porch are slippery when wet. I found that out the hard way."

The best lies are the simplest ones, which is where a lot of people mess up. They think spinning something elaborate makes their story sound more legitimate, but it does the opposite. Details get harder to remember.

"Please tell me you got this checked out."

I guilty-shrug. "It was late and I wanted to go home. I'm fine."

"You could be concussed. That's a nasty-looking cut."

"I know. But I'm fine, really."

Her brow furrows. "If you say so." She doesn't look convinced, and I know it's just as hard to fool a crime scene photographer as it is me. Tiffany notices details. I fake a smile and make my way into the captain's office.

"You wanted to see me, sir?" I hesitate in the doorway, not sure if I should close the door or not.

"Yes, come in."

He doesn't say to shut the door, so I don't. Maybe he doesn't know my gargoyle friends ripped the heads off three vampires last night after all.

God, I sound crazy.

"I want you taking the lead on these murders," he says, and opens a laptop. "Word has gotten out on social media about a victim whose blood was drained from 'strange bite marks,' and now we have a swarm of people crying vampire." He rolls his eyes. "We need to shut this down."

They're right. "Yes, the sooner the better. Was the post taken down?"

"It was as soon as I became aware of it, but not before screen shots were taken and shared."

"Oh, of course."

"And let's try and keep this as discrete as we can. The brutality of the murder has people in enough of a panic. If word gets out there was a similar murder the day before, they're going to be crying serial killer before we can confirm it."

It's not just one serial killer, and it's much worse. I look at my boss, a respected man of the law with years of war combat under his belt, and wonder what he'd do if I told him the absolute truth.

Laugh and think I'm joking, most likely. Then send me for a mental health evaluation when I keep a straight face. And then it hits me that even when I do find the master vamp and shove a wooden stake through its non-beating heart, I'll still have an unsolved case.

"Right," I agree. "We can't have that. I'll get right on it."

"I know you will." He dismisses me with a curt nod and I do my best to keep my cool as I walk away, going back to my desk and sitting heavily in my chair. A new headache forms on top of the one I already have. Allowing myself ten seconds, I put my head in my hands and close my eyes, taking a slow, deep breath.

This isn't a normal case, and I can't go about it the normal way, even though my norm is pretty damn effective at solving crimes. I already know the motive: the baby vamps are hungry and need to eat.

I pull up a Word doc on my computer. Finding it neater, I usually take digital notes. But for this, I don't want any sort of electronic fingerprint left behind. I pull an old notebook from my desk drawer, flip halfway through until I find a blank page, and start writing out notes. I don't have much to go on and won't be able to talk to the gargoyles until tonight when they wake up.

I start with what I do know: the victims. Finding similarities is something normal, and something I task out for the time being. We know who they are. But what we don't know is who the vampires are. *Were.* They might be responsible for the murders, but they're victims, too. Something killed them. Turned them.

Thinking back to last night, I recall the vampires. It was dark and I was certain I was going to die. My memories of them are fuzzy, and I close my eyes to try and recall their faces.

Red eyes.

Fangs.

The stench of sulfur.

I rub my temples. *Come on, Ace...there has to be something.*

Brown hair. Not one was more than a few inches taller than my five-foot-six-inch frame. They all appeared to be in their early twenties. I log onto the computer and pull up missing persons reports, and search for men aged eighteen to twenty-five, under six feet, and with brunette hair. A handful come up, and I flip through the reports until I see a familiar face.

Bryan Porter. Reported missing by his mother two weeks ago.

My chest tightens. I hit him over the head with a rock and then plunged a knife through his heart. Hasan ripped his head off and I felt relief.

I wish I could think of them as faceless monsters, but the baby vampires are just as much victims as the bodies we found yesterday. I close my eyes in a long blink and look away for a moment before reading the rest of the report. He went missing after coming home from college over spring break. He's twenty-three and working on getting his master's degree in social work. His mother reported seeing him the afternoon before and didn't think much when he didn't come home one night since he was going out with friends and often stayed with a "lady friend" after a night out at the bar.

She called him the next morning to tell him she had leftovers in the fridge and went to work. When she still hadn't heard from him throughout the day, she began to worry and called the police. It was too early to file an official report, and she was brushed off until the "right" amount of time passed.

A ball of dread starts to form in my stomach. I've told mothers about their murdered children before. I've informed parents their precious child has carried out horrific crimes. Yeah, it's hard, and yes, it gets to me. But I compartmentalize. It's part of the job.

But this…how the hell do I handle this? Mandy Porter will forever hold onto hope her son will come home. Which, again, isn't different than a good number of other family members who filed the rest of these missing persons reports, but I know what happened to Bryan. And I can never tell her.

I go through the rest of the missing persons files, trying to ID another vampire. I find another who's a possibility—he's been missing for nearly a month—and try to make connections between the rest of the missing men. I print out files that could be of interest and arrange them on my desk in order of when they were reported missing.

I look them over, sighing. Brunette hair and being of average height might just be a coincidence and I'm wasting my time.

Speaking of time...I add up the remaining hours until sunset. I could sit and fire questions at the gargoyles all day about the curse, how I'm connected, why did whoever cursed them choose gargoyles over turning them into frogs...but I need to stay focused on the vampires, starting with Bryan.

"You think he's gonna be next?" Officer Beasley's voice almost startles me. I get jumpy when I'm tired.

"What?" I look up, blinking from the bright sunlight streaming in from the windows behind him.

"Those reported missing. You think they're gonna be the next victims?"

In some sense or another. "Maybe. Want to cover all bases."

"Right. Good thinking." He smiles. "I'm headed to get myself a cup of coffee. Do you want anything?"

"Thanks, but I'm already on cup number two. I probably shouldn't have any more."

He laughs. "Yeah, it's early for two cups." He hesitates, waiting for me to say something else. I'm not the most social person, but I try, and I'm usually good at it. Being able to read people and acting in accordance to how they expect me to act is a talent that comes in handy in my line of work.

But right now, I don't have time for this. Vampires are out there, murdering innocent people. Beyond that, an older vampire is taking people off the streets and turning them into killers.

Officer Beasley mutters an awkward goodbye, and I go back to work. An hour later, I've still got nothing. Since I'm waiting on the full lab and toxicology report to come back on our most recent victim, I grab Bryan's report and get in my car, driving half an hour away to Mrs. Porter's house.

My heart is in my throat as I walk up the porch steps. I've done this before and never felt nervous. I've never flat-out lied like this before. I've kept the truth, stretched a few details before, but it was all for the sake of the case.

I ring the bell and step back. A minute passes and I think no one is home. I turn to leave, and then hear the lock click back.

"Can I help you?" someone inside says, opening the door only two inches.

I hold up my badge. "I'm Detective Bisset. Are you—"

"Is this about Bryan?" The door swings open and who I'm guessing is Mrs. Porter steps out. "Did you find him?" Her eyes fill with tears.

"No," I lie. *I not only found him, but I also fought him off, bashed his head in, stabbed him in the heart, and then somehow summoned my new friends to come protect me and rip your son's head clean off his body.* "But I think he might be connected to a case I'm working on and wondered if you had a few minutes to answer some questions."

"Yes," she says, and steps back, opening the door. My heart aches for this poor woman, and I hate how I can never tell her what happened. Even if she did believe me, I can't imagine what it would do to her to know her son was murdered, turned into a vampire, and then became a murderer himself. "Come in."

We move inside and she motions to a couch in the living room. I pull a notebook and pen from my bag and take a seat.

"I read over the report," I start, "but was hoping you could give me your recollections of the last time you saw him again."

She takes a deep breath and nods, blinking rapidly to keep the tears from coming. Fuck, I hate this.

"It was Wednesday afternoon. I came home from work for lunch and he was here. I made him and myself a sandwich and sat with him while we ate. He mentioned going out with friends that night, and not to wait up for him. When he didn't come home, I assumed he had stayed the night with Rebecca."

"Who's Rebecca?"

"An old girlfriend. They had a bit of a Ross-and-Rachel situation going on, and he ran into her earlier that week. I called on my way to work, not expecting an answer since it was early. But by ten o'clock...I knew something was wrong. He's a good kid. He checks in, especially when he's home from school like this." She breaks down, and I give her a few minutes to collect herself before pressing on.

"Did you talk to Rebecca?"

"Yes, and she never saw him that night. They were supposed to meet for drinks, but he never showed."

"What about the friends he went out with?"

"They were at the same bar with Rebecca. He...he never made it."

"Do you mind if I had a look in his room?"

Mrs. Porter wipes away her tears. "No, I don't mind if you think it'll help." She leads me down the hall into his room. "I haven't touched anything. It makes me feel like he'll come home this way." She stands in the threshold, unable to step foot into her son's room. "I just want my baby back."

I can't get him back, but I can stop the undead asshole who turned him. Going into work-mode, I look around the room. The bed is unmade and clothes lie in a heap on the floor. An open suitcase is in front of the dresser, with clothes and shoes spilling out. At first glance, nothing seems out of the ordinary.

And then I notice the folded piece of red paper that's fallen between the nightstand and the bed. Carefully, I pull it out and unfold it. The word "Delirium" is at the top, in bold letters. It's a flyer for the bar, advertising "half-off hump-day drinks."

I've never been to Delirium, but it's a bit notorious with the law. Gothic-themed, dark, and hosting interesting party nights, the place has been of concern to us as cops because it's rumored people go there to buy drugs and hook up in the private rooms in the back. It's been looked into a time or two before, but nothing has come out of it.

The owners—three brothers from Russia—pay their rent and utilities on time, keep everything up to code, and have all the proper licenses to run the place. They've never given anyone any trouble, and pay their employees nearly double the standard rate.

I take a photo of the flyer, look around for a few more minutes, then head out to leave. I get Rebecca's number from Mrs. Porter, trying as hard as I can not to externalize the guilt I'm feeling for lying to her, and call Rebecca as soon as I'm in my car.

She's at work but can talk, which is good news. It's also good news that she works at a coffee shop. I'm feeling that lack of sleep again, which doesn't make sense now that I think about it. There have been many nights where I was up late working, or binging something on Netflix, staying up three or four episodes past my bedtime. It sucks, but I drink coffee, get my shit together, and I'm okay.

Right now, I feel like I'm coming down with something and it zapped all my energy. I inhale deeply, taking in a lungful of crisp air, and mentally shake myself. I have to stay on my game.

The Starbucks where Rebecca works is twenty minutes away. The early morning rush has come and gone, and I get in line behind the two people in front of me. I order a white chocolate mocha with an extra shot of espresso and ask the barista to get Rebecca.

She's the manager and is in the back. I take a seat by the counter and wait for both my coffee and Rebecca. My coffee comes first.

I log onto Delirium's Facebook page, looking through photos and lists of people who've checked into the location. I mentally roll my eyes at every single one of them. Just go ahead and make it easy to be stalked, why don't you? It's almost as bad as posting you're going on vacation and leaving behind an empty house.

"Detective Bisset?"

I look up, finding a timid-looking young woman standing near the table. Her hair is dark black streaked with red, pulled back into a perfect French braid. Her ears are full of piercings and her hazel eyes are lined in heavy black pencil.

"Yes, please have a seat, Rebecca," I say, eyes going to her name tag. "Thank you for meeting with me."

"Of course. Did you find…"

"No," I once again lie. "I'm working on a lead and have just a few questions."

She takes a seat, holding her arms in close to her body. She's nervous, which isn't unusual. People who are completely innocent with nothing to hide still get nervous when talking to cops. With all the shit we've been given on social media lately, I can't say I blame them.

"Bryan's mother told me he was supposed to meet you Wednesday night at a bar."

"Yeah. We were going to The Grasshopper. He was supposed to meet me there around eleven."

"Did you talk to him beforehand?"

She nods and spins a ring around on her finger. "We'd texted throughout the day. The last text I got from him was about seven. I was working here until we closed and didn't get to check my phone right away. He said he might be late."

"Did you text him back?"

"Yeah. A few times. Then I called him and when he didn't answer, I got kinda mad and thought he was brushing me off again. He does that a lot, which is why we keep breaking up."

I nod, trying to analyze her. "Have you heard of a bar called Delirium?"

"The vampire bar? Yeah. Everyone's heard of it."

"Do you think Bryan would go to it?"

"It's not really his thing, if you know what I mean."

I set my coffee down. "Enlighten me."

"I've never been, but I've heard people go there to, you know… have sex with vampires."

"Vampires?"

"People dressed up as vampires. One of my friends likes to go there and—oh, uh, I forget."

"Look," I say, and lean forward. "As long as your friend isn't selling organs on the black market, I don't care what sort of freaky things he or she is into."

Rebecca nods. "She said if you pay extra, they'll bite you. Until you bleed." If I'd spoken to her last week, I'd brush off the paid vampire sex as a fetish thing. But now that I've seen vampires with my own two eyes...

She wrinkles her nose. "I don't get it, but, I mean, some people are into that, and the whole vampire thing is taken seriously at Delirium." Letting out a shuddering breath, she looks back into my eyes. "Was Bryan there?"

"I found a bar flyer in his room. I'm considering all options right now." I pull a card from my pocket. "If you think of anything else, please give me a call."

"I will." She takes my business card, and tears fill her eyes. "Please find him."

It's like part of me dies at that moment, and the reality of living a double life hits me like a wooden stake to the heart. It's been less than twenty-four hours since I learned that demons and magic exist.

And I hate it already.

9

I set my phone down and lean back on my couch. I've been home for only half an hour, and have been on the phone the whole time, setting up appointments to get the old house in working order. Someone is coming to check out the furnace tomorrow, another to clean out the chimneys the week after, and I left a message with an electrician to check on the old wiring.

The thought of paying for all that makes me cringe, but taking care of things properly has always been the way I roll. And I'd rather not have the furnace burst into flames or die from toxic fumes filling the fireplace. Rubbing my temples, I lean back on the couch, pulling a blanket up from the floor. The sun is setting soon, and I need to pack a bag, get food, and find a place that sells firewood.

I'll get up in one minute, after I rest my eyes for just a moment. I don't mean to drift off to sleep, but I do. My dream takes me to a weird and foreign place, where I'm running over rocky ground.

Rain falls around me, and red eyes glow from the trees in the forest behind me.

Time is running out, and though I don't know what's going to happen, dream-Ace does, and she's desperate to get to him before it's too late. The vampires emerge from the trees. There are hundreds and there's no way I can escape.

Something flies overhead, making the vampires slink back. Strong arms wrap around me, lifting me off the ground and out of harm's way. I don't need to look up to know it's Jacques. There's something familiar about his touch, about the way his arms fit around me perfectly.

He's held me like this before.

We fly over a lake, past an unkept field, and land on the edge of a cliff. He takes my hand, leading me into the woods to a small cabin. His large wings hardly fit through the door. As soon as he's in, his monstrous appearance gives way and he's a man.

Just a man.

A good-looking, half-naked man, and the dream sets the perfect mood.

"Braeya," he breathes, taking me by the waist. This is why his touch felt familiar. We *have* done this before. My arms fasten around his neck, and he leans in, putting his lips on mine. The kiss burns all the way through me, making my heart skip a beat and warmth tingle between my thighs.

We fall back on blankets laid before the fireplace, and Jacques moves on top of me, pulling the laces on my bodice. So many emotions surge through me, with the main one being lust.

But I also feel sadness, both his and my own. And overwhelming longing starts to take over, to have him sexually and to just be together. Slowly, he unlaces the bodice until it falls to the sides and pulls the chemise under it down. Licking his lips, he looks down at my bare breasts. I feel his cock begin to harden against me, and heat grows inside of me.

Bringing his head down, he takes my breast in his mouth, tongue flicking over my nipple. I moan softly and buck my hips, pressing myself against his hardness. His mouth goes to mine again, kissing me harder than before. The feeling that time is running out presses down on me again, and I put my hands on his chest, moving him away.

He sits up and I move, shoving him back onto the blankets. I hike up my skirts, part my legs, and straddle him, hands going to the tie on his pants. Keeping my eyes on his, I move his pants down, freeing his large cock. I look down at it, body aching to have him inside me.

I run my hands up the smooth shaft of his cock and move down, taking him in my mouth, licking the salty pre-cum from the tip and sucking him hard. Jacques groans with pleasure, reaching down and taking a tangle of my hair in his fingers. I cup his balls in one hand and take him in as deep as I can, then move up and swirl my tongue over the tip. His breathing quickens and I feel his balls tighten in my hand. I suck hard again as he comes, swallowing everything he gives me.

Wiping my mouth, I lie back, craving my lover. Jacques swiftly removes my skirts and rolls me over onto my stomach. Starting with my shoulders, he massages his way down, then runs one hand over my ass until his fingers sweep over my clit.

Pleasure explodes from his touch. I'm so turned on. I need him. Now. His gentle touch gives way and he flips me over and parts my legs, bringing his face to my pussy. His tongue lashes out against me and I moan loudly. He closes his mouth around me and sucks, while at the same time rapidly flicking his tongue over my clit.

I've never felt anything like it. The pleasure builds inside me, winding so tight I know it's going to feel fucking amazing when it finally springs free. He puts a finger inside me, finding my G-spot right away. He presses, rubs, and I'm just about to—

My phone rings, jolting me awake. I'm disoriented, having to look around to remind myself where I am, and turned on. It's been a long time since I've been with a man, and I crave the touch as much as that girl from my dream.

Braeya. It's not the first time I heard the name spoken from Jacques's lips, and—oh my god. I just had a sex dream about a gargoyle. Heat rises to my cheeks, but it's in second place compared to the heat that's still going strong a little lower. Dammit. Why did I wake up?

Oh, right. Phone. Shit. I really am out of it.

I reach over and pick my phone up from the coffee table. I have a missed call and a message from work. Sitting up and working hard to ignore the way my jeans are rubbing me in just the right way, I hit play on the message.

It's Samantha from the lab, telling me the reports are in on our victim from last night and I'll want to call as soon as possible to hear. I stand, still feeling like I'm in a fog, and go into the kitchen. I've had vivid dreams before, but this felt more like a memory.

I call Sam back and go into my small bedroom, getting another overnight bag ready for myself.

"Hey, Ace," she says in her usual upbeat tone. The girl is way too peppy for someone who slices open murdered bodies on an almost daily basis. "You got a minute?"

"I do. What's going on with my vic?"

"Dude. It's weird." I can hear her moving around the lab in the background. "So, official cause of death is blood loss. Looks like he's been slowly bleeding for a week. The puncture wounds on his neck are all in various stages of healing. They're bite marks, and we got different hits on human saliva. If I didn't know better, I'd say someone took fang-banging a little too far."

"What about the bones?"

"You mean the lack thereof? That's even weirder. They were chewed from his arms. The flesh was cut along his inner arm, a relatively clean cut, but not clean enough to make me think it was done by a surgeon or anything. The skin was peeled back, muscles and tendons torn. And the teeth marks on the bone: human."

I'm not surprised, because I knew that's how vampires work. "We've gone past weird to fucked up," I say.

"Right? I don't even know where to start with this one."

I do, and I already have a good idea where to go next. "Yeah, it's a mess."

"You're telling me. I'm going to run some tests on the newest vic and see if I can get any DNA matches. I'll call you if I get a match."

"Thanks, Samantha." I hang up and close my eyes again. Images from the dream flash before me. "Stop it, Ace," I mutter to myself. I need a shower. A cold one. Or maybe a hot bath, take care of myself and get it out of my system.

Unless that makes it worse.

I PLUNGE my hands into the warm soapy water and scrub a plate. The old estate doesn't have a dishwasher, and though the dishes in the cabinets looked clean, they've been collecting dust for years. While I'm not a clean-freak by any means, giving the dishes a quick wash before I use them is a must.

Leaving a stack of clean dishes to dry on the counter, I check the time on my phone. It's seven-fifteen, minutes away from sunset. I rushed to get here in time and arrived not long ago. Feeling restless, I needed to do something productive other than sit around and wait for the sun to go down.

Plus, my mind kept drifting back to that stupid dream. Which is all it was: a dream. I've had my fair share of sex dreams. They're usually about celebrities or some fictional guy I read about in a book. I wake up hot and bothered, reach into my nightstand drawer and pull out the trusty B.O.B., and give myself a quick orgasm—or two, if I'm being honest—then go back to sleep.

I dry my hands and go onto the porch, walking up and down the path in front of the old house, feeling a bit anxious and nervous. I know next to nothing about these creatures, yet here I am, waiting for them to awaken. My gun is loaded and strapped to my hip, just in case, but I don't think I'll need it.

They helped me last night when they didn't have to. And I feel… something. Something I can't explain. A bond? It's stupid and doesn't make sense. Though nothing about this makes sense.

I spend my time waiting for the sun to set searching through social media, using hashtags commonly associated with the Delirium crowds. I scroll past selfie after selfie, sighing. If Bryan was at Delirium on Wednesday, he's not in the background of any of these pictures.

A timer goes off on my phone, letting me know it's officially sunset. I stand in front of the porch steps, staring at Gilbert and Thomas.

Nothing happens.

"Guys?" I ask, and raise my arm, reaching for Thomas. The energy in the air shifts the moment my fingers make contact with the smooth stone. It's warm again, like human flesh. An electric spark jolts me, and I jerk my hand back.

A tiny crack in the stone starts to form in the center of his chest, webbing out with impressive speed. A piece of rock crumbles to the ground, disappearing in a cloud of dust as soon as it lands.

I stand back, watching with wide eyes as the rest of the rock crumbles, giving way to the man behind the stone. The hideous, demonic sneer on his face falls apart, revealing Thomas's handsome face. He blinks dust from his eyes and stands tall to stretch.

"Acelina," he says, and my name rolls off his tongue like velvet. He jumps down, wings opening to slow the landing. "Wasn't sure if you'd be back."

"Why wouldn't I be?"

He gives me that famous cocky grin and shrugs. "I thought maybe you'd find us too grotesque."

Gilbert jumps down next to him and brushes dust from his dirty blond hair. I look each brother over slowly.

"Actually, you aren't." I narrow my eyes. "You look more…more human than yesterday."

Thomas turns to Gilbert. "You don't look any different to me. Still ugly. Maybe you can get a pity fuck from the blind whores at the brothel."

"Shut up, we both know I've always been the pretty one," Gilbert quips.

"There are no brothels anymore," I tell them. "And most people get cured from chlamydia before they go blind. I thought Templar Knights took vows of chastity."

"Oh, we did." Thomas gives me that grin again and dammit, it's doing bad things to me right now. "Doesn't mean we upheld them." He takes another step toward me, biting his bottom lip. He knows exactly what he's doing and how good he looks doing it. "How's your head?"

He pushes my hair back, deft fingers sweeping over my skin, making me shiver. He looks at the wound and lets his hand fall down my neck and over my collarbone. I really want him to break some vows with me right now.

Dust falls from the roof, and Jacques and Hasan jump, gliding down. They, too, look more human than before, with their skin being more of its natural color, and shortened claws.

"Ace," Jacques says, and his eyes meet mine. He's looking at me the same way he did in the dream, when I was someone named Braeya. I step back, finding him too close for comfort.

"Good morning," I say awkwardly. "I brought food. It's inside."

"I like this one," Thomas whisper-talks to his brother. "She has her priorities in order."

I roll my eyes and motion to the door. "Then get your asses inside before the food gets cold." They step aside, letting me in first. "I got Mexican food today, though I skipped the margaritas. I'm not much of a drinker, though the last twenty-four hours have been almost enough to turn me into an alcoholic."

I turn and am greeted with blank stares from all four gargoyles. To be fair, not a lot of people get my sense of humor to begin with.

"Do you even feel hungry?" I ask, going into the living room.

"Yes," Thomas tells me, cracking that smirk again. I think he knows he looks damn good when he does it. "And I'm feeling other things I think you can help with."

Jacques narrows his eyes ever so slightly in Thomas's direction, causing Gilbert to snicker at his brother getting scolded.

"Use your upstairs brain," I retort, and open a Styrofoam box full of tacos. "And eat, because we have work to do."

"Work?" Hasan curiously pokes at a taco.

"The vampires. I need to find them and I need to kill them. I have a theory on how they're picking their victims, albeit a rough, not-based-on-any-proof theory that I'm going to look into. Though I'm still not sure how to kill them. You didn't give me a straight answer yesterday. Do I need to cut their heads off? What about sunlight? Having them burn into a pile of ash would be too easy, right? I've never dumped a body before."

I can feel the collective incredulous stare. "What?" Turning my head up, I look at each gargoyle.

"They almost killed you yesterday." Jacques, who's standing next to the chair I'm sitting in, turns, large wings brushing against the wall, and moves my hair back. "You're still hurt."

"It's not as bad as it looks." I shrug off his touch, hating and loving how familiar it feels at the same time. It was just a dream, but it's like he really had his head buried between my legs an hour ago.

"Going after the vampires is what you want to do?" Gilbert questions, and I know they are all wondering the same thing.

"Look," I start. "I know there are a lot of questions, with the biggest one still being *what the fuck,* but people's lives are at stake here. I have to find the vampire nest and get to the sire. I don't want to be forced to lie to another mother about why her son has gone missing."

Hasan's stance changes and he looks at me with what I can only describe as respect. "What is your theory?"

"There's a bar in town called Delirium. It's vampire-themed, and, until yesterday, I thought it was just a hangout for people with an undead fetish."

One of Hasan's eyebrows goes up and I sigh.

"A bar is a place people go to drink alcohol and a fetish is sexually enjoying something kind of weird."

"People enjoy sex with vampires?" Thomas asks, reaching over the table for another taco. He and Gilbert are the only ones who sat down. Hasan and Jacques seem on guard.

"Not with real vampires. After seeing—and smelling—those baby vamps, I don't think they'd go for the real deal. Vampires have been romanticized a lot and some people are into being bitten. There are some pretty realistic fake fangs you can wear nowadays, too."

Thomas parts his lips, showing off his fangs. "Do you like being bitten?"

Blood rushes through me, but I'll be damned before I let him know he's throwing me off guard. I haven't had a boyfriend in a long time. There's no denying the physical attraction I'm feeling to the guys, but it's more than that. And I like it even less than how attractive I find them.

I don't want to have romantic feelings for them. It won't end will for my heart.

"I prefer to do the biting." I twist the cap off my water bottle and look back up at Hasan. "I was able to identify one of the vampires. I think he went to the bar the night he disappeared. It's obvious, I know, but what's better than hiding in plain sight? Especially when the world doesn't believe you exist." I lower my eyes. "You guys did. You spent years on the house and no one blinked an eye over it."

"Your theory has merit," Jacques says, finally picking up a taco.

"Thanks," I tell him, and notice a long, thin scar on his hip, just like the one in the dream. I noticed it yesterday. I had to. "I didn't get good enough looks at the other vampires to properly ID them, but I did bring a stack of missing persons files for you to look through. If I can get names for the other vampires, I can see if they were at the bar, too."

"And if they were?"

I look into Jacques's deep, chocolate eyes, knowing all four of them will object. "Then I'll go."

"You could be walking into a trap."

I take a drink of water and set the bottle on the table. "I know."

10

"What if you get hurt?" Gilbert asks.

"Then I get hurt." I grab my water again. "I don't want to force you to do something you don't want to do. But I..." Admitting I need help isn't my forte. I'm used to going at things alone, and even more used to having to prove myself. It doesn't make sense and I know it, but I've developed the unhealthy habit of thinking asking for help means I'm weak. "But I need to know how to kill the vampires."

"Wooden stake through the heart," Thomas blurts, and the others look at him with annoyance. "What?" He shrugs and goes for yet another taco. "The sooner she kills the sire, the sooner we can break this fucking curse. I don't know about you, but I'd like to feel the sun on my face again."

"You shouldn't encourage her," Hasan says gruffly. "She's human. She can't go up against a nest of vampires. It's a death wish."

"She seems capable," Gilbert agrees with his brother.

"Guys, stop." I stand. "I'm right here, and I'm not asking for permission or advice. If you don't want to help me, fine. Don't help me. But I'm doing this, and if I die, good luck breaking the curse."

"I don't want you to get hurt," Jacques says softly, and he looks at me with the same familiarity as before.

"Trust me, I don't want to get hurt either. But if I don't stop the vampires, someone else will get hurt. Unless Sam and Dean Winchester are out there ready to swoop in and save the day, I'm the only person who knows the murderer is actually a bunch of vampires. I'm the only one who can stop them."

Hasan, who seems to have an ever-present scowl, tips his head down to me. Even on my feet, he towers above me, standing at least a foot past my five-foot-six-inch frame.

"I will help you."

"You will?"

He smiles. "Yes. Helping the less fortunate is why I became a Templar."

Behind the pounds and pounds of muscle and the rough exterior he wears like armor, I see him, and know he means it. We're not that different.

"That's why I became a cop. Part of it at least…to make the world a better place, even if it's just a little bit better than it was before."

"To help people."

"Yeah." I cast my eyes down. "To be there, bringing light to the dark and all that lame shit." I put the torn napkin on the table and reach for a taco. I need to eat. "Anyway, back to the vampires."

"You need to be careful, Ace," Jacques starts. "Vampires are stronger than humans and they are going to be drawn to you even more since you have magic."

"I don't have magic."

"You woke us. You summoned us. There is magic in your blood."

I blink, not even trying to process it. "I'll figure it out later."

"I just told you that you have magic and you're not at all curious?" Jacques questions. I know enough about human psychology from my years interviewing suspects to know what he's doing. He's trying to figure me out, to see if I'm full of bullshit or not.

"Oh, I am." I peel back the flour tortilla and add hot sauce. "Super curious. But like I said, the vampire issue is time-sensitive. Once I kill the sire, you can bet your ass we're sitting down for a lengthy conversation."

"Fine." He eyes me suspiciously, not able to make up his mind. He's good at hiding his emotions, but I'm good at reading them. And right now, he's trying to decide if he wants to hate me or fuck me.

Maybe both.

"Not just any wooden stake will do. You need a priest to bless it."

"A priest?" I haven't set foot in a church in years, and while I'm sure there are a good deal of Christians who believe in demons, I know I'm going to have a hard time finding a priest to bless a pointy stick. "Well, fuck."

"Can't you do it?" Thomas asks Jacques.

"You're a priest?" I ask in disbelief.

"I was." He turns, looking out the window. If I wasn't in a life-or-death rush to kill the vampires, his brooding might be sexy. But right now, it's just annoying. "Being cursed has stripped me of whatever connections I once had."

"Holy water," Hasan suggests, looking at Jacques. "Soaking the stake in holy water should work."

Jacques considers it. "Yes, it should. As long as the wood retains the water. Once it dries out, I'd imagine the power would be gone."

"Good to know. And, if all else fails, I'll cut off their heads."

"Have you ever cut off a head?" Hasan asks, completely serious.

"I can't say I have." I let out a breath and take a bite of my taco.

"The neck is hard to cut through. Swing hard the first time."

"THIS ONE," Gilbert says, pointing to one of the missing persons reports.

"Are you sure?"

"Yes." He looks at Thomas, who nods in agreement.

"It was him." Thomas slides the paper across the coffee table. We're in the living room, and my back is to the fire. With proper firewood, the fire is roaring and brings much-needed warmth into the house. "I remember his face clearly."

"And the rest?"

"None look familiar." Gilbert hands the papers to Hasan, whose large hands crinkle the pages as soon as they are in his grasp.

"No," he says.

"Two out of three is really good." I tap the screen of my phone and log onto Facebook.

"Technology." Jacques looks at the glowing screen of my cellphone. "Are you using radio waves?"

"Not quite, but I am using up all my data." I enter the name "Gavin Black" and filter through several profiles before I find the right one. It's set to private and there's nothing more I can do until I get into work tomorrow. I consider explaining Facebook and the basics of social media to the gargoyles, but stop, not having the energy to start.

"You can contact anyone with that," Jacques tells Hasan, and for some reason, the sentiment is absolutely charming.

"It's a phone," Gilbert says.

"How do you know?" I ask.

"I don't know. But I do."

Thomas leans in, resting his large hand on my shoulder. "It looks familiar."

"You two were on the front porch. You were around people more than the others who were on the roof. If my sleep theory is correct and you were able to process and retain info you heard while sleeping, it makes sense you'd know more."

"Hear that?" Thomas shoots a look at Jacques. "We're the smart ones."

"Don't get used to it," Jacques retorts dryly, making me wonder about their relationship before they were cursed. He turns his attention from Thomas to me. "Can the phone tell you if Gavin was at the vampire bar?"

"No, I'm limited to what I can access from my personal account. I'll start by questioning the person who reported him missing and go from there."

"And if he was there, you'll go in. Alone?"

"I think that's my only choice." I bite my lip and lean back toward the fire. "It's not like I can bring backup."

"You can bring us." Hasan's voice resonates inside of me. "We took an oath to fight in God's name."

In my peripheral vision I see Gilbert roll his eyes. "I'm up for ripping heads off. What about you, brother?"

Thomas grins. "I never say no to a fight."

"You guys know you can't just walk in there with me, right?" I ask. "You have wings." I let out a breath and roll my neck, trying to stretch out a knot in my shoulder. "It's pretty isolated out here. But in town…it'll be culture shock." I unfold my legs and yawn. It's a little after ten and I'm ready for bed.

"Magic," Jacques starts. "It takes a lot out of you."

I'm still not convinced I actually possess magical powers, but it would explain the total depletion of energy I've been feeling.

"You should rest."

"Probably. I have to work in the morning again too."

"We'll guard the house." He eyes the couch. "Are you sleeping here again?"

"Yeah. It's too cold for me upstairs." I get up, muscles aching from my scuffles with the vampires yesterday. "Do you want me to show you how things work around here? Like the water and lights? I brought more food, too, in case you're hungry later."

"Sure." Jacques follows me into the kitchen. I turn on the water, showing him which way to turn the faucet to get hot or cold. The bathroom is next, and his fascination with indoor plumbing makes me realize how much I took it for granted.

We walk past the library, and Jacques slows, looking inside. "I used to read every night." I'm not sure if he's talking to me or himself.

"You can read tonight," I gently offer, and step in, going to the lamp near the window. I pull the chain and the bulb flickers on. "Don't take this the wrong way, but can you read English?"

"Yes, and I think you were right about absorbing information we heard over the years. Though back when I was a man, I could read and write in several languages."

If what I know from the few historical movies is correct, highly educated men came from rich families...and didn't turn to the priesthood.

"Why did you become a Templar priest?" I ask, running the risk of being too frank.

"I believed in the message of the church."

"Believed?"

He lowers his gaze. "I don't anymore."

"Because of the curse?"

"No," he says, and turns away. "I stopped believing before that."

Away from the fire, I'm cold again. Jacques steps to the bookshelf, scanning the volumes in front of him. He pulls one down and runs his finger over the title.

"*Emma*," he reads, and the word sends a chill down my spine. Out of all the books he chooses that particular one. "Have you read it? It's a strange title."

"I have. More than once." I curl my fingers in, pressing my nails into my palms. "Jane Austen is a great author. She's pretty well-known now."

Jacques's lips move into a smile, almost mirroring the one from my dream. "I'll start with this one then. Maybe I'll learn something of value."

I smile back, kicking around the thought of leaving a copy of *Fifty Shades of Grey* lying around for him to read next.

"There's another light by the fireplace."

Jacques tucks the book under his arm. "I can see in the dark."

"Really?"

"Really. Part of the curse."

"Oh, right. You're only awake at night."

His gaze goes to the dark window. "I forgot the feel of sunlight."

"If I can break the curse, I will."

"You should rest," he says, acting as if he didn't hear me. Maybe he doesn't think I'm capable of breaking it. We leave the library, and I grab my bag to change into pajamas for the night.

Hasan has gone back outside to keep watch, Jacques is in the living room with the book, and I'm not sure where Thomas and Gilbert are. I unfold my blanket, fluff up my pillow, and settle in on the couch.

This time around, it takes me a good hour before I finally fall asleep, despite my exhaustion. I wake up not long after with a cramp in my neck. The couch isn't comfortable at all.

The house is quiet and the fire has died down some. The room has retained enough warmth to keep the chill away, but not enough to shed my blankets. I press my fingers into the base of my neck, massaging my sore muscles.

Something shuffles behind me, and I jump up.

"It's just me," Thomas says, leaving the shadows. "Are you all right?"

"Yeah." I sit back on the couch. "I woke up with a stiff neck, that's all."

"Let me help you." He stands behind the couch, putting his hands on my shoulders. "You're very tense."

"I usually am."

"Why?" With one hand, he moves my hair to the side, then starts kneading my muscles.

"Work, I guess."

"Then why do you do it?"

My eyes fall shut. For a man with fangs, claws, and wings, his touch is gentle. "I like my job."

"You like a job that makes you tense?"

"It doesn't make sense, I know." I let my head fall to the side. Thomas slides his hands down my shoulders. "I guess I just like getting the bad guys."

He brings his hands back up and moves one forward, tracing my collarbone with one finger. I shiver from the sensation. The last time a man touched me like this was, well, never. I'm not a virgin, but the relationships I've had in the past never amounted to much.

I bring my hand up, placing it on top of Thomas's. He feels human. Warm flesh, tender touch, and deft fingers. He might have vowed to keep it in his pants, but I know these hands have pleasured many women. He knows what he's doing.

I tip my head back and open my eyes, looking at him. In one swift movement, he jumps over the couch, landing next to me. I angle my body toward him, studying his wings.

"Go ahead. Touch it," he whispers.

Tentatively, I bring my hand up and feel the top of the wing. They're much like bat wings, just sized for a large man. The bones beneath the webbed flesh are ridged and bumpy, with rough patches of thick skin along the top. The edges are outlined in barbs, reminding me a bit of the back of a stegosaurus. Gilbert's wings look similar, much unlike Jacques's, which are as detailed as a carefully carved statue, artfully formed with Gothic beauty. Even the razor-sharp talons at the top of his wings have Celtic symbols engraved into them. Hasan's wingspan is the biggest, and his wings are plain and dark with no hooks, barbs, or talons.

"You all look different," I start, then realize how stupid that sounds. "I mean, of course you do, but your wings vary a lot."

"They're based on our personalities. Well, the opposite of them. Gil and I prided ourselves on our looks and we got the ugliest wings. Hasan loved his weapons and has the least defensive wings of us all. And Jacques didn't believe in material wealth and he looks like the King of Hell with those ornamental wings."

I swallow hard, getting a better sense of the curse. Whoever cast it wanted the men to suffer in every way possible.

"What did you do to get cursed?"

Thomas stiffens and looks into the fire. "We were blamed for a murder we did not commit."

"Who died?"

"The daughter of a pagan sorcerer. Her father cursed us."

"Braeya?"

"Yes, that was her name."

I think back to my dream. The intensity in Jacques's eyes. The feeling of time running out. He said he stopped believing in everything he fought for before he was cursed. Was this woman the reason why?

He was a priest for the Templars. Braeya was the daughter of a sorcerer. If they had a thing going on...talk about forbidden love.

My head spins and I yawn. Thomas takes my hand in his and motions to the stairs.

"If the couch isn't comfortable, you should take one of the beds upstairs."

"I need the fire," I remind him. "It's too cold up there for me, but hopefully I'll be able to turn the heater on tomorrow. It's like a built-in fireplace in the walls. Kind of. It keeps the whole house warm."

"Sounds dangerous."

"This old one probably is, but upgrading to a new system would cost a lot more than I can afford." I resituate my blankets. "The couch will be good enough. I have to get up in a few hours, anyway."

"I'll stay with you," Thomas offers, and puts his arm around me. As enticing as his touch is, there's nothing sexual about it. I'm sure he'd jump into bed with me if I offered, but right now, he's comforting me. Keeping me warm.

My heart flutters again and I put my hand over his, making him pause for a moment. Then he envelopes his other arm around me, massaging my back again. My eyes fall shut, and if it wasn't for the feel of his wings against me, it would feel like I'm snuggled up next to a normal man. A man I could date. A man I could fall for.

He pulls me to him and lies back, bringing me with him. My head rests on his chest, and I listen to his heartbeat. He continues to run his hands up and down my back, lulling me to sleep. The fire crackles next to us, casting long shadows across the room.

"I always thought I'd have this," he whispers.

"Have what?" I whisper back, not opening my eyes.

"A wife. And then a family."

His words are enough to jolt me awake. I sit up and look into his sky-blue eyes. "You wanted a family?"

"Yes," he confesses, and his famous cocky grin is nowhere to be seen. There is sadness and longing in his eyes. My heart aches for him.

"But you joined the Templars."

"It wasn't my choice to join." He starts rubbing my back again, both wanting to comfort me and needing to distract himself. I rest my head on his chest again, splaying my fingers over his broad shoulder. "Gil and I are the youngest of six. Our eldest sibling is—was—our sister, Mary. She was married to a Duke before I was even born. Then came John, set to inherit the family's fortune. Elizabeth came after him, and shortly after we swore into the Templars, she got engaged to a banker. Paul was everything my father could have wanted in a son and was the spare in case John died. With two heirs and two daughters married into rich families, he didn't want or need us."

"Oh, wow. I'm sorry."

Thomas shrugs. "It's how things were back then. And it'd be lying if I didn't say Gil and I got into our fair share of trouble and used the family name to get what we wanted. I think we both knew it would come to this if we didn't settle down. And I wanted to, but I refused two arrangements set up for me by my father."

"You wanted to be in love."

"Yes," he admits. "When I refused the second marriage proposal, I was told I brought shame to the family. Our father tried to offer Gil instead. He refused too, and off we went, as expected."

"But you never expected to be turned into gargoyles."

"No," he laughs, and that smirk is back. "That was not something I ever expected." His hand moves down to the curve of my lower back. I crave more of his touch. I want him to make me feel. "I don't believe in all the godly shit Jacques and Hasan do, and I can tell you don't either. But I'm starting to think maybe they were onto something about destiny and fate."

I lift my head, eyes locking with his. "I'm starting to believe it, too."

11

I run a brush through my hair, eyeing the time. I woke up fifteen minutes before my alarm went off and was alone, missing Thomas the moment I realized he was gone. He opened up last night, showed me there's very much a man behind the mask, and I almost wish he hadn't.

I have no idea how to break the curse.

I have no idea how to use magic.

And I'm still not sure I actually have powers.

I set my brush on the bathroom sink and messily braid my hair, then go back into the living room and poke at the fire in an attempt to put it out. Thomas must have put another log on before he had to go take his place on the porch in the morning. The fireplace is large, with a wide stone hearth, but leaving with a fire burning isn't something I want to risk.

Once I'm dressed, I go into the kitchen to throw away the leftovers, but discover there is nothing left. Making a mental note to get even more food tonight, I bag up all the empty containers to take with me and toss in the recycling at work. I gather up the rest of my stuff and put it on the couch in the two-story living room.

As I'm leaving, I see *Emma* on the coffee table in the front sitting room. I stop, thinking of Jacques.

And Thomas and Gilbert.

And Hasan.

The more I get to know them, the less I see them as monsters and the more I see them as the men they used to be. The men they want to be again. I move into the foyer, taking one last look around the house before stepping out onto the porch.

"I'll see you guys tonight." I put my hand over Thomas's. Turned to stone, his handsome features have taken on a monstrous appearance once again. The sun is glowing behind hazy clouds, and the air is humid. I get in the car and fiddle with the air conditioning before taking off. I watch the house disappear in my rearview mirror, missing the estate already.

Obviously, I can't sell the place. But I can't pay rent on my small apartment and cover the cost of owning such a large piece of property. The utilities alone will be a lot, and the property tax is pretty insane. I'm locked into three more months at my current dwelling, though there might be a chance I can get out with at least one month's fee given back.

I've lived in the same place for the last seven years and have never been late on rent. I've never had an issue. No one has complained about me. It's worth a shot to at least ask. Though the estate is far from livable for every day.

My head starts to spin. Moving into an old house is a big enough project on its own, and I'm going to have to wait on it. Vampires first. Curse-breaking second.

Streaming 4K Netflix will be my reward.

I get drive-thru coffee and breakfast again and arrive at the office a few minutes before I need to be there. We have a meeting this morning, and it's afternoon before I'm able to call Gavin's girlfriend, who's the one who reported him missing. I leave a message, go down to the lab to go over DNA evidence with Sam, and then fill out reports as I eat my lunch at my desk.

Gavin's girlfriend calls back, and I arrange to meet her at her house once she's home from class at three-thirty. She lives on the other side of town, and I have the guy coming to look at the furnace at five.

Shit. I don't know how I'm going to fit this all in. Whatever. I'll make it work. I have to.

"Checking out another lead?"

I turn, following the sound of Beasley's voice. He eyes the folded missing person's report in my hand. "Oh, uh, yeah."

"What ever happened to the one from yesterday?"

"Dead end," I lie. It's not like me to not check in with everyone working on the case. I'd been in such a rush to get out of the office I forgot. "No sign of foul play, but no sign of him running away either." What I said is true to an extent, but I still feel like the world's biggest ass. "I got another one to follow up on, and I'm trying to catch her as she leaves work."

Officer Beasley smiles, eyes lingering on my face too long for comfort. "All right. See you tomorrow then."

"Yeah. See you."

I GET to Francine DeBoy's house at three-fifteen. I'm early and was hoping she'd be early, too. The sooner we talk, the sooner I can get to the estate. I have no idea how long it will take to fix the furnace, and I can't have the guy there once the sun sets.

Twenty-five minutes later, a car parks in front of the house and a twenty-something-year-old girl gets out. I'm leaning against the door of my car, scrolling through social media again trying to find something—anything—to tie the vampires together.

"Are you Detective Bisset?" the woman asks.

"Yes. Francine?"

She nods. "That's me."

I push off the car and follow her into the garage. "My roommate's not home yet," she starts. "She gets home around four."

She doesn't have to tell me she's hoping I'll be gone by then. A fast interview works for both of us.

"Did you find him?" Her voice shakes as she unlocks the door. "He's not dead, is he?"

"No," I flat-out lie. Yes, I found him, and yes, the man I cuddled myself to sleep with last night ripped your boyfriend apart and enjoyed it, called it "fun," actually. "I have just a few questions for you."

"Okay."

We sit at the kitchen table. "Have you or Gavin ever been to the bar Delirium?"

"Yeah, I went once. Does this have to do with him disappearing?"

"It might." I open my notebook. "When did you go?"

"A couple of weeks ago."

"Did you two go together?"

"Yeah." She brings her hand up, subconsciously rubbing her neck. "It was Gavin's idea."

"You say that like you didn't want to go."

"I didn't." She shakes her head. "We have friends who like to go and they're always trying to get us to join. I'm not...I don't like... that stuff freaks me out."

"What stuff?"

Heat colors her cheeks. "You know...freaky stuff."

"Are you referring to the Gothic theming?"

"Kind of."

I know exactly what she's referring to since I now know what goes on behind closed doors, but I'm not going to egg her on. How the story unfolds can be just as telling as the words themselves.

"Can you explain?"

"I don't know." She looks at the floor.

"It might help me find him." Another lie. Though I really *don't* know where his body is.

"It's like a meet-up for people into BDSM. Like hardcore into it."

So vampires like it rough. "And you two went?" I put my pen down and do my best to do that girl-to-girl bonding thing. I'm not good at it. "Look, whatever you're into is your business. Going there to partake in whatever kind of sexual acts you want isn't against the law. I don't even need to put it in my report." That part is true. Mostly because I haven't decided if I should even write up reports on this yet. The fewer paper trails, the better, right?

"We tried it once. For Gavin's birthday. It wasn't my thing, and I got mad at him for liking it. He thought it would be fun, you know, and bring us closer together."

"Did you go back?"

"No. It freaked me out too much."

Her body language tells me there was more going on than freaky sex between her and her boyfriend. "Francine," I say gently. "I need you to tell me exactly what happened to freak you out."

She lifts her eyes, surprised I was able to pick up on her thoughts, and nods. "When I agreed to go, I thought it was like going to one of those couples' getaway sort of things. You know, where they set the mood with a romantic room, a bottle of wine, and have chocolate-covered strawberries on a silver plate on the bed."

"And it wasn't like that?"

"No, not at all." She shudders. "It was like a strip show, and the strippers encourage the couples to make out and go backstage with them. There were two people fucking in the back. Just out there in the open. And the strippers…they're not just stripping. They're, uh, involved."

"Was it only couples watching?"

She shakes her head. "It was mostly men."

"Did Gavin ever go back?"

"Not that I know of. He agreed it was way too intense for the both of us. Nipple clamps in the bedroom…yeah, I'll try it. But getting naked in a dirty room full of strangers…no thank you."

"Tell me about the night he disappeared."

"The night he disappeared," she repeats, and her eyes gloss over. "He went out to pick up Chinese and never came home. I had him on Find My Friends and tried to search for his location, but his locations had been disabled. I was told his phone couldn't be traced, that whoever stole it knew what they were doing."

I nod, having read the same thing on the report. Bryan Porter's phone couldn't be traced either. "You said you went to Delirium for Gavin's birthday. Did you go out on his actual birthday?"

"No, the week after."

That makes their first trip to the bar about a month ago, and Gavin was reported missing nineteen days ago.

"Was he acting weird before his disappearance?"

"No," she says, becoming defensive. "He didn't leave me. I already told the police this ten times and no one will listen! Somebody took him, and he's….he's…" Tears roll down her face.

"Francine." I speak her name slowly, keeping my tone calm. "I believe you. That's why I'm trying to piece things together, and I need you to answer my questions."

She takes in a deep breath. "Okay, and no, he wasn't. He was busy with work, and I had an exam that week. We didn't see each other much the days before he went missing."

I make a note of the dates and, getting all the information I need, offer my condolences to Francine and lie through my teeth when I tell her I'll do everything in my power to find Gavin.

The guy from the repair company is parked in front of the house by the time I pull into the driveway.

"Sorry!" I call, getting out of my car. He steps from the van and looks at his watch. I'm only five minutes late, and I did call on my way to let him know.

"It's all right," he gruffs, eyes going to my gun and badge. He hesitates by Thomas and Gilbert, and the weirdest sense comes over me and I have to work hard not to burst out laughing. "Those things are creepy."

"I kind of like them." I fish the key from my pocket and let us into the house.

"What's going on with the heater?" He pulls shoe covers from his bag and slips them over his work boots.

"It hasn't been run in years, and, when I tried it, it made a weird noise and smelled bad." I lead him to the basement, pulling the string light at the top of the stairs. "I went down to take a look and realized I have no idea what I was looking at and didn't want to mess with anything."

"Good idea. Old units can be tricky. Have you considered upgrading to something newer? They're more energy efficient and would make sense in this big house."

I hadn't considered it because I was set on selling this place and sleeping naked on a bed of money after I collected. "If this one can't be repaired, I guess I have no choice."

He goes to the old furnace and gets to work. I step back, not really sure what the etiquette is in situations like this. Do I hang around and make small talk? I have no water or coffee to offer him, and I'm starting to feel weird just hanging around.

Other than looking at the furnace, I haven't really explored the basement. It's divided into several rooms, and packed full of shit. Old furniture, broken dishes, boxes and boxes of tattered books...I didn't want any of it and the thought of lugging it all upstairs to dispose of it made my muscles ache.

But I don't have to do it, not on my own. I have four very strong and very capable men living in the house. I bet they could get this place cleared out in an hour or less. Deciding to make the most of my time, I quickly flip through the boxes, making sure everything I label as junk really is junk.

My aunt used to live here, and although she and I were never close, she was family. My parents were taken from me when I was young. I didn't get a chance to get to know the rest of my family, and it's seared an empty hole in my heart that's gradually grown bigger and bigger every day of my life.

I not only miss my parents, but I also miss the idea of what could have been. Had my mother and aunt been on speaking terms, I could have moved in and grown up here. She could have helped me with school, offered me friendship and guidance.

After my parents died, I was bounced back and forth between my dad's brothers for a couple of years. Neither wanted me, and it was obvious I was a burden. Uncle Chuck, Dad's older brother, was married for a short while before he cheated on his wife, Katie. She and I got along well, and she welcomed me into her small apartment after the divorce went through.

I was twelve then and knew it was fucked up to be living with my dead father's ex-sister-in-law. Over the next few years, things seemed okay. Normal, even. She taught at the school I attended, and we rode to school together every morning. She was quiet, taking the divorce hard. Dad was never fond of his older brother, and to this day it's hard not to have a seething hatred for the man who refused to raise his flesh-and-blood niece and who cheated on someone as kind-hearted and caring as Katie.

I stayed with her until college and was even in her wedding when she finally remarried. We kept in touch, but then she relocated to Texas and our communications lessened. I haven't heard from her in years.

Dad's family...I knew and didn't like. But Mom's side was a mystery, one she'd always tell me we'd talk about later. I saw pictures from her childhood and thought she must have lived the most glamorous, exciting life. My grandpa was a pilot, and my mom traveled the world with him.

Her own mother died of cancer when she was young, so it was just her and her dad, taking on the world. I'd seen a handful of photos of them in all sorts of exotic locations. I knew my grandfather only through his work. The plane he'd flown. The trouble he faced while in the air. The famous people who boarded his plane.

And that was it.

I didn't know anything else. Aunt Mary, who owned this house, was my grandfather's younger sister. Why she never came up in conversation was beyond me, though I do remember my mom saying she was "off her rocker" more than once.

I move a heavy box to the floor and peel back the cardboard of the one beneath it. It's full of old romance novels, ones that apparently didn't make the cut for the upstairs library. Continuing to quickly look inside each box, I find most are full of junk too old and crusty to be garage-sale worthy. I'm not the kind of person who stops a project once it's started. I wipe dust from my face and grab another box from a new row, expecting it to be heavy like the rest.

But it's empty.

So is the one next to it. And beneath it. *That's strange.* The boxes were neatly arranged in rows in one of the storage rooms, with the last row being against the exterior basement wall. I move two more empty boxes and discover they've been stacked around a small table, but it's the wooden box under the table that grabs my attention.

I take a quick look behind me at the repair man, who's busy taking the old furnace apart, and take the flashlight off my belt. The lighting is dim down here, and I've moved farther away from the overhead light.

Cobwebs stretch over the lid of the wooden box. Brushing them aside, I flip open the latch. My heart starts to beat rapidly. The hinges creak and the wood groans, not having been opened in years. Slowly, I open the lid, eyes wide in wonder at what I might find.

It's another box.

"That was anticlimactic," I mumble to myself, and shine the light in. This next box is prettier than the first, which was more utilitarian than decorative. I reach in and pick up the smaller box. It's heavy, much heavier than I expected. And it's also locked. I think. If that crazy steampunk-looking thing is indeed a lock.

Tucking the box under my arm, I slip back upstairs and into the kitchen and turn on the lights.

"What the heck?" I mutter, examining the lock. There's no place for a key, and, upon further inspection, it looks more like a puzzle. I spin a dial and a sharp piece of metal shoots out, stabbing my fingertip.

"Son of a bitch!" I pull my finger back, wiping away a drop of blood. Did the thing malfunction or— "No way." I lean in, careful not to get too close in case something else pops out at me, and look at the needle. There's a tiny hole in the metal, and I watch as a small drop of my blood rolls inside.

I bring my finger to my mouth, sucking away the blood. The lock clicks and something inside moves, sounding like metal sliding across metal. The gears spin, and suddenly the lid pops up.

Knowing better than to reach in barehanded again, I use a spoon from the kitchen to pry the lid off. It falls with a clatter onto the wooden table, and I step in, eyeing what appears to be a leather-bound journal. I poke it with the spoon.

Nothing happens. Still, my throbbing finger tells me not to reach inside. I get another spoon and awkwardly pull the book out. It's the only thing in the box. It's on the small side, no bigger than an average fiction novel, and the leather is worn and scratched. Slowly, I unwind the leather tie from around the book and open it.

I don't know what I was expecting, maybe for the lights to dim and a breeze to blow my hair back dramatically like it does in the movies, but I wasn't expecting this. I wrinkle my nose and flip through the pages. Everything is written in what I think is Latin and there's no clue as to what I'm reading. A journal or diary? There are no dates at the top of each page, and hardly anything to separate one entry from another.

I flip through the pages, and a neatly drawn vegvisir catches my eye—an Old Norse symbol believed to help the bearer find their way when traveling. My knowledge of the occult is impressive, or so I always thought. I know a good deal of magical symbols, what they mean or represent, and their origins. The symbols were just symbols before, marked on bodies or the site of crimes to illicit fear, or to appease what I thought were false deities.

And now…now I'm not so sure everything was false.

"Ma'am?"

I jump, almost dropping the book. Dammit. I don't startle easily. I shouldn't startle easily. Not in my line of work.

"Yeah?"

"I found what was wrong." He holds up a part of the furnace that means nothing to me. "I might have a spare in the truck. If not, I'll call a guy I work with and see if he has one. It's an old part and we might be able to order one. I just replaced a unit like yours with a newer one before I came here and kept some of the working parts. Lucky, right?"

"Yeah. Lucky."

I go back to the book the moment he goes outside, madly flipping through the pages. It's full of other occult symbols I recognize. I don't let myself get too excited, but I have a feeling this is a book of shadow.

I shift my gaze to the ceiling, imagining Jacques and Hasan up on the roof. If this book is full of magic spells, then maybe, just maybe, I can break the curse after all.

12

"God, I'm such an idiot." I rub my temples, looking at the mess I created in the kitchen. Why I thought cleaning out the cabinets was a good idea is beyond me. Seeing that I have no other choice than to pick this shit up, I stand and step over a pile of rusted pots and pans from my "throw away" pile.

The repairman is still working away on the furnace downstairs in the basement, and I have about an hour until sunset. Having flipped through what I think is a spell book probably fifty times, I needed to do something productive to keep occupied, and cleaning the kitchen sounded like a good idea at the time.

On the surface, everything in the house appeared clean. There was no clutter, the counters had been wiped down before the house was abandoned, and the cabinets were in good condition. Upon further inspection, I found a lot of the dishes to have been lazily washed, the pots and pans to be old, rusted, with flaking Teflon making it not safe to cook in anymore. Not that I cook.

But I think I'm going to have to start.

I stack the old pots and pans in an empty box I brought up from the basement and slide it to the back door. I washed most of the plates and silverware yesterday and finished the cups and glasses today. This kitchen must have been impressive at one point, and my mind drifts to Great Aunt Mary. Did she host dinner parties at this house? Her friends would have come in and looked around in awe.

A bigger question burns inside, one I desperately wish to know the answer to. Did she know about the gargoyles? The house was built roughly a hundred and twenty-two years ago. How the hell did four gargoyles from the Templar time period get here? Maybe they were bought as art pieces, set on the house to make it stand out more than it already does. Digging into the history of the house is yet another thing on my ever-growing list.

"Ma'am?" The basement door opens and the repairman steps out, moving into the kitchen. He eyeballs the giant mess I've made. "You're all set."

"It works?"

"Yep. It'll take a while to heat the whole house, and the farther the rooms are from the unit, the colder they will be. I recommend getting a newer unit sooner rather than later. I don't have much confidence that old one will hold up much longer. You might get one more winter out of it."

"Great. And thanks. I'll, uh, look into new units."

I fork over my credit card, cringing inside as he processes the payment, and finish cleaning the kitchen, feeling the most domestic I've ever been. With a few minutes left until sunset, I get out my notes, trying to make sense of what I know so far.

Which isn't much.

Bryan and Gavin were both turned into vampires. Gavin has been to Delirium at least once, and Bryan might have been there. It's a shaky foundation to build my theory on, but it's all I have for now.

The body in the ditch had been slowly drained of blood over the course of a few days, and the body in the park was ripped into like it was done by a starving animal. Desperate. Messy. They got caught.

The first body was far from fresh, making me think it had been a few days since the vampires had eaten, hence the attack in the park. I'm certain if the gargoyles hadn't killed the vampires, they'd be out again tonight and I'd have another dead, bloodless victim to find in the morning.

If Gavin, Bryan, and the unknown vampire were the only three new vamps in town, did that buy me some time? I might very well have pissed off someone as old and powerful as Hasan himself, and that might work in my favor. People do stupid things out of anger. I'm sure vampires do, too.

I TURN off the alarm on my phone, grab my jacket, and go outside to wait for the gargoyles to wake up. I saw the transformation yesterday and it amazes me just as much again today. They wake at the same time, and all jump down to the ground around me.

Jacques is a foot in front of me and, like the others, looks more human than ever today. His chocolate eyes are so vivid I could drown in them. I blink, and a vision of him naked and on top of me flashes through my head. He looks away at the same time. Did he see it, too?

"Hey," I say.

"Hey?" Hasan asks.

"It means 'hi.' Not hay like what horses eat."

Hasan raises one eyebrow. "Then why not say 'hi?'"

"I don't really know. We just say 'hey' now."

"What'd you bring to eat?" Thomas asks with a smile.

"Nothing," I say guiltily, feeling the intensity of his gaze. It felt so good to be wrapped up in his arms last night, listening to him talk about his past. The more time we spend together, the more I realize he's exactly the kind of guy I've dreamed about. "I can order takeout to be delivered. Chinese food sounds good."

"China," Jacques mumbles with familiarity.

"That place is actually old enough you might remember it. But not from the food. The takeout I get has been Americanized a lot." I wave my hand. "Let's go in." The four men follow me inside.

"What is that God-awful noise?" Gilbert looks around.

"The heater." I take his hand and hold it over an old radiator. "Feel."

"It's warm!"

I laugh. "Yeah, it fills the house with warm air."

They all take turns feeling the heat. I stand back, watching, and then start laughing.

"Are you all right?" Jacques looks at me like I've lost it.

"Yeah." I wipe away a tear. "It's just this whole situation is so not funny that it actually is."

Jacques looks at his brothers in question. They don't get it either. "So why are you laughing?"

"To keep myself from crying." I shake my head. "I'm fine, really. I'll order the food."

Going into the kitchen, I take my jacket off and hang it on the back of the chair and order the food online.

"The other vampire—Gavin—had been to the bar," I start, pointing to his photo. "I talked to his girlfriend and she said they'd gone to Delirium a few weeks before he went missing. Can just anyone be turned into vampires?"

All eyes fall on Jacques. "If the sire is strong enough, yes."

"And if not?" I ask.

"They'd die. The actual process of going from human to vampire is full of dark magic, and I don't know exactly what happens. There's an exchange of blood, and the sire has to bury himself under the earth during the three days of the new moon."

I blink. "I was not expecting that. And we have like what...ten days until the next new moon?"

"You keep track of the moon cycles?" Thomas asks.

"Yeah, well, kind of. Crime rates go up around the full moon. Even before, when I didn't think magic was real, there was no denying something about the full moon made people crazy."

"At least there's one thing that hasn't changed." Gilbert picks up a full-page photo of the body found in the ditch. "This is a very impressive drawing."

"It's a photograph." I dig my phone from my back pocket. "Watch this." I lean in next to Gilbert and take a selfie, then flip the phone around to show him. "Don't worry, I'll delete it. Though if anyone saw it, they'd assume it was fake."

"Delete?" Gilbert asks distantly, enamored by the picture.

"Get rid of." I rack my brain trying to think of the best way to explain this and come up short. It's confusing enough to explain it to elderly folk who at least already know what a phone and a camera are. "The phone has memory and can store things like photographs. But don't worry about it. I'm sure you'll get used to everything."

Hasan scowls at the phone. "Is it magic?"

"The opposite of magic."

"Technology," Jacques quips.

"Right." I stifle a laugh. "But back to the vampires...how do they decide who to, uh, eat?"

"From what I understand," Jacques starts, "they go for what is easiest. Which is basically any human. You are no match for a vampire."

"Yeah." I subconsciously bring my hand to the side of my head. "I know."

"Are you still in pain?"

"No, but I still feel drained of energy. If I really am using magic, how long will it take to get used to this?"

Jacques shakes his head. "I do not know."

"Why do you know so much about vampires, but know nothing about magic?"

"I didn't typically deal with magic."

I wait for him to elaborate. He doesn't. "But you typically dealt with vampires?"

"No, not often."

"But sometimes?" I press, not sure if he's purposely ignoring the shock in my voice or if he really doesn't understand the rarity dealing with vampires is.

"Yes, sometimes. Mostly, we were called upon to handle demonic possession and assist with exorcisms."

"Exorcisms," I echo. "Was this before or after you were cursed?"

"After."

I inhale. Exhale. My mind goes back to *what the fuck* mode. "So you four were like the supernatural police."

Thomas laughs. "Being cursed exposed us to other monsters. Physically, our humanity was gone, but in here"—he taps his head—"we still knew what was going on."

Gilbert makes a face. "And we were bound to the sorcerer. We didn't have much of a choice other than to do his bidding."

"And his bidding was to kill other monsters?" I ask carefully.

"Yes." Hasan's voice booms through the large house. "Who better to kill monsters than other monsters?"

I sit at the table and start gathering up my papers. The guys were cursed, blamed for a death they had nothing to do with, and the curse turned them into medieval Robocops. The curse had a purpose. I twist a loose strand of hair over my shoulder. Understanding the reasoning behind the curse might help me break it.

"Are you all right, Ace?" Jacques asks quietly.

"I'm trying to deal with everything, mentally." I pull the hair tie from my wrist, gathering my long locks into a messy bun at the nape of my neck. "And not feel overwhelmed in the process." I let out a breath in an attempt not to overthink. From finding the vampire sire to deciding what to do with this house and my apartment, I'm close to a nervous breakdown.

"I'll help you," Thomas offers. At first his words surprise me, then I remember they want this curse broken. The sooner I get through my other shit, the sooner I can work on breaking the curse. "Whatever you need, I'll do it. And right now, I think you need to relax."

"If I relax, someone else dies. There's not much time left until the new moon, and if I don't find and kill the sire before then, that means more vampires. I need to get to the bottom of this sooner rather than later. It's fucking everything else up." I look up at the guys. "I never lie at work, and I've done a lot of it the last few days. The longer it takes to kill the vamps, the more likely I am to get caught in a lie."

A few seconds of silence tick by and I can feel all four men staring at me. Finally, Jacques speaks.

"The bar you mentioned earlier...is it open during the day?"

"No, and the hours change with the seasons. It's only open after sunset."

"That is compelling."

"I know, right?" I put the rest of the files in their folders, stacking them neatly on the table. "I should go tonight. Scope it out and see if I can find anyone who looks like a vampire."

"Vampires can look like normal people if they desire. The three you came across were young and didn't know how to use their powers."

"Hold up." I raise my hand, holding up a finger. "Now vampires have magical powers?"

"Not quite," Jacques answers. "They can make you spellbound for a few moments at a time, usually just long enough to not feel pain when they first bite you. And they can hide their appearance from humans. Though some of the older, powerful sires could kill you without touching you."

"Great. What about the sulfur smell?"

"They can cover it up, but it's there. All demons smell like sulfur."

"So, basically, you're telling me I need to go around sniffing people."

"Even in our time, that wouldn't go over well," Jacques replies.

"I'm joking. Maybe. I think." I let out a sigh that turns into a yawn.

"You really should call it a night," Gilbert urges. "You haven't gotten much sleep lately and going up against vampires requires quite a bit of stamina."

I hate that he's right. I've always had a bit of an obsessive personality, which worked in my favor as a detective, giving the case I was investigating everything I had. And while I've worked on my fair share of "big" cases with high-profile victims, nothing has been bigger than this.

"Fine. I'll sit down and relax until dinner gets here." I look at my watch. "Which should be in twenty minutes."

Getting up from the table, I grab my large overnight bag and go upstairs. It's still chilly, but I can feel the warm air seeping from the furnace, slowly heating the master bedroom. I set my bag down on the dresser and go to the bed, stripping off the old sheets and blankets and replacing them with clean ones I brought from home.

"I thought you were resting."

I turn to see Thomas standing in the doorframe. His large wings take up the entire space, and I'm pretty sure he'll have to turn sideways to enter.

"I will be resting after I make the bed. Sleeping on an old, used mattress kind of grosses me out."

"At least you get a bed," he jokes.

I toss the old pillows to the corner of the room, frowning. "You're right. There are a lot of little things I've taken for granted. Like showers and not turning to stone when I sleep."

Thomas laughs and I slip a corner of the fitted sheet around the mattress. It pops off when I pull it to the other side. Too lazy to go around, I climb onto the mattress and try again.

"That's an interesting concept." Thomas brings his large frame into the room.

"Interesting is a good word to use."

"What's the purpose of it?"

"It keeps the mattress clean." I get the last corner of the sheet on the bed. "Come here." I sit and pat the space next to me. "This mattress isn't the best, but it's probably better than anything you've experienced before."

I watch how he moves his wings as he sits, and the look of surprise on his face makes me smile.

"Comfy, isn't it?"

"Better than the couch," he says, and lies back. A few seconds pass before he grabs my arm and brings me back with him. My head settles on his chest and he trails his fingers up and down my spine. "You need to learn how to relax. I've seen many strong men drive themselves to a breaking point by trying to do it all. You're different, Ace. Obviously not a man, but it's so much more than that. So much has happened to you in the last two days and you haven't hesitated once."

"I have a few times, just not long enough for anyone to notice."

He brushes my hair out of my eyes and smiles. "I like you, and it'd be a damn shame if anything happened before I got to know you better."

His brazen words send a shock through me, and I find it almost hard to believe. "You like me?"

He smiles. "What, is that hard to believe?"

"I don't know. I mean, I know I'm a total catch but you…"

"I'm a gargoyle, yeah, yeah. I get it."

I shake my head. "That's not what I was going to say."

He runs his hand through my hair and my heart speeds up. His eyes meet mine. "What were you going to say?" He tips his face toward mine, and for a split second, I think he's going to kiss me.

And I want him to.

"You're not like anyone I've ever met before either," I start, suddenly feeling shy. I'm not good at sharing my emotions, especially ones like this. "You're funny and brave and any modern guy that's as attractive as you would be a womanizing jerk, I'm sure of it."

Thomas laughs. "I might have been one before." He gives me a wink and smiles. We click in a way that makes no sense. A wave of heat goes over me, and I find myself craving his touch from last night. But more of it.

I run my fingers through his wavy blond hair. "Besides, I have so many questions. If I died now, I'd come back as a ghost and annoy the shit out of all of you."

Thomas laughs and rests his hand on the small of my back, fingers inching toward my ass. "As long as you looked as good dead as you do alive, I won't complain."

Laughing, I hook my leg over his. "Your skin isn't gray anymore." I trace a vein with my finger on his muscular chest. He shudders from my touch, and he quickly brings his hand up, fingers wrapping around my wrist. For a split second I think I crossed a line, that my touch offended him for some reason.

And then I see the lust in his eyes.

In a sudden movement, he rolls over, moving on top of me. My heart is in my throat and heat burns between my thighs. He looks at me with such intensity it makes me squirm beneath him, and he likes it. I gently push his golden locks out of his handsome face and inhale deeply, crushing my breasts against his chest.

His wings are slightly spread above me, shielding everything from sight. Heart racing, I part my lips and slide my hand to the back of his neck. My eyes fall shut as he lowers his lips to mine. Every nerve in my body comes alive the moment he kisses me.

Soft.

Wet.

Warm.

Desperate.

My heart swells in my chest and it's in that moment I realize how much I need this, how much I've missed something I've never had. I can deny it all I want but I know what I'm feeling and I'm pretty sure Thomas feels it too.

I've been closed and guarded before, always feeling the need to put up a front and hide my vulnerabilities. But I don't feel that way with Thomas. My heart races and I pull him closer, needing to feel him against me. But it's more than physical; being with him fills the void in my heart, the emptiness I've had inside me since the day my parents died.

I widen my legs and feel his cock begin to harden against my stomach. Red-hot desire washes over me, and if he was wearing a shirt, I probably would have ripped it off. Thomas mirrors my desperation, kissing me with a fierceness I've never experienced before. His tongue slips into my mouth and he wraps his arms around me, sliding one hand under my shirt.

His kisses move from my mouth to my neck, and I throw my head back, a moan escaping my lips. I curl my legs around him and feel every inch, every ridge of muscle on his torso. With deft fingers, he undoes the buttons on my blouse, pulling back the material and gazing upon my breasts.

"It's a bra," I pant, sitting up just enough to unhook it.

"It's quite nice." He leans away, licking his lips. "I prefer it off, though."

"You and me both." I scramble to get the clasp undone and let the straps roll down my shoulders. Thomas takes it off and tosses it on the floor, then dives back on top of me, kissing my lips again before working his way down, taking one of my breasts in his mouth. His tongue swirls over my nipple, sending waves of pleasure right through me. I've never been one to particularly get off from nipple-play, but whatever the hell he's doing to me is just about enough to make me come right here and now.

Out of habit, I go to wrap my arms around him but my hands hit his wings. Instead of moving my hands to another, smoother part of his body, I run my hands along the rough bones of his wings, remembering how he said he thought they were ugly and unattractive.

"I'm...I'm sorry," he says, casting his eyes away.

"Don't be." I run my hand over his wings again. Thomas cups my face, bringing my face to his. He closes his eyes and rests his forehead against mine, and for a brief moment, the dominance is gone. Like the others, he puts up a front, acting as if he's okay with the curse and optimistic about me being able to break it.

But right now I know he's scared of being like this forever.

Feeling so much for him, I run my hands through his hair and kiss him hard.

"I want you, Ace," Thomas growls, but it's almost as if he's asking permission.

"Have me," I order, lifting my head off the mattress just enough to look at him. He moves his head down between my legs, taking off my pants. He moves to the floor, kneeling before the bed, and I get a glimpse of the outline of his big cock, hardly hidden beneath the thin brown fabric of his pants.

He lifts my legs, wrapping them around his neck, and kisses his way up my thigh. Soft and gentle at first. And then he nips at my skin, sending a shock through me. He runs his fingertips along my leg, mouth hovering over my core. I can feel his warm breath on me, and I realize he's teasing me on purpose.

He knows exactly what he's doing to me, and I am so fucking glad he didn't take his vow of celibacy seriously. Slowly, he grabs the sides of my panties and rolls them down my thighs. I lift my ass off the mattress and he groans with need at the sight of my pussy. Unable to wait any longer, he rips them in two and dives between my legs, mouth against my clit.

I ball the sheet with one hand and bring the other to the top of Thomas's head, fingers tangling with his hair. His tongue lashes against me in a fury, and he licks and sucks relentlessly. My breathing quickens and the muscles in my thighs tighten as pleasure winds inside me.

He slides one hand under my ass, bringing me closer to his face. My grip on his hair tightens the closer I get to coming, and he slips a finger inside my tight pussy. A loud moan escapes my lips.

The door is open.

The others are downstairs.

And for some reason, I don't care.

Thomas bends his finger ever so slightly, rubbing furiously against my inner wall. I press myself against him, and he hits my G-spot.

"Don't even think about stopping," I pant. "Not until you make me—" I cut off as an orgasm hits me, hard and fast, like the way Thomas is eating me out. He slips another finger inside, pressing against my G-spot, while at the same time flicking my clit with his skillful tongue.

I shudder as I come and every muscle in my body goes rigid for a few seconds. I'm panting, heart racing and ears ringing. Thomas slowly pulls away, cocky smile on his face. Blinking away the stars floating before me, I feebly reach for him, eyes going to the glistening wet tip of his cock that's sticking out from the top of his cloth pants.

I lick my lips. My body is still rolling with pleasure from the orgasm he just gave me, but I'll be damned if I don't feel turned on all over again from the sight of that thing. It's big, and not just long.

But thick.

The perfect combination of girth and length. The kind of cock I'll feel long after he's done fucking me.

"Pants," I huff. "Take them off."

Thomas stands, eyes on mine, and undoes the tie on his pants, letting them drop to his feet. He steps out, and I welcome him between my open legs.

"Your cunt is so wet," he groans, grabbing my hips and positioning himself to enter me. I prop myself up with one arm and reach forward with the other, taking hold of his big cock. Slowly, I pump my hand up and down the shaft, swirling my thumb around the tip and bringing the pre-cum down to the base.

Thomas's eyes close and he practically melts in my hand. For a man who hasn't had sex in over a thousand years, he has impressive stamina. His mouth goes to mine, and I can taste myself on his lips.

"I need to fuck you, Ace. I need to bury my cock inside of you. Now." He kisses me again. "I can't wait any longer."

He throws me back and moves on top of me. Legs apart, I grab his hips and guide him to me, then slide one hand down and take hold of his large cock. My heart skips a beat when the tip presses into me. It's been a while since I've had sex, and I've never had a cock as big as his inside of me.

"Are you ready, Ace?" he growls. "Are you ready for me to fuck you?"

"Yes," I pant.

"Once I start I won't be able to stop until I'm done." He wraps his hand around mine, pushing his cock into my core. Anticipation tingles through me and the need to have him take me is all-consuming.

"I'm ready, Thomas. I need to feel you inside of me."

Without any warning, he plunges that big cock in. I cry out, both from the shock of the tight fit and from how fucking good it feels. He thrusts in deep, moaning as he pushes his cock inside me before pulling back and pushing in again.

It's basic and animalistic. His need to come is so strong it's all he can think about. And then he suddenly slows, circling his hips and hitting me at another angle. One that feels fucking amazing. He leans back, fucking me slow, and rubs my clit with his thumb in time with his thrusts.

I curl my nails into his muscular biceps, breath hitching as another orgasm rolls through me. I cry out as it hits, pussy contracting wildly around Thomas's thick cock. He lowers his head, kissing me ferociously as he fucks me hard and fast. His wings spread open and he buries his cock as deep as he can, bending his head down to kiss me as he comes.

His cock pulses, spilling warmth inside me, and he lets out a shuddering breath. My arms fall back onto the mattress, and I cannot catch my breath. Thomas pulls out and lies on the bed, bringing me to him.

"That was amazing," I pant.

Thomas pushes my messy hair out of my face. "That was. We should do it again sometime." He grins and wiggles his eyebrows, making me laugh. He's already dangerous, with his wings and fangs and inhuman strength. Add in his good looks, ability to make me laugh *and* make me come twice in a row…he could be a stone-cold killer.

"Give me a couple of hours."

"I'll be waiting." He's hopeful and I know he will be ready for round two in probably a few more minutes instead of hours.

"We'll see."

Thomas trails his fingers along my body, exploring every curve. "You're beautiful, Ace."

Despite the fact that this half-man, half-gargoyle was just all up in my personal business, I blush from the compliment. I don't get complimented like that very often, and I let myself get close to people even less.

"You're not too bad yourself, even if you don't think so."

"Oh, I know I'm good-looking." Thomas's eyes glimmer behind his smirk. "Even with the fangs. Though you did say some women get off on the fangs."

"Some do." I smile back.

"Can you promise me something?"

I lift my head to meet Thomas's gaze. "What?"

"Don't go after the vampires alone." The cockiness is gone again, and I'm seeing the real Thomas once more. His jaw tenses and his hold on me tightens. "I've never…" He trails off and shakes his head.

"What?"

"I don't want anything to happen to you," he says, and I know that's not what he was originally going to say. I don't press him. He'll tell me in time. "So don't go after them alone."

He knows I can't promise that. He knows I won't. And then I realize he doesn't want me to. I cup his cheek with my hand and move in, lips brushing against his as I talk.

"I don't make promises I can't keep."

"Neither do I."

I shiver and he spoons his body around mine, using one of his wings to keep me warm. I'm so tired. Mentally and physically worn. I could easily drift to sleep, but right as I'm dozing off, Thomas sits up and tips his head toward the window.

"Someone is here."

13

"Here?" I echo.

"Yes. In a car."

Why would someone—oh, right. "The food." Begrudgingly, I get up and look around for my clothes. Skipping my bra, I pull a T-shirt from my bag and slip it over my head on my way to the bathroom. The doorbell rings right after I flush. Shit. I pull on underwear and grab sleeper shorts, putting them on as I go down the hall.

The doorbell rings a second time. I break into a jog, not wanting to miss our food. I almost slip on my way down the stairs, catching myself at the last minute. Gilbert is at the door, eyes narrowed with distrust. I hesitate when I see him. There's no way he didn't hear what just went on upstairs.

"It's just the guy bringing our food," I say, diverting my eyes.

"Can you be sure?"

"No, but I'm hoping."

"I'm sure you're hungry," he says with a grin. "Sounds like you worked up an appetite."

"Oh my god." I turn away, cheeks turning red. "Yeah, I, uh...we..."

"You don't have to explain, Ace."

I nod and hurry through the foyer, then grab my purse and throw open the door. God, this was awkward.

"Hi," I say to the young man holding my bags of Chinese food. "Sorry. I was upstairs."

His eyes nervously shift around and he tries to look inside the house. I can feel Gilbert's presence behind me, but trust he has enough sense to stay out of sight. I pay for the food and give him a generous tip. He hands over the bags and turns to go but stops before he gets to the first porch step.

"You should leave." His voice is barely a whisper. "Something doesn't feel right about this place." He looks around and shakes his head. "Sorry." He turns and runs back to his car, peeling out of the driveway as fast as possible.

His words unnerve me, but only for a second. I shut the door and find all four gargoyles standing in the foyer, both waiting for the food and making sure I'm safe. Things might not feel *right* here because what we've been forced to believe is right is actually all wrong.

I wave them all into the kitchen and set the food on the table. Thomas and I just hooked up, and the others had to have heard us. Yet none of them are acting like it's weird.

Jacques gets plates from the cabinet. Hasan fills a glass with water from the tap. Thomas and Gilbert open the bags, curiously looking at the containers of takeout. We're like a dysfunctional family.

"Are you going to the vampire bar tonight?" Hasan asks, breaking an egg roll in half.

"I feel like I should." I take a seat closest to the radiator. "Though it kinda just occurred to me I have nothing to wear. I need to fit in, not look like an undercover cop who may or may not have magical powers."

"You wear less clothing than the women of our time." Hasan runs his eyes over me, and it's like he's stripping me naked right now.

"Yeah, we do. Women's clothing has been revolutionized over the last few years, though we're still working on the whole free-the-nipple thing."

"Your nipples look free."

I turn my head down, remembering I'm not wearing a bra. The flush is back to my cheeks, but instead of embarrassment, I feel empowered. "I still have to cover them in public."

"That's a shame," Thomas quips, giving me a wink. I smile and blush, wishing we could go back upstairs. Not for more sex, but just to lie in bed again together. Being close to him is comforting, physically and emotionally.

I shake my head. "It'd be nice to be all equal and everything, but we have bigger problems."

"Like the vampires," Jacques says.

"Right." I dig into my fried rice, suddenly realizing how absolutely starving I am. "I need to go to the bar and scope it out. It might be a dead end, but I at least need to look." Going off the photos I saw on social media, the dress code for Delirium is black, tight, and slutty. My one black dress won't cut it. I have to go shopping, and I'm not entirely sure where to go for clubwear. And how the hell do I hide my gun if I'm wearing a short dress? Plus running in heels...forget it. I'll find something in my closet and make it work.

"I DON'T LIKE THIS." Jacques crosses his arms, eyes narrowing.

"Too bad." I lean back on the couch, pulling the blanket over my legs. "To be fair, I don't like it much either. But like I said before, we don't have much of a choice."

"We do." He paces back and forth in front of the large windows in the living room. There's a fire going again, and the flames illuminate his wings, highlighting the detail. My mind goes back to what Thomas said about him and how he rejected material wealth. Jacques can read and write in several languages. He had to have come from a rich and noble family.

He turns, eyes zeroing in on me. My heart skips a beat and the memory of him making love to me comes rushing back. I'm still tender from having Thomas's large cock inside me, yet my body craves another.

"Care to elaborate?"

"Yes. Don't go in alone."

"That's not a plan." I throw out my hands, exasperated. We've been going 'round and 'round in this loop for the last twenty minutes. "That's the exact opposite of a plan."

"Plans are carefully formulated."

"This plan *is* carefully formulated. I'm going to go back to my apartment, find something sort of sexy to wear, go to the bar, look for anyone with fangs, and be back here by midnight." I look at the time. "Okay, one AM. I'll still get five hours of sleep before getting up for work."

"And if you see a vampire?"

"I'll leave."

Jacques raises an eyebrow in question.

"Really," I tell him. "I haven't had a chance to make any wooden stakes yet anyway, let alone soak them in holy water. Cutting off heads might be effective, but it's not really my thing." I pull my hair into a ponytail, accidentally catching my fingers on the scab on my head.

"Are you all right?" Jacques takes my hand, pulling it away from my head. "That doesn't look good."

"I know," I admit with a sigh. "I don't think it's infected. Yet. I kinda forgot about it."

"How did you forget about that? It's not like you have anything going on."

"Are you making a joke?" I bring my hand to my mouth, feigning shock.

"Was it funny?" A lightness takes over his dark eyes and he walks away from the windows. The others are outside, stretching their wings and patrolling. I'm not sure what they're worried about finding, and I don't want to ask. Not yet.

"Yeah, it was," I say with a smile.

"I like seeing you smile."

My smile grows. "I like smiling."

He lets go of my hand and sits on the couch next to me. I haven't seen Jacques smile—really smile—anywhere other than my dream. Speaking of the dream, my eyes go to the scar on his waist. Apprehensively, I reach out and touch it, tracing the thick line of scar tissue down to the waist of his pants.

"How did you get this?"

He turns his head, looking down to see which scar I'm talking about.

"I was a knight," he says, like it's obvious. "I fought."

I continue tracing the scar, pushing past the waist of his pants. Jacques inhales deeply, muscular chest rising.

"You're definitely nothing like the priests I knew growing up."

"What about this?" His hand lands on my thigh and slides down to my knee. "How'd you get this scar?"

"I fell off a bike when I was twelve years old. Scraped the hell out of that whole leg but that's the only scar that remains. A true testament to my wild childhood, that's for sure."

Jacques smiles along with me, then shakes his head. "I have no idea what a bike is."

"A horse on wheels. Wait, no." I laugh. "That's a terrible description. Tomorrow I'm bringing my computer. I can use my phone as a hotspot and we're watching a movie. I think that's the best way to expose you all to the modern world. Lots and lots of movies."

"I don't know what those are either."

"I'll bring you newer books too. Though *Emma* is a good one to start with. Taking a couple hundred years off might help with the shock that'll come from the digital age and all."

Silence falls between us, and every time I blink, I see Jacques as a man—a naked man—before me.

On top of me.

In me.

I let out a breath, trying to cool off. But there's no escaping the heat quickly building inside.

"Are you scared?" he asks.

"Of what?"

"Vampires."

I bend my legs up onto the couch, resituating so I'm leaning closer to Jacques. "Yes and no. I try not to let myself think ahead to the 'what ifs' in life. Because at the root of it all, that's what's scary. *What if* the vampires attack me? *What if* I can't fight them off and I die?" I quickly shake my head. "I'm not proving my point very well."

"I think I know what you mean," he says. "The unknown is what we fear. What if something bad happens? The more likely we are to get hurt in an unknown situation, the more likely we are to feel fear."

"Right. And the more comfortable we are, the more we assume we're fine, the less fear we feel." I grab a loose string on the hem of my sleeper shorts and pull on it. "Though, in my line of work, I know that's all bullshit. Being comfortable doesn't stop the bad things. Terrible shit can happen in the best settings, you know? So, I guess, no, I'm not scared of the vampires. I'm scared of what could happen, but if I'm prepared, I'll be okay. And, really, I could die in a freak accident any day. Living in fear robs you of life."

He looks at me with admiration. "I understand. I didn't when I was...when I was human."

I study his handsome face, trying hard not to fan the fire that's burning inside me. "It's not too late. And it's not like I'm some inspirational chick living life to the fullest with amazing Instagram pictures to prove it. I do nothing but work and justify it to myself that I'm making the world a better place. Yeah, my life might be empty and unfulfilling, but the dead guy in the alley had a great life and I owe it to him and his family to find the low-life who killed him." The words rush out of me, and the raw honesty almost feels as good as sex.

Almost.

"You fear fear."

"Yeah, I guess I do." I bring my arms close to my body, fighting off a chill. I'm convinced this house is never going to heat up. "And clowns. I am absolutely terrified of clowns."

"What's a clown?"

"A horrible, terrifying, and most likely soul-sucking creature meant to entertain children." I take my phone from the coffee table and do a quick Google search for clowns.

"They are terrifying," Jacques agrees, eyes wide. "They're for children?"

"Theoretically."

"What is their purpose?"

"They're supposed to be funny, but most people disagree."

"I'm one of them," Jacques says so seriously it makes me laugh.

"A really creepy clown movie came out a few years ago and I wanted to watch it, you know, to face my fears. But I couldn't do it." I smile and roll my eyes at myself. "Maybe someday, right?"

"Right." He angles his torso in toward mine and brings his hand up, gently cupping my cheek. "You look so much like her," he whispers, and I think he's talking to himself and not me.

"Who?"

His hand falls and his dark eyes cloud over with emotion. "No one."

"Braeya?"

Jacques turns away. "You should go if you want to make it back around midnight. There's not much time left."

"Right." I shake myself and stand, going upstairs to change out of my PJs and back into the clothes I had on earlier. It's a bit too chilly to go out in shorts just yet. Jacques isn't in the living room anymore when I come back down. I take a lingering look through the house, finding everything to be quiet. I'm almost to the front door when the floor creaks behind me.

"He's not going to talk about her."

I whirl around to find Gilbert casually leaning against the wall. He was so not there a second ago.

"Braeya?" I ask.

"Yes. I don't even know the details."

"Who was she? Did they have a thing going between them or something?"

Gilbert pushes off the wall, large wings blocking out the light behind him. He's just a shadow in the dark right now, a large black shape looming near me.

"It started as a spell."

"A spell?"

"I just said that, didn't I? Keep up, Detective."

I make a face. "She cast a spell on him?"

Gilbert nods. "Jacques held a high position within the Templars. There were many who opposed us, hell, even I opposed us, and they'd do whatever they could to break us down. All I know is Braeya—and her father—came from a long line of pagan magicians. She cast a love spell on Jacques to get information on the Templars. When she discovered that not all of the Templars were assholes, she lifted the spell. But whatever he felt during the spell didn't just go away. They saw each other after."

"That's fucked up."

"I know. I think she felt bad for doing it to him. He and Hasan were some of the few who truly believed in the mission, in making the world a better place or some bullshit like that."

"Then what happened?" I ask, hanging onto his every word like he's reading a paranormal Nicholas Sparks novel. Only, I know this story doesn't have a happy ending.

"I don't know. We got blamed for her death and turned into monsters."

"He said I look like her."

Gilbert shrugs. "Maybe. I never saw her. I only heard about her bewitching beauty. Going on that alone, yeah, I could see how you look like her. You're quite beautiful, Ace."

Just like his brother, he's blunt with his comments. "You're only saying that because you haven't seen any other women in the last thousand years."

He laughs, eyes glimmering. "True, but I know what makes my cock hard, and that's *you*."

On their own accord, my eyes drop to his crotch. The bulge in his pants is obvious even in the dark.

"Though what I'm more concerned with, Ace," He moves across the hall, stepping in front of me. One hand lands on my waist and he pushes in, pinning me against the wall. "is if you want me as much as I want you."

My heart speeds up and I lose the battle not to reach out and touch him. I flatten my palms on his chest, feeling his heart beat beneath my fingers. He moves my hair aside and puts his mouth to my neck. His touch is different than what I felt earlier.

Patient.

Gentle.

He's going to take his time.

And he said it himself: he's more concerned with me being turned on.

"But I just..." I start, feeling that flush come back to my face. I was naked and under Thomas not that long ago. I'm more than ready to have a go at round two, but will Thomas care? We didn't establish anything, because the sex happened naturally between us. Nothing needed to be established.

"I know," he says softly.

"You don't care?"

"Not if you don't. Thom and I…we're used to sharing everything. We like it. As long as it's okay with you." His lips brush against me as he talks. "Are you okay with it, Ace?"

"Yes," I breathe, and feel a rush of excitement go through me. I've never done anything like this before. Slowly, I slide my hands down to his waist, then slip them behind his back. I'm a little nervous and hope I'm able to please him as much as I'd pleased Thomas. I urge him closer, wanting to feel every inch of him against me.

I plunge my hand inside his pants. My fingers brush over his cock, hard and thick, just like his twin. I run my hand along his inner thigh, slowly dragging my fingers back up. I cup his balls and he trails kisses along my collarbone.

Suddenly, he grabs my wrists in his hands and brings them over my head. His gentle kisses turn rough, and the boyish charm has vanished from his face. I stand there, ass pressed into the wall, body on fire. I need him to touch me.

But the moment his skilled fingers go into my pants, a long and harrowing scream comes from the porch.

14

"Stay here." Gilbert's fangs show as he snarls, going into protective mode. He jerks away, leaving me against the wall. I blink and push off, going after him.

"No, you stay here. I'm a cop, remember. You can't be—"

Another scream, high-pitched and feminine, reverberates off the house, followed by someone yelling "There's something on the roof!" and a clamoring of footsteps on the porch.

"Seen," I finish, knowing it's too late. Gilbert hasn't been seen, but someone else has. I grab my gun and throw back the front door. "Hey!" I yell at two running teenagers and jump down the steps. The cobblestone is cold under my bare feet. "Stop before I call the police!"

The girl slows, but her male partner in crime keeps going. He steals a glance back at me and notices the gun in my hand. "Faster!" he shouts to the girl, and I roll my eyes. You can't outrun bullets, idiot. And he's running in a straight line down the driveway, which is their only option unless they want to take a chance in the tangle of trees and weeds that line the property. I'm pretty sure there's a broken fence in there somewhere, which will definitely slow them down.

Hasan flies overhead, high enough to be just a shadow in the dark. The girl drops down, screaming.

"That thing is back! Jared, stop!"

"She's right, Jared. You should stop." I don't mean to sound as creepy as I do, but it's working in my favor.

Jared, a red-haired, freckle-faced boy who can't be any older than fifteen, comes to a stop and slowly turns, raising his arms to the side. He's holding a camera in one hand.

"Don't shoot us," the girl begs. She has long blonde hair and vivid eyes and is way too pretty for Jared. "We didn't know anyone lived here."

Hasan stands at the end of the driveway, ready to stop the kids if they start running again, and I can feel the others behind me, ready if I need them.

"What the hell are you doing on my property?" I ask.

The girl's eyes widen in fear. "We...we...wanted to see—"

"Shut up," Jared mumbles. "We were looking for our dog."

"With cameras?"

"Night vision. To try and see him better."

God, this kid is a pompous ass. "You are still trespassing, and whatever footage you recorded previously will disprove your lost dog story."

He shrugs. "What are you going to do about it, lady? Arrest us?" He lets out a snort of laughter.

"Actually, I might." I lower my gun and pull my badge from inside my shirt.

"Shit, Jared!" The girl starts to cry. "My dad's going to kill me!"

"Tell me what you're really doing here." I let go of my badge, chain swinging over my breasts. I don't want to press charges against these kids, even though I'm annoyed as fuck right now. That would take too long. They need to leave, and I'm pretty sure if the threat of being arrested isn't enough to scare them away for good, having my gargoyles ominously fly overhead a time or two will be.

"What you're really doing here," I press, feeling the presence of the gargoyles move in.

"This place is supposed to be haunted," the girl admits. "I saw the light on but didn't know anyone moved it. I am so, so sorry."

"Give me your camera." I hold out my hand.

"No way. You can't take it from me. I know my rights." Jared snubs his nose at me.

"And I know mine." I flash a fake smile. "I'm going to have to call this in. Trespassing and an attempted break-in."

"Break-in?"

"You were on my porch in the dark. Pretty suspicious, if you ask me."

"But we weren't—we were just looking," he stammers.

I shrug. "It didn't look like it to me, and when the cops take your camera and phone for evidence, it'll be up to the court to decide."

"Just give her the camera," the girl says through gritted teeth. "If he gives you the camera, will you let us go?"

"Camera first." I extend my hand and Jared gives me the camera with a huff. I delete the three minutes of footage he recorded. The little shit lied and he wasn't even recording in night vision. Everything is dark, blurry, and hard to see. "I don't have time to deal with little assholes like you. I have real work to do. Murderers to catch. Drug dealers to arrest. Go home to your iPads and Netflix." I hand him the camera back. "And if I ever see you put a toe on my property again, I will have you arrested for trespassing, okay?"

"I am so sorry," the girl says, and tugs on Jared's sleeve.

"And the house is haunted," I tell them. "With lots of dangerous, angry spirits who don't take kindly to strangers."

"Or gargoyles?" Jared loses a bit of his attitude as his eyes flick behind me. Something spooked them *before* I got out here. How much of the gargoyles had they seen?

"What are you talking about?"

"There were four gargoyles on the house. I've seen them before."

I raise an eyebrow. "So you're admitting to trespassing previously?"

"I took my sister door to door selling Girl Scout cookies. Is that against the law, too?"

"Depends on the mood the judge is in," I admit. "I had the gargoyles removed to be restored." I say the first thing that comes to mind. It's an expensive lie, but not a terrible one. "Now, unless you want to find out how competent minors can be tried as adults, I suggest you leave." I look down the driveway, wishing I could see in the dark like the gargoyles. "How did you get here?"

"I live up the street, about half a mile away. We walked."

I let out a sigh. "You shouldn't do that. Walking around a rural road at night isn't safe for adults, let alone a couple kids. The world is unforgiving. I'm a homicide detective, and I'd hate to stumble upon your bodies in the ditch."

The wind blows dry branches overhead, and the distant flapping of wings can barely be heard over the rustle of the trees. Both kids startle, looking around with fear in their eyes.

Good.

Shivering, I watch them hurry down the driveway.

"Should we follow them?" Thomas asks from the shadows. He and Gilbert are only yards away.

"Yeah, but only to make sure they get home okay."

"You're worried about their safety?" Gilbert gives me a look. "After they came onto your property, poking around, looking for *us*?"

"They're just kids. Annoying, entitled kids, but kids. And I'm actually not surprised this place is rumored to be haunted. I doubt they're the first to come poking around, either, and probably won't be the last. I need a fence." I rub the goosebumps on my arms and head back into the house to grab my shit. I'm not leaving until those kids are back inside their house. If they saw me take off down the road right after they left, they might think they'd rattled me.

And because I meant what I said about the night being dangerous. Though with Thomas and Gilbert keeping watch, I have no doubt they'll make it home safely. I brush dirt from my socks and take a seat on the couch in the front living room.

The front door opens, and I know it's Jacques before I can see him. Each gargoyle has a different energy about them, and I'm starting to be able to tell each one apart.

Maybe there is some magic in me after all.

"You look tired, Ace." Jacques's voice is low. "Maybe you should stay home tonight."

"This isn't my home," I blurt.

"Do you want it to be?"

"I don't know." I'm resisting this place. I'm resisting what could very well be my destiny. I'm resisting my growing feelings. I'm resisting *them*.

Relying on people, getting close and opening myself up emotionally always ends one way, and it's never good. Once the curse is broken, what's stopping the guys from leaving?

"It's not mine either," he says softly, and his words surprise me.

"What do you consider home?"

He slowly shakes his head. "I don't know anymore. Though, if my years of travel have taught me anything, it's that home isn't always a place."

I give him a small smile. "People still say that, even after a thousand years. There's a difference between a house and a home, and if I'm honest...it's been a long time since I felt like I had a home too."

He doesn't have to say it for me to know we're both longing for a place to lay down roots and call our own.

"I LITERALLY HAVE NOTHING TO WEAR."

I sort through my clothes one more time, looking for anything remotely sexy. Thinking back, I cannot recall the last time I tried to dress up for anyone, actually. And I'm well aware how pathetic that is. I haven't had a boyfriend in three years, and, until tonight, it had been over a year since I had sex with something other than rubber and plastic.

I have a lot of workout clothes, a decent number of jeans, and just enough professional wear to look presentable for meetings and conferences. The few "going out" clothes I had were dated and I donated them to Goodwill last Christmas.

The curling iron I plugged in starts to smell hot, reminding me of how little time I have. I grab a black silky camisole and put it on. It's something I wear under a blouse, and it's too loose-fitting to work. It *looks* like an undergarment and not in the sexy way.

I fiddle with the straps on my pushup bra, propping the girls up as much as possible. Finally, I settle on tight jeans, a black V-neck T-shirt that shows off a decent amount of cleavage, and the only pair of heels that I own. Then I quickly curl my hair and put on makeup before I head out the door, nerves growing the closer I get to the bar.

With my gun, badge, and phone in my purse, I swallow my pounding heart and get out of the car. Unable to find parking out front, I'm parked a block down. People mill in and out of the bar, most dressed to fit the Gothic theme. The bouncer stands just inside the door, checking IDs. He doesn't smell like sulfur, his eyes are brown, and I don't see any evidence of fangs.

For a weeknight, the bar is packed. Loud music thumps in my ears, and I take a moment to observe the other patrons to try and clue myself in to how to act in this type of social setting. Being out of my element makes my usual I-don't-give-a-fuck-what-others-think-about-me personality falter and I feel a tad self-conscious. Knowing I can't just stand here and look around, I go to the bar, grab the first stool I can, and order a vodka and cranberry.

I sip it, turning in the stool to watch the crowd. *You're a sexy young woman here to have fun. Act like it.* My gaze zeroes in on a group of girls who look to be about my age. All three are in skin-tight leather dresses, with their hair teased and curled to perfection, and just the right amount of black eyeliner to look edgy and cool.

They're talking, drinking, and dancing, and look totally at ease. Being here alone limits me, and I have to force myself not to think about how I don't even have friends to invite out with me even if I wasn't on a secret mission to gather vampire intel.

"Hey." A short blond guy saunters over, leaning onto the bar next to me to order another drink. He's also dressed in all black and has fake fangs fitted over his teeth. "First time here?"

I take another sip of my drink, waiting for the "because I would have remembered you" line.

"Yeah. How can you tell?"

"You look nervous." He rests his elbow on the bar and lowers his gaze from my face to my breasts, letting it linger there for a few seconds. "And I wouldn't forget a pair of tits like those."

I grind my jaw. He's an asshole. A pig and an asshole, who probably has a small dick. Hating myself just a bit, I fake a smile, acting flattered and shy at the same time.

"I take it you come here often?" I take another sip of my drink. I don't intend on finishing it.

"I'm a regular," he says proudly, flashing the fake fangs, which are several shades whiter than his normal teeth. "It gets addictive."

"The bar?" I ask, since I can't come out and say "the vampire sex" without raising alarm.

"It's more the camaraderie here. We all have something in common and we don't judge each other's freaky interests."

"That's actually really awesome."

"I've met some good friends through this place." He gets his drink but doesn't leave. "What brings you here?"

"Curiosity." I flash a smile, watching his body language. I'm going to give him whatever he wants—without ever touching him, that is. This guy could be my ticket to the back room.

"I like curiosity." He takes a big gulp of his drink, then offers me a hand to shake. "My name's Darrell, by the way."

"Emma."

"Beautiful name for a beautiful woman." He downs the rest of his drink. "So, Emma, what are you curious about?"

I lean closer. "A friend came here not too long ago and told me she had the *best* night, if you know what I mean." I touch my neck then sweep my fingers down over my breasts.

"Oh, I think I do." He looks me up and down. "You're into that?"

I fake a high-pitched laugh. "Are you judging me, Darrell? I thought you said this was a safe place to be myself."

"It definitely is, baby."

It takes effort not to cringe. I do not like pet names, especially when they come from stout little men wearing Halloween-costume-quality fangs. I take my straw between my lips, pretending to take a drink. I catch sight of the three girls in all leather again. They're at a table now, taking selfies and sucking down margaritas.

"Want to watch a show with me?" Darrell asks.

"Uh, sure. Yeah. Definitely yeah." That was easier than I thought, and I'm both grateful I don't have to schmooze him anymore and taken aback from the ease at which he asked me to watch a strip show with him.

"Follow me." He steps forward, holding out his arm. I loop mine through, leaning in to smell him for good measure. He's in need of a shower and to lay off the cigarettes, but he doesn't stink of sulfur. We weave our way through the people on the dance floor and go behind a black velvet curtain that leads to a narrow hallway and down a set of stairs into the basement.

I'm a cop with a loaded gun in my purse and this is making me nervous. What the fuck were some of these women thinking, going to a place like this?

"After you," he says, holding out a hand. I push open a blood-red door, emerging into what looks like the typical strip club you'd see in movies. Three girls are on stage, bending over and shaking their asses in the faces of horny men. A male couple is making out at one of the booths, and the fat old man who's getting a lap dance seems to be having a hard time controlling himself. A few other couples are here, looking like they're pretty damn into this as well.

I follow Darrell to a small table near the front, and I try to quickly scope everything out before taking a seat. Along with the door we came through, there's one behind the bar, probably leading to a kitchen, and a third on the side wall, and it's labeled as the emergency exit. There are rooms behind the stage, of course, and who knows where that leads.

Only seconds after we're seated, a cocktail waitress who must double as a stripper on stage brings us complimentary glasses of champagne. Darrell drinks his down and I look inside my glass for any sort of remnants of a pill not yet dissolved. I don't see any, but I don't risk drinking it.

Darrell gets right into it, pointing to each girl and telling me their names and their special talents on the stage. He keeps elbowing me, telling me not to be shy and to relax and enjoy myself. *Lives are at stake. Lives are at stake.*

"Come on, Emma." He slides the flute of champagne in front of me, sloshing some down the side. "Drink and have a good time." If he doesn't shut the fuck up, *his* life is going to be at stake.

A large group of women come in, here to celebrate a bachelorette party. Darrell is way too excited about it and I can tell he's debating leaving me to go socialize with them. They look more his type, at least.

A male stripper comes out next, to appease the bride, no doubt. He's tall and muscular, with weird-looking tattoos all over his dark skin. Could he be my vamp? I sit up straighter and lean in.

"Ahh, you see something you like." Darrell laughs to cover up his disdain. "I'm not surprised. Joe gets all the ladies."

"His name is Joe?"

"I don't think it's his real name," Darrell explains. "He hardly speaks any English."

Ding-ding-ding, we have a winner. Would it be too much to get a lap dance from this guy solely so I can smell him? I bet he'd make me pay extra for that.

"I need to use the ladies' room." I stand, keeping my purse close to my body, and look around. I don't really have to go, but I need to get a closer look at the stripper, and one more minute with Darrell might lead me to becoming a murderer myself.

"By the bar," Darrell says, fishing a dollar bill from his pocket. I take my drink with me, dropping it in a trash barrel as I walk by. Joe leaps off the stage, making the bachelorette partygoers scream and squeal. I slow to watch him go to the bride, thrust his hips in her face a few times, and then take her hand, leading her up onto the stage.

She's a pretty girl, wearing a black and red corset that squeezes her already thin torso. Laughing, she sits in the wooden chair on the stage and holds up a handful of cash. Joe takes it, then drops it behind him, seemingly uninterested. Lights from the stage reflect off his eyes. It's hazy in here already from the smoke, making it hard to discern if there's something off about his eyes or if that reddish hint is from the red and pink lights flashing above him.

I go around a table, headed for the ladies' room. And then I see her, one of the tight-leather-dress girls, wobbling through the back of this place to the private rooms. She's drunk, hanging all over the guy and laughing loudly as she trips, hardly able to talk anymore. He slips his arm around her, nervously looking around.

Vampire or not, the guy's a creep. She's obviously had too much, and even if he's not planning on drinking her blood, I'm willing to bet my badge on him not getting consent for anything he's about to do.

I hurry down the hall after them, and my stupid heels catch on the carpet. I throw out my hand to catch myself, but me tripping over my own fucking feet doesn't go unnoticed.

The guy dragging tight-leather-dress girl jerks his head back, startled. The lights flash, reflecting off his eyes like an animal in headlights. For a split second, he just stares at me, and then he starts forward again, probably assuming I'm just another drunk girl who can't walk a straight line to save her life. He picks up his pace, needing to practically lift the drunk girl off the ground so she can keep up.

I'm narrowing in, planning on pulling my badge from my purse and having him arrested for sexual assault. And then I smell it, and it's getting stronger and stronger the closer I get to the private rooms.

Sulfur.

15

I freeze, eyes going wide. My heart skips a beat, and every muscle inside me twitches in response. I want to run after him. I want to pull tight-leather-dress girl from his arms and bring her back to safety. I want to hit him hard in the face, harder in the dick, and end this once and for all.

But I can't.

Because I know from the strong smell of sulfur coming from the looming room in front of me, he's not the only vampire here. I went up against three vampires before and didn't make it. I promised I wouldn't take my chances, and I'm not even prepared. If I go in that room, there's a good chance I'll never come back out.

I lean against the wall and let out a breath, trying to stay calm and think clearly. I need a plan, and fast. Who knows what's going to go on behind closed doors. Either way, I'm sure it won't be in tight-leather-dress girl's favor. She'll be assaulted and violated in at least one way, and I cannot stand here and let that happen.

I'm not a betting person, but I'm willing to bet at least ninety percent of the people here at Delirium are humans. The bar is known for being dark, sexy, and obscure. Not murderous or dangerous. Reputation is important for places like this, but I don't think that's enough to work in my favor. I'm in the basement moving farther and farther away from the majority of the patrons.

The music is loud. Loud enough to drown out screams.

Taking another breath, I push off the wall, cursing the stupid heels, and move swiftly down the hall. It ends in a T, and they go to the left. I pause, slowly inching forward to see what I'm walking into. To my right is an exit that I'm guessing leads to the alley out back. To my left—and the way the vampire and tight-leather-dress girl went—is another hall. The lights are low and there are several doors on each side.

Low moaning comes from behind the closest door, followed by the distinct sound of an ass getting smacked.

"Harder, baby," a muffled male voice cries. Someone's ass gets smacked again and the moaning ensues. The door to room number five shuts and I continue down the hall, trying to see if the smell of sulfur is coming from one specific room.

It seems to be coming from all of them.

I stop before door number five and listen for a beat. I don't hear anything, which is both good and bad, and I'm hoping it means there's only one vampire in there. One I can handle.

Maybe.

Probably.

I fucking hope so.

I unzip my purse, making sure my gun is easily accessible, though I'm really hoping I'm not going to need it. Bullets won't kill the vampire and explaining why I shot someone is not something I want to do right now. Or ever.

I blink, force my shoulders back, and grab the doorknob. It opens with a twist, and I stumble in, doing my best to appear wasted. The door hits the wall behind it, and the vampire jolts up. The room is set up much like a hotel room, with a bed in the center, lame decorations, and a dresser on the adjacent wall.

Unlike a regular hotel room, there are chains on the wall over the bed and bloodstains on the carpet. The guy is sitting on the bed, with the drunk girl on his lap. Her head droops down and I know she's close to passing out.

"Josh?" I call, stumbling into the room. "Are you in here, Joshy? I'm sorry I got mad at you," I slur, and stop a few feet from the door.

Tight-leather-dress girl looks up, blinking rapidly. She's so drunk she has no idea what's going on. The guy narrows his eyes and I'm still not sure if he's human or a vampire. The entire room stinks like sulfur, cigarette smoke, and bleach. The scent is so strong it makes me nauseous. He narrows his eyes and his glare gives me a chill.

"You're not Josh." I put out my hand, acting like I can hardly stand. "But hey!" I point to the girl. "I know you! We went to McKinley High together. Allison, right?"

"No, I'm Marissa, and I...I..." She leans over the bed and pukes. The guy on the bed shoves her to the floor, and her hands land in her vomit.

"Stupid bitch," he sneers, and I think I see a flash of fang under his lips. He looks down at his feet, worried there might be puke on his expensive-looking shoes.

"I got her," I say, trying to keep up my drun- girl pretense. "Come on, Marissa. Let's go to the bathroom and get you cleaned up."

She grabs onto the bed, needing to pull herself up. I take her arm and start to lead her out the door. My heart is racing and I know I'm only seconds away from my cover being blown. The guy moves closer behind me and the source of the smell of sulfur is undeniable now. It's coming from him.

"Come on," I say again, and urge her to move a little faster. I've only been this drunk once before, and it was in college. I spent the night puking into my dorm's toilet and was convinced I was dying. If I give her one second to hesitate and sit down, I probably won't get her back up again.

We're almost to the door when the guy grabs my arm.

"Looks like your boyfriend left you," he coos in my ear. "Why don't you stay and play with me?"

"In a room full of barf? No thank you." I push Marissa out the door and jerk my arm back. He tightens his grip and tips his head down to mine, flashing red eyes.

He expected me to scream in shock and fear. He didn't expect me to bring my knee up to his balls, then shove him back. He hits the door and opens his mouth. A row of fangs drops down from his gums.

"Run," I tell Marissa, and give her another push. She takes a few quick paces then falters, sliding against the wall. I grab her wrist and pull her up. "Keep going."

I turn back just in time to duck out of the way of a punch from the vampire. His fist hits the wall, and his hand goes through the drywall, getting momentarily stuck. I turn my attention back to Marissa and help her get a few more feet away before the vampire grabs a handful of my hair, yanking me back.

I whirl around, already prepared, and deliver a hard blow to his nose with my elbow. The pain does little to stun him. My heart is in my throat as my mind races with what to do. Shooting him in the head might work. But it might not. And then there will be mass chaos from a gunshot and people could get hurt.

He advances on me again, and I move out of the way, sending him crashing into the wall. He might be stronger than me, but I'm quicker and more skilled in my movements. As a woman, I've learned over the years that blunt force and brute strength aren't necessary to win. Years and years of self-defense classes and belts earned in various martial arts have given me a leg up, and, thankfully, this vampire hasn't figured it out yet.

He hits the wall hard and I reach inside my purse for my gun. Holding the barrel, I crack him over the head with it, and then kick him in the chest.

Marissa hasn't gotten very far, and, with another kick to the knee, the vampire goes down. He'll be back up in seconds, I know, but seconds are all I've got.

"Come on!" I shout at Marissa and put the gun back in my purse. Her eyes are wide and she's blinking rapidly, trying to process what the hell is going on. There's a good chance she'll remember this in the morning, but I'm hoping she'll chalk up her memories of the fangs and glowing eyes to having a few too many margaritas.

We get to the end of the hall and I gently shove her around the corner.

"Keep going," I say. "Find your friends."

I watch her take a few shaky steps down the hall, going back to the strip club, and turn, holding my gun out at my side. But the vampire isn't there. My heart thumps away, too loudly in my chest. The people in room three are fucking away and all the other doors are closed.

I narrow my eyes, looking in the doorways. He's here, I know it, and it's too damn dark to make anything out for sure. I risk a glance back down the hall at Marissa—she's wobbling and going slow but is still on her feet, thank God—and then look back and find myself face to face with the vampire.

Suddenly, he appears from the shadows and lurches forward, arms out. His hands strike me hard and the blow shoves me back into the wall. Everything happens so fast, and the blunt blow to the back of my head leaves me a little stunned. The vampire opens his mouth, showing off his fangs, and slowly lowers his mouth to my neck. His grip tightens on my arms and his nails dig into my flesh, breaking the skin on my arms. His teeth make contact with my neck.

And then he stops, jerking away as if I'm offensive.

"Malefica," he snarls, nostrils flaring. His red eyes are wild with rage, and his grip on me tightens. I fight against him but he's so fucking strong. "Malefica!" he shouts, but not at me. He turns his head and says it again, as if he's calling to someone.

The one-second distraction is all I need. I bring my arms up with as much force as I can muster, breaking his hold on me. I drop down, extending my leg and kicking him, knocking him off balance. I scramble away as he hits the floor, kicking him hard in between his legs before twisting away and rushing down the hall. I need to get out of here.

I'm not equipped to kill the vampires.

I'm having a hard time moving in these fucking heels.

And I'm mad as hell right now, making me act out emotionally instead of logically.

I can hear the vampire sputtering behind me. The smell of sulfur gets strong but I don't risk a look behind me. I don't have time. I need to get to the club and hope they don't follow. They ran away from the crime scene. I don't think they want to be caught.

They don't want people to know they exist.

Lights and music dance through the hall, and my heart beats faster the closer I get. I'm almost to the corner. If I can just make it around, make it to where I'm close enough to be heard, I'll—

Shit.

Another vampire rushes forward, coming around the corner with his mouth open in a hiss. I come to a halt, almost tipping over in these stupid fucking heels. At this point I think taking them off and being barefoot is a better bet.

Heart in my throat, I take a step back, fully aware there is another vampire encroaching only feet behind me. The new vampire is tall, with dark eyes and even darker hair. I move away and my back hits the wall. *Motherfucker*.

The new vampire tips his head down, inhaling deep. A smile creeps over his face, revealing yellowed fangs. He shudders with pleasure and smells me again.

"Creep," I huff, and push off the wall, punching him as hard as I can in the face. He blinks, the pain there and gone in just a second, and snarls at me. The other vampire is drawing near, and the tall one with the dark eyes springs forward. I jerk away, subsequently twisting my ankle. I'm never wearing heels again.

I slip back into a doorframe and slide down, my head hitting a doorknob on the way. It would hurt, regardless, but I hit my head in the same spot I'd been bashed with the rock. Pain sears through me, bringing little stars to my vision and a twist of nausea to my gut.

I blink rapidly, trying to clear my vision. The scab was scraped off and blood seeps down my hairline and onto my face. As much as I try to ignore the pain, it winds through me, blinding me and making me unable to move.

And that's all the vampires needed. That one second where I'm stunned.

One of them grabs my ankle and yanks me forward. I fly back, desperately lifting my neck to keep my head from hitting against the hard floor. I thrash and kick, doing everything I can to get away. The sharp bottom of my heel clips one of the vampires in the face, tearing the skin on his cheek.

He recoils, letting go of my leg. His hands fly to his face, and I know it's not the pain he's reacting to. He's concerned about his looks and doesn't want a mark. I press my hands onto the floor and push myself up, spinning and kicking the first vampire who attacked me. I use every ounce of strength I have to shove the other away.

Using the doorknob above me, I hoist myself up, but the vampire I kicked in the face grabs me by the waist and throws me to the floor. Hard. So hard, it knocks the wind out of me, leaving me gasping for air on the floor.

His hands go around my neck and he licks the blood dripping from my torn-open scab, shuddering the second his tongue is against my skin. He laps up more and lets out a moan. The other vampire is on the floor next to me now, putting his mouth over the small punctures in my arm made from his nails.

I only have a few seconds before I run out of oxygen. It doesn't take long to be strangled to death, and I don't know how I'm going to break free from the vampire's grasp. Desperation rises inside of me, and watching the vampires get off from drinking my blood makes me mad.

Really fucking mad.

I raise my hand and grab the face of the vampire on top of me, digging my fingers into his eyes and nose. Heat burns in the palm of my hand, almost as if I'm touching a hot iron. Only it doesn't hurt. Suddenly, the heat bursts into a bright ball of light, radiating out from under my fingers and glowing a fiery red.

I dig my nails into the vampire's face, and the smell of burning flesh fills my nostrils. I don't let myself think about the how or the why. All I know is I'm holding fire in my palm and it's not burning me.

But it's burning them.

The vampire screams, jerking his head back. Charred and blackened skin falls in flakes down on me. He lets go of my neck and brings his hands to his face, cradling his burns. He pulls away, flesh still glowing from the fire. I bend my legs up and kick him hard in the chest. He falls back, reeling with pain from the burn.

The vampire next to me scrambles away, mouth open in a hiss. On shaky legs, I get up, holding my hand out in front of me. My ears are ringing and exhaustion threatens to take over.

Using magic requires a lot of energy.

Jacques's voice rings in my ears. Magic. Motherfucking magic. I look away from the vampire for half a second to glance down at the flames surrounding my hand. My heart jolts again and I lurch forward, causing the vampire to jerk away.

"You picked the wrong girl," I spit, not caring I just said the most cliché thing possible. Along with the exhaustion comes a high, and I'm riding it to the top right now. I make a move toward the vampire, ready to press my hand to his chest and burn him until there's nothing left.

The other vamp is still on the floor, madly hitting himself in the face to try and put out the flames. I curl my fist and the flames intensify.

Holy.

Shit.

I'm controlling it. A wicked smile takes over my face and I round on the other vampire, holding out my hand.

"Not so scary now, are you?" I taunt, narrowing my eyes. "I know all about you and how you're turning people into vampires. And I'm going to stop you."

His snarl disappears and his eyes widen in fear. I advance, squinting from the bright light emanating from my hand. The power flows through me, intoxicating. Something clicks inside of me, and it's like a missing part of myself—a part I've always been looking for—is suddenly unveiled.

I've fought tooth and nail to find my place in the world, and no matter how good I was at my job, how successful I became in my field, it wasn't enough.

Now I know why.

This is who I'm meant to be.

I raise my other hand, staring at my fingers, and feel a spark hit the palm of my hand. I inhale and will the fire to spread. Holding flames in both hands, I look from vampire to vampire.

"You're fucked now. Tell me who's turning people into vampires and I'll make it a quick death."

The vampire with the burned face pushes up onto his knees, lips pulled back. He growls, but doesn't dare come at me, not when I'm holding some sort of unexplainable magic fire that I conjured out of thin air.

Slowly, I move away from the wall, still not liking being pinned against it even though I have the upper hand right now. Though as long as I can keep the flames going, I'm safe.

The unscathed vampire lunges for me but stops himself before he gets close enough to get burned.

"Hah. Nice try, asshole," I leer. "You're not so tough now when—"

A wave of exhaustion hits me and the fires dim, flames dying down to embers, falling from my hands. I blink, suddenly dizzy.

And then the fires go completely out.

16

Goddammit.

I flick my fingers out, desperately trying to reignite the fire...the fire I have no idea how I started in the first place. The vampire with the burned face is still a few feet away, and the other is looking at me apprehensively, not sure if I intentionally quenched the fires or not. I can't waste time letting him figure it out.

Not if I want to live.

I turn and sprint down the hall, but instead of turning and going back toward the club, I go the opposite direction to the door labeled exit. It could lead me into a dark storeroom for all I know.

I take my chance and push on the bar. The door swings open on rusty hinges and yellow light from the streetlamps spills into the building. I race outside, up a few cement steps, and emerge into the alley behind the bar. The sounds of the night go on around me. No one in the city knows there is a network of vampires hiding out inside Delirium. They're completely clueless to all that lurks in the dark.

Panting, I reach inside my bag and pull out my gun. If one follows me out, I will shoot. I know a bullet can't stop a vampire, but it can at least slow him down enough for me to cuff him. And then what? Take him back to the estate and ask Hasan to rip his head off, too?

Something moves overhead. I stumble back, loose gravel rolling under my heels. I steady myself, flick off the safety, and raise my gun. The streetlamp a few yards from me shatters, raining glass down on the pavement and bringing the dark back to the night.

My breath leaves in a huff, and the chill of the spring night sets in, awakening every nerve in my body. The hair on the back of my neck stands on end and goosebumps prickle down my spine. I inhale, trying to summon the strength to start the fire, but I feel so depleted inside. I spin, hearing something scuttle down the alley and behind a dumpster.

And then I feel it. Or more specifically, *him.*

"Were you following me?" I lower my gun and stare at Hasan. His large frame takes up most of the alley and his wide wingspan blocks everything from view.

"Maybe."

"Maybe?" I cock an eyebrow and put a hand on my hip. "Someone could have seen you!"

"I know stealth."

"Yeah, maybe years ago, but now we have night vision and infrared cameras…it's risky." I step closer. "And I don't want anything to happen to you." Saying it out loud makes me realize how deep of a fear it is. So many bad things can happen if they're seen.

They're not human. It wouldn't go over well. Hasan can rip vampires apart with his bare hands, but how will he stand up to a military-grade machine gun? Or worse. And losing him…it would kill me.

"Nothing happened to me.", He strides over. "But I can't say the same about you."

I let go of the front I'm holding up and the exhaustion hits again. Using magic took everything out of me. "I've been better. Good news is, I found the vampires." I motion to the door. "They're down there. I thought they would come out after me, but…" My vision starts to fade and the world spins. Hasan's strong arms wrap around me, and he cradles me to his chest.

"If they come after you, I will kill them."

"I know." I look up, eyes fluttering. I'm close to passing out and I cling to Hasan, fighting to stay conscious. "I'm hoping they do come out."

"I need to get you home."

"Home…the estate."

He spreads his wings. "Hold on."

"Wait," I protest. "No, no way." I won't say I'm scared of heights, but I will say I'm not their biggest fan. "Someone could see us. Get a five-second-long clip of video on their phone and it'll go viral overnight. Then everyone will know you're awake, and correct me if I'm wrong, but something tells me there are people —or things—out there who won't be happy about it."

Hasan stops, turning his head down to me. I'm still in his arms, feeling a bit like a child but needing his protection right now.

"How do you travel?"

"In a car. Just, uh, give me a minute to get my head on straight and I'll drive us. Unless..." I look at the door.

"Ace," Hasan says sternly. "You can hardly walk. You cannot fight vampires now. And, trust me, they're long gone."

"Yeah, I bet you're right and they ran away with their tails tucked between their legs."

"Vampires don't have tails."

"It's a figure of speech." I let my eyes close and my head fall against Hasan's chest. God, he's so muscular. And warm. It feels so damn good to be nestled in his arms right now. He's more rigid than the others, but we're alike in more ways than one. Knowing that makes me feel close to him, which confuses me as much as it comforts me. How can I feel the same for him as I do for Thomas? My heart speeds up again, though this time it's not from danger.

"Rest," he instructs, and moves deeper into the alley, finding a turned-over crate to sit on. He keeps me in his lap, holding me with one arm and using the other to run his hand through my hair. "You're bleeding again."

"It's the same wound busted open. I'll be fine."

"It doesn't look fine."

"It doesn't now, but it will. It's fine, really."

"If you say so." He rakes his large fingers through my hair again, then sweeps them over my arm. "And you're bleeding here."

"Fucking vampire cut me with his nails. And then licked my blood."

Hasan's body tenses. "They drank your blood?"

"Not so much drank as tasted. Why?" My heart races and I feel like someone just dumped a bucket of ice water over my head. "Am I going to turn into a vampire now?"

"No, but once they get a taste for your blood, they'll stop at nothing to track you down and kill you."

"Good, they'll come to me. And I'll be ready this time."

"This is serious, Ace. You are a human. How you went up against vampires and lived is a miracle."

"No miracles...but it *was* magic." I carefully sit up, head still spinning, and hold out my hands. "I have no idea how I did it, but I was holding fire in my hands. And the fire burned one of the vampires pretty badly for the little I hit him with it."

Hasan takes my hand, running his finger over my palm. It makes me shiver, longing for his deft fingers to touch more of me.

"It didn't burn me." I look at my hands, as well, and see no signs of fire. "Or hurt."

"And you have no idea how you did it?"

"None. Things were bad...like I was pinned on the floor with a vampire trying to bite my neck bad. And then my hands felt hot, and suddenly they burst into flames."

"Jacques might know. We need to go back to the estate. Now." His eyes shift to the basement door.

"They called me something...right before one was going to bite me. He stopped and said 'malefica,' I think."

"Witch." Hasan's dark eyes meet mine, his handsome face serious. "It means witch."

A chill runs over me, and the second I shiver, Hasan pulls me to him. I shift my weight, straddling him instead. He pushes his shoulders back, suddenly tense, then relaxes and holds me close.

"You have magic inside of you, Ace."

"I can't really deny it now." I rest my head on his shoulder, needing one more minute before I get up and get my car. Hasan's hands run down my back and over my hips. He hesitates, then slides them under my ass, lifting me just a bit. I pitch forward, breasts crushing into his firm chest.

Despite the fear and the danger—or maybe because of it—the feelings I have for him grow stronger. I hate being afraid. I hate being made to feel helpless and defenseless. I like to be in control, and I know he understands. He gets it, and isn't going to tell me otherwise. And having someone understand a deep, dark part of you is one of the best feelings in the world.

I slowly lift my head, lips parting. Hasan tips his face down to mine. I can feel his heart racing beneath the pounds of muscle on his chest. I move a hand up, tracing a tattoo on his pec. He moves his hands to the small of my back, pressing me down against him. His cock begins to harden beneath me, and already I can feel it is just as large and impressive as the rest of him. The thought of it exhilarates me and I begin to grow wet.

"We should go," he murmurs, lips brushing against mine as he talks. "I took vows, Ace."

"Right," I say, shaking myself. Thomas and Gilbert might not uphold their vows, but that didn't mean Hasan and Jacques don't. "You did. And I don't want to make you break them if you don't want to." I slide back, and his massive dick rubs me through my jeans. And fuck, it feels good. I grip his shoulders tight, trying to summon the willpower to stand.

"I do want to," he admits with no shame at all. "But I shouldn't."

"Then don't," I say, hating the words coming out of my mouth. "Not if it means a lot to you."

"Not everyone wanted to become a Templar," he says, and I assume he's referencing the twins, who had no say in the matter. "But I did. I still do."

A car goes by, headlights illuminating our faces. Hasan and I both freeze. As soon as it drives away, Hasan stands with me in his arms.

"Where is your car?"

"A few blocks away." He sets me on my feet but doesn't let go until he's sure I have my footing. "Stay here and I'll get it."

"Ace, you—"

"I'll be okay once I'm on the street. The vampires didn't come out after me. I don't think they want to be seen by the public." I fish my keys from my purse. "Give me five minutes."

"Be careful."

"I will be." I meet his eyes, smiling. "Besides, I have a feeling you're going to be watching, right?"

He smiles back. "I will."

Taking a deep breath, I force myself to focus. I feel a bit like I've been drugged, and going out into the hustle of the nightlife helps to clear the fog. I get in my car, slide the passenger seat back as far as it can go, and go to the alley.

Hasan hardly fits and sits awkwardly inside. He's never been in a car before. This has to be weird.

"How do you operate this thing?" He peers over at me.

"Honestly, I don't know exactly how it works. You put fuel into a tank, and it uses that to propel the car. I control it with the pedals on the floor and turn it with this wheel. It's a rather complicated procedure now that I think about it, but I'm so used to it I don't stop and wonder."

He moves his gaze to the touchscreen glowing on the dash and brings his hand up, touching the little music note. The radio turns on, blasting a Spice Girls song. He jerks his hand back and tips his head.

"What is this?"

"I call it music, but I'm sure others disagree," I say with a smile, and turn the volume down some. "I like '90s music. 1990s, that is."

Hasan doesn't speak for the rest of "Wannabe." Another song comes on, one I don't like, so I change the station to one that plays current music.

"Music has changed."

"I'm not sure what was popular in your time. Organ music, maybe?"

"I didn't listen to music often."

"Right," I say, and slow for a stoplight. "It had to be live in order to hear it. No offense, but I'm glad I was born now. Mostly because as a woman I'd have no rights back then and I really enjoy being able to vote and work and wear pants." I yawn and fight the urge to close my eyes. "How weird is it being here? You guys basically time traveled. I know technically you were here the whole time, but you went to sleep a thousand years ago and woke up to this."

"It's a lot to take in," he starts, "but the world seems like a better place now."

I make a mental note not to let them watch the news. "Things have come a long way. Human rights, healthcare—well, that's debatable, but the ability to care for health issues is better." I shake my head. "Sorry, getting off topic."

Hasan carefully touches another button, bringing up the navigation system. I spend the rest of the drive back to the estate trying to explain GPS and satellites. I've confused myself by the time we pull into the driveway.

The others are outside waiting. Gilbert and Thomas are sitting on the roof, and Jacques is in front of the porch. His arms are crossed, face set with anger. It's a look I know well because it's one I've worn a time or two.

He's not really pissed.

He's scared shitless and fighting his feelings. He doesn't want to care about me, because when you care about someone, you open yourself up to a world of hurt. I know it, and he knows it. We've both been hurt before.

I falter on my way up the porch, and Gilbert swoops down to help me.

"Jesus, Ace, what the hell happened to you?" He slips his arm around me, hoisting me up.

"She used magic," Hasan answers. "And faced vampires."

"Good thing you were there," Gilbert says to him, helping me up the porch steps.

"I didn't do anything. She fought them on her own."

"And got away?" Thomas opens the door for us, stepping aside. My body begs to lie down and let my eyes shut. And this time, I don't want to fight it. I need to sleep. I need a few hours of slipping into the black, dreamless nothing and not worrying about vampires or magic or how the hell I'm going to make things work at the station in the morning.

The house is warm, thank God, and I go to the couch in the sitting room since it's the closest. The first thing I do is take off my shoes.

"Tell me about the magic." Jacques sits next to me.

"Give her a fucking break," Thomas says, coming into the room with a bottle of water. I take it and chug half of it down, feeling a little better already.

"I'm okay," I insist. "There were two vampires at the bar. I caught one trying to drag a drunk girl into a back room, I think to feed." I blink, and the scene replays before me. I hope tight-leather-dress girl got back to the bar okay. I shouldn't have left like that. But I was in no condition to keep fighting.

My stomach hurts with regret. I've made one bad decision after another since finding out about the gargoyles and vampires. I can't think like a cop when I'm fighting the supernatural, and I hate it.

"I got her away, and the vampire attacked me. He called me a 'malefica' and shouted for another. They cornered me and somehow I started the fire. I burned one vamp and it hurt him. That's how I was able to get away."

The guys all look at me, and several beats pass before anyone speaks.

"You need to rest," Gilbert says, breaking the silence. "I can turn on the shower for you."

"You know how to do that?"

He gives me a crooked smile. "What do you think we do when you sleep?"

"Oh, right. And yeah, a shower sounds great."

His eyes slide over my body, then he disappears up the stairs.

"They tasted her blood." Hasan's deep voice rattles through the small room. The look on Jacques's and Thomas's faces says it all.

"They're going to come for you," Thomas says, sullen.

"I know." I sit up, eyeing the three men in front of me. "And this time, I'll be ready."

17

"You said you'd be ready the next time you saw the vampires, and clearly you weren't," Jacques reminds me.

"I know." I don't argue. There's no point when he's right. "And if the vamp hadn't been dragging that girl back with him, I wouldn't have gone after him. But I couldn't stand back and do nothing when someone was in danger."

"This is serious, Ace. *You* are in danger."

"Trust me, I know. But they won't come out during the day. I'll be safe at work. Plus, I'm a cop, after all. I know how to handle myself. And, yes," I add, holding up a hand, "I know they aren't human and are stronger, faster, and have the whole undead thing going for them, but I'm going to steal some holy water from a church tomorrow and soak wooden stakes in it. Stakes that I still have to make." I shake my head. "My point is, they're only a threat at night. You guys are awake at night."

As soon as the words leave my lips, I realize just how much I need the gargoyles, and how I just admitted it to them. Though I suppose it's not like they couldn't have figured it out.

I am human.

I have limitations.

But I also have magic, and it will take time to get the hang of it.

"We will keep you safe," Hasan vows, and knowing he'd do anything to protect me sends a rush right through me. "Starting with rest. You need to sleep. It's late, and you get up not long after dawn, correct?"

"Right."

"I will stand guard." Jacques stands and my eyes travel down the strip of hair below his navel, in the middle of the sharp V his muscles make over his hips, to the scar on his side, the one that disappears down into his pants.

"Is there any food left?" I ask.

"No."

"Dammit."

Jacques's face softens and I can tell he feels bad. "I'd offer to get you something but I don't know how your currency works."

I smile. "That's the least of your problems. I'll go grocery shopping tomorrow. We have these things called supermarkets here where all your eating needs can more or less be met in one place. You can get bread, milk, meat, wine...all that fun stuff in one place."

"I was born in the wrong century," Thomas says under his breath, and I laugh. He probably would have done well in this century. Life tends to be easier when you're good-looking and born into a rich family. Throw in having a twin and he and Gilbert could be Insta-famous or something.

I stretch my arms over my head and yawn. A dull headache pounds, spurring me to finally get up off the couch. I take my purse—the basically empty one I carried tonight—and put my badge, gun, and wallet into my regular bag. I don't know why I like to carry such a large bag. Maybe it's the part of me that likes to always be prepared? I dig through it until I find a bottle of Advil and go into the kitchen to down the pills with a glass of water.

I can hear the shower running overhead, and just the thought of warm water soothes my sore muscles. The front door opens and shuts and the downstairs falls silent. I fill up my cup once more, forcing myself to drink another glass of water, then go up the back stairs and into the master bedroom.

Steam billows from the open bathroom door, and Gilbert stands next to the shower, holding his hand under the water. I remember his touch from earlier when he almost kissed me. Funny how that seems like so long ago when, really, it was just hours.

"How long does it stay warm?" he asks.

"Probably not too long in this old house. The water at my apartment stays warm forever." The bathroom looks like it was updated sometime in the '80s, based on the black and white tile pattern in the shower. While the decor is awful by today's standards, whoever renovated it knew luxury. The shower is large and tiled, with a bench, a glass door, and two shower nozzles overhead, creating a wonderful cross-stream of hot water.

"It must feel nice." Gilbert shuffles closer to the shower. "The water all over your body." A few drops spatter onto his chest, slowly rolling down the ridges of muscle.

"It does." I lean against the sink. "You'll have to give it a try." I reach up to run my fingers through my curls and wince.

"What's wrong?"

"Nothing. It's nothing…just my shoulder's a little sore. I guess I didn't realize how hard I got shoved into the wall when it happened."

"Let me help you." Gilbert turns and strides over. His hand, still wet and warm, goes under my shirt, taking hold of my hip. He brings me to him and I rest my hands on his chest.

He's over a thousand years old, yet has a youthfulness to his eyes, one not many people are able to retain these days. Slowly, he combs his fingers through my hair, separating the curls. I've always been a sucker for having someone run their fingers through my hair. I rest my head on his chest, arms around his neck.

My heart starts to speed up and suddenly I feel like I should push him away. I already had sex today. With Thomas. Sleeping with two guys never crossed my mind before.

Not until today.

Because I'm equally attracted to all the guys. All four of them. And I know for certain at least two are attracted to me in the same way.

"Are you all right, Ace?" Gilbert asks. "You're tense."

"Yeah," I tell him, letting out a breath. "I just...I don't know."

"If you're not comfortable with this, we'll stop."

"No, I am."

Gilbert raises an eyebrow. "Then what's the problem?"

"I feel guilty for feeling comfortable, which I know doesn't make sense. But being with more than one person isn't exactly common, even today."

Gilbert considers my words for a moment, then runs his hands down my back. "I actually have no idea what to say to that, Ace," he says with a chuckle. "Don't feel guilt over doing what you want. You're not hurting anyone. You're not doing something wrong. In fact, you're making others rather happy."

I trace a vein on his chest with my finger. "And by others, you mean you."

"Yes, and I'm a very important person."

"Yes, yes you are." I smile, feeling some of the tension leave me. "It's not going to be weird to see Thomas after this?"

"Only if you make it weird." Gilbert brushes my hair back. "I told you, we're no strangers to being with the same woman, separately or together."

Together? My heart skips a beat as a scene of both brothers naked and in bed with me flashes through my mind of its own accord.

"I like you, Ace," he says softly. "And there's something about you that makes me feel human again."

I smile, looking into his eyes as he runs his hand through my hair again.

"You are human," I say back. "That's what I see when I look at you."

"You're the only one, then. I'm cursed, that's all I am."

I put my hand on his chest, feeling his heart beating beneath my palm. "There's so much more to you, and I don't know how you can't see it. Is weird to say I wish I met you years ago?"

He blinks, eyes glossing over. "No, it's not weird. I wish I met you years ago too. And if you were on the other end of an arranged marriage, I would have said yes."

I laugh, curling my fingers in and running my nails down his chest. He suppresses a shiver and steps in closer, hand going to the small of my back. He kisses my neck, taking his time. I relax even more and start to forget about how taboo it is to have more than one partner. I like Thomas, and I like Gilbert just as much. What I'm feeling is starting to surpass *liking* and I'm not sure what to think about it. I'm scared of getting hurt, but being with them feels so right.

His hands run down the length of my back and onto my ass. He slips one between my thighs and I part my legs, willing. I bring my own hands down his chest, fingers slipping inside the top of his pants.

His perfect body is marked by one imperfection, and I gently run my finger over the birthmark. He moves his hands to my front and pops the button on my jeans. Then he slides a finger through a belt loop on either side of my waist and tugs my tight jeans down. My panties go down with them. I bend a leg up, freeing my foot, then do the same with the other.

Gilbert's dick is getting hard, and I take it in my hand. There's something so fucking hot about feeling a guy's cock harden and knowing I'm the one causing him to get turned on.

He pulls my shirt over my head and groans at the sight of my breasts. I have on my best pushup bra, and even I have to admit my tits look fan-fucking-tastic. Gilbert takes me by the waist and buries his head in my breasts. I steady myself with my hands on his shoulders, enjoying the sensation of his hard cock rubbing on my stomach. He kisses me all over, reaching up and sliding the straps of my bra over my shoulders.

Not wanting to spend a single second without his lips on me, I unhook my bra myself and shimmy the straps all the way down. Gilbert stares at me, a hungry man looking at a feast, then picks me up, pressing me between his body and the wall. My legs wrap around him, and desire burns deep inside me. I'm so turned on, so wet and ready for his big cock to push inside me. My pussy quivers in anticipation and I don't want to wait any longer.

I push him away and drop to my knees, yanking the ties on his pants. Once undone, they fall to the floor around his feet. Wrapping my hands around his thighs, I rake my fingers up, slowly lifting my gaze to his cock. Big, thick, and so fucking hard. Precum drips from the tip, glistening under the bright lights above us. I lick my lips, cup his balls with one hand, and move in, starting slow.

I put my lips just around the tip, sucking gently. Gilbert puts one hand on the wall behind me and the other on my head, tangling his fingers in my hair. Keeping one hand on the base of his cock, I get to work, swirling my tongue around the tip before taking him in my mouth. I suck hard and pull my head back, then repeat the same motion over and over, sucking him off until his legs begin to tremble.

"Ace," he pants, hips moving in rhythm with my head. He's close to coming but doesn't want this to end yet.

And neither do I.

With a final hard suck, I take my lips off his cock. He grabs me under the arms and hoists me up against the wall again as if I weigh nothing at all. His cock rubs against my clit, and I moan, rocking my hips so it'll hit me in the same spot again.

"You like that?" he pants, thrusting his hips against me. I close my eyes, head going back against the wall. Still holding me, he takes a step back and goes into the shower. Hot water rains down on us, and for a moment, Gilbert turns his head up, stunned.

God, I've taken hot showers for granted.

I shut the glass door, watching water roll off his wings. I tip my head up, needing the hot water on my face. Gently, Gilbert moves my hair from my face, rinsing the blood from my face, and watching it go down the drain. His hands run the length of my body and he urges me to sit on the bench. As soon as my ass is down, he's on his knees, spreading my thighs.

Hot water cascades down on me as Gilbert brings his lips to my pussy. His mouth covers me, tongue lashing out at my clit. Hard and fast. Over and over. Moaning, I bring my leg up, hands going to his wet hair. I look down, watching him eat me out, and feel my inner walls begin to contract. I'm so hot and he's winding me up so tight, I'm going to come hard.

The pleasure builds up until I'm about ready to burst. And then Gilbert stops, breaking the contact. I exhale, heart hammering, and blink water out of my eyes.

"Touch yourself, Ace," he orders. "Make yourself come so I can watch."

My heart flutters. I've never touched myself in front of anyone before. I'm teetering on the edge of orgasm. I need to come before I implode.

"Don't be shy."

I nod, push a strand of wet hair out of my face, and drag my fingers down my chest and over my pussy. The second I touch my clit, red-hot tingles go through me. I close my eyes, let my head fall back, and begin to rub myself. Gilbert's hands are still on my thighs as he watches. I shift my weight so I get hit with hot water, enhancing my own pleasure.

I start to move my fingers in a circular motion. Slow at first, then faster and faster. Using my other hand to further spread myself, I'm on the brink of coming once again. And as soon as I'm there, Gilbert takes my wrists, moves my hands to the side, and dives down, tongue flicking my clit again and again.

My pussy spasms against his hot mouth, warmth spilling from inside of me as I come harder than I ever have before. He slows his movements but keeps his mouth on me, gently licking and sucking at my sensitive clit until it's too much. Writhing with pleasure, I try to push him away, but he's relentless.

His mouth goes to my thigh, biting my tender flesh, and he pushes a finger deep inside my pussy, going right for my G-spot. He taps it, stops, and taps again. Oh. My. God. My ears ring and my toes tingle. I lean back against the shower wall so hard my butt starts to slide forward. He holds me steady, fingering me for another moment, before turning his face back in to eat me out again.

I come for the second time, and my whole body reacts to the orgasm. Gilbert holds me, keeping me in the warm water until I stop shaking. Panting, I let out a heavy breath and feebly reach for him.

Still on his knees, he comes closer and moves my wet hair out of my face. And then the water starts to get cold.

"Shit," I pant. "We're running out of hot water."

Gilbert stands, shuts off the water, and reaches for the towels he'd gotten out from under the sink. He quickly dries himself off, then wraps one around me and carries me into the bedroom, sitting on the bed with me in his lap. He takes another towel and pats at my wet hair, catching the water that's dripping off the ends.

His cock is still hard and pressing against my bare ass. Still riding on ecstasy, I nuzzle against him, needing another minute to recover.

"You're shivering," he whispers, and stands with me still in his arms. The towel falls to the ground, and he holds me with one arm and turns down the blankets on the bed with the other. We get in bed together and he spoons his body around mine before bringing the blankets over us both.

His erection presses against my ass. I wiggle closer to him and his hands find their way to my breasts.

"Are you tired?"

"You wore me out," I say with a smile on my lips. I turn in his arms, facing him. He's on his side, with one wing tucked under his body and the other slightly above. I reach out and run my fingers along the rough edges. "But I'm not too tired to take care of you."

"Sleep if you're tired, Ace."

I hook my leg over him and his cock rubs against my pussy and I start to get wet all over again. "You don't want to fuck me?"

"I do. You know I do, Ace." He cups my face and kisses me hard. "I want nothing more than to bury my cock inside your tight cunt and fuck you so hard you feel me inside you even after we're done. What I want to do to you won't be quick. When I fuck you, I'm going to take all night."

"Holy shit," I whisper, breath catching.

"So rest, Ace. You need your strength."

I WAKE WITH A START, having heard the floorboards creak. Gilbert is still next to me, naked, with his arms wrapped around my waist. His breathing is slow and steady, making me think he's asleep. Someone grabs the doorknob and twists. My heart is in my throat and visions of the vampire flash before me.

"Thomas?" I whisper, seeing a winged man move into the room. Shadows are over his face and I can't discern who it is.

"Yeah."

"Is everything okay?" I ask, hyper-aware I'm naked in bed with his brother. Gilbert said they've had threesomes together, but I can't help the frisson of nerves that goes through me, as if I got caught doing something naughty.

Which I am, I guess.

But there's also a thrill to it, a tingle that warms my skin and makes deep, dark fantasies dance through my mind. I find myself wanting to pull Gilbert closer with one hand, and Thomas with the other. To see just what it would be like to have sex with two men at once.

Thomas nods and puts his finger to his lips, eyes going to his twin. "Yes. I wanted to check on you."

"I'm fine."

He shoots me a dubious look. "You keep saying that, but you've taken one hell of a beating several nights in a row."

"I know," I say, and sit up, keeping the blanket over my breasts. Thomas has seen them before. They've been in his hands...his mouth... There's no point in being shy. And, like Gilbert said, I shouldn't feel guilt or shame over doing what I want. "I have to use the bathroom." I throw back the covers and get up, knowing he's checking out my bare ass as I walk.

I pee, wash my hands, and go back to the room, finding Thomas sitting on the edge of the bed. I want this. I want *them*. I get back under the covers, brushing Gilbert's hair out of his eyes. I settle against the pillows and extend a hand to Thomas.

"Aren't you tired?" he asks, moving closer.

"Yeah, but I can't sleep."

"What's bugging you?" he asks. "And I mean other than almost dying tonight."

"I feel like I have no idea what I'm doing, or if I'm even doing the right thing anymore." The confession is like a weight off my chest.

"What do you mean? You're fighting vampires. How is that not the right thing?" He lies back, sandwiching me between his body and Gilbert's. I lean back, too, pulling the blankets over the three of us. In his sleep, Gilbert snakes an arm around me. I nuzzle against him, finding his presence calming. I'm happy being here with them, feeling like they're old friends turned into my lovers.

"The girl at the club...I made sure she got back to the crowd and just assumed she'd find her friends and get home safe. The old Ace wouldn't have done that. I've always been thorough. Followed through with everything and made sure the small details were taken care of. I might not have rid the world of crime, but I felt like I was making the city a safer place, little by little. Now...now it feels like I'm poking the dragon, and once he wakes up, innocent villagers will be burned alive in his fury and it'll all be my fault."

"That's a common misconception, you know. Dragons are rather friendly."

"Dragons are real—never mind. I can't get into that right now, especially if it's true."

"You're not doing the wrong thing, if that helps." Thomas resituates his wings under the blanket.

"It kinda does. And kinda doesn't. It's stupid, I know."

"Sleep, Ace."

I yawn. "You guys keep telling me that. Do I look that bad or something?"

"No," Thomas says with a laugh. "But we know how little you've slept, and how much energy it takes to do magic. Even when you don't mean to."

"Yeah, true. By tomorrow I'm guessing I'll be so exhausted I won't be able to lie awake and agonize over how much I've screwed up. I'll pass out as soon as I'm in bed."

"I think you're joking, but it's not funny." He cocks an eyebrow. "Roll over."

I turn, facing Gilbert, and bring my leg up over his. My back is to Thomas, and he starts rubbing my back, kneading my sore muscles.

"Mmmhhh," I moan. "That feels good."

"What feels good?" Gilbert mumbles, eyes slitting open. He pushes his hips forward against mine. "Oh," he says when he runs his hands down my back and feels Thomas's fingers working away at a knot.

Instead of turning away, he brings his hands up to my face, tips my chin to his, and kisses me. His tongue slips into my mouth and his cock grows hard, pressing into my thigh. I arch my back, nipples rubbing against his chest. Thomas keeps rubbing my back and Gilbert deepens the kiss.

"Is this all right?" Gilbert whispers, and knowing he's concerned with me enjoying this in every single aspect only makes me want this more. I feel safe around them. They're not going to push me further than I want to go.

His hands travel down my body, moving me over just enough to stroke my clit. Having two men do everything in their power to please me at the same time is in-fucking-credible.

Gilbert pushes a finger inside my pussy, spreading my wetness. I'm about to come, and he doesn't stop this time. I cry out as I come, body shuddering from the overload of pleasure.

Once my heart stops racing, I reach down and take a hold of Gilbert's cock, slowly stroking him. He lets out a moan and moves so he can kiss me as I jerk him off. I circle my thumb around the tip of his cock and gently bite his lip.

Then he pushes me back and moves down under the covers. I roll onto my back, heart racing at the thought of what's coming. Gilbert is skilled with his tongue.

He spreads my legs and moves between, keeping the blankets over me so I don't get cold, though what he's doing is so fucking hot, I don't think that'll be an issue. I moan when his tongue runs over my clit. Thomas gets up and shuts the door, then comes back into bed. He leans over me, lips on mine, and stays out of Gilbert's way while sparing no attention to me.

They really have done this before.

Gilbert works his tongue and my breathing quickens, making it hard to kiss Thomas. He moves his mouth to my neck, kissing and sucking at my flesh as Gilbert continues to pleasure me.

Feebly, I reach for Thomas, trying to untie his pants. He brings his hand to mine, helping me find the tie to pull. He moves up and his hard cock presses into my hand. As soon as I start stroking him, Gilbert flicks my clit with his tongue and I lose control as I come.

Gilbert keeps his mouth on me, not stopping until my body is shuddering. Then he moves up, kisses me, and goes back to my side. Gently, he pushes me away and onto my side so that my ass is against him and I'm facing Thomas, who's patiently waiting out of the way before getting into bed along with us.

He's facing me and pushes my damp hair over my shoulder. Gilbert's hard cock is pressing against my bare ass, and Thomas's is against my thigh. This is really happening. Two guys who want me enough to take me at the same time. I've never felt more desired in my whole life.

Gilbert's hand settles on my waist, and I arch my back, offering myself to him. He lines up my hips to his cock, and slides one hand down to the back of my thigh. I part my legs, willing his large cock inside. Nerves still on end from the orgasm he just gave me, every thrust and movement feels so fucking amazing.

I sweep my hand down Thomas's body and push his own hand away. Wrapping my fingers around his cock, I start pumping my hand up and down at the same time Gilbert is fucking me. Pleasure builds in all three of us at a rapid pace, and we finish at nearly the same time.

I fall back, exhausted, heart hammering and blood pumping. Nothing has ever made me feel more satisfied, more alive, more *empowered* than that. Thomas takes my hand and traces circles in my palm with his thumb. Gilbert wraps his large frame around mine again, kissing the back of my neck. Nestled against him, I'm safe and warm.

The circumstances aren't ideal, glad they're here. My heart feels full inside my chest, and for the first time since my parents died, I don't hear the wind whistling through the emptiness deep in my bones. When I'm with them, I feel like I've found the thing I've been searching for my whole life.

Maybe this curse isn't so bad after all.

"Son of a bitch!" I throw the covers back, blinking in the bright sunlight. I just woke up and have no idea what time it is. I'm alone in bed, obviously, and, judging by the amount of sunlight streaming into the room, sunrise was well over an hour ago. Probably more.

Which means I'm going to be late for work. With everything going on last night, I forgot to bring my purse upstairs, which has my phone in it. The house is too big to hear my alarm going off and I overslept.

I get up, body sore both from being attacked by vampires...and it's not like I got much rest last night. A smile springs to my face when I think about the twins, and my head turns to the window of its own accord. I can see the top of Thomas's and Gilbert's wings from up here.

Before I get dressed, I hurry down the stairs to get my phone and check the time. I pull it from my purse and tap the screen, cursing again when I see it's seven thirty-three. I'm supposed to be at work at eight. If I leave right now, I might be able to make it as long as traffic isn't too bad. I stand too fast and get hit with dizziness. I throw my hand out to keep my balance, blinking away the spots that are clouding my vision.

Thank God I have this weekend off.

I scramble back up the stairs, take a shower, brush my teeth, and get dressed in only five minutes. I rake my fingers through my hair as I rush to my car. I never brushed the curls out, and went to bed with it wet. My hair is a horrid mess. Twisting it into a messy bun at the nape of my neck, I deem it good enough and speed off to work.

Since I'm the lead detective on the murders ironically dubbed the "vampire murders," I don't have a chance to grab coffee or a stale donut from the break room until after I meet with the other investigators and officers working on the case. I fumble through everything I want to say, finding it hard to give a halfway decent report when I can't tell them the truth.

I'm tired enough to be sloppy, and I know it's a matter of time before I slip up and say something that'll give everything away.

Only, they won't assume vamps are real. They'll know I've been investigating on my own—alone—and withholding information. I could get fired for that.

Or worse.

"Hey, Ace," Tiffany says, coming up to the coffee pot. I fill my mug almost to the top and put the pot back.

"Hey, Tiff." I add cream and sugar, then take a big gulp.

"Are you all right?" She looks away from her coffee for a second to inspect me.

"Yeah." No one is going to believe that lie. I sigh and shake my head. "I'm tired. I haven't gotten much sleep the last few nights."

"This case is really bothering you, huh?"

"Yes, it really is." At least that's not a lie.

She takes a sip of her coffee and leans against the counter. "It's been over forty-eight hours since we found the first victim, and we've got nothing. Honestly, it's a little scary."

My jaw tenses. "It is scary."

"I don't mean that in offense to you, you know. Saying we've got nothing…I'm not implying anything against you."

"I know." I offer a smile. If only she knew… "Whoever is behind the murders is taking extra care not to be found." Some of them *won't* be found. They died. Twice.

Tiffany sighs. "We haven't had a good old-fashioned serial killer in a while. That didn't come out right." She rolls her eyes at herself. "You know what I mean. I think. I hope."

"I do." I chug more coffee, needing the caffeine high to kick in, and look at Tiffany. I want to tell her to stay inside at night, to keep her doors locked and to carry a wooden stake soaked in holy water just in case.

But I can't, and *not* telling the few people I care about how to protect themselves leaves me with a nasty taste of guilt in my mouth. If something happens to the members of my team, I'll never forgive myself.

18

I grab a bottle of red wine and add it to my shopping cart. It's the last thing I have on my list, and I think I got enough food to last the guys a few days. Well, nights, technically. Having been single my entire adult life, I've never bought this much food at once. It's weird.

After taking two steps forward, I come to a sudden halt and backtrack. Two more bottles of wine go into the cart. I look at my phone—I'm making good time—and head to the checkout lane. I get in line and a familiar voice calls out my name.

"Hey, Ace!" Tiffany pushes her cart up behind me.

"Tiffany, hey." I turn around, eyes going to the car seat snapped into the front of the cart. "And Mavis. I can't believe how much bigger she is since the last time I saw her." I smile at the sleeping baby.

"I know. She's growing so fast. Everyone told me how fast it would go by, and it turns out they were right." She laughs.

"Go ahead of me," I tell her before I move up in line . "I have twice as much."

"Are you sure?"

"Yeah, I have a lot and you don't."

She peeks into my cart. "You do have a lot. Stocking up?"

"Uh," I start, glancing down into my cart. Is it even possible to keep all this stuff for that long? I don't know. My cooking skills are close to nothing. And I hate lying to Tiffany. I've lied so much the last few days, and I know the more I lie, the more likely I am to get caught. And what happens if she sees me here again next week? "Actually, no. My cousins are in town."

"Oh." Her eyes widen and she leans back. "I didn't know you had any cousins in the area."

"I didn't either." I pull my cart back to let her through. "I just found out about them, and they're not from around here."

She starts putting her groceries on the conveyer belt. "Oh my God, was it because of the house?"

"The house?" The blood might have drained from my face just a little.

"Are they trying to take it from you?"

"Oh, right. And, uh, no. They heard about my aunt—*our* aunt— passing and we got in touch. Now we're just catching up."

Mavy lets out a cry, taking Tiffany's attention off me. She puts the rest of her groceries up and moves down toward the register.

"That's great. Are they staying long?"

"A while."

"I love my cousins. More than my sisters at times, but don't tell my sisters that." She pulls her wallet from her purse. "Hopefully you guys get along and stay in touch."

"I have a feeling we will." I unload my groceries.

Tiffany takes her bag and pushes her cart forward. "Thanks again for letting me go ahead. Mavy's at her limit. See you tomorrow."

"Bye, Tiff."

I pay the biggest grocery bill I've ever had in my life and make it to the estate with an hour to spare. The closer we get to summer, the later the sun sets. It's usually something I enjoy, but right now I find myself missing the short days and longer nights, for obvious reasons.

I put the groceries away and go upstairs, unpacking the rest of my stuff that I brought over, which is basically everything I could fit inside my bags. I take a few minutes to straighten up, then head back to the kitchen to start dinner. My alarm goes off on my phone at sunset. I left the front door slightly ajar so the guys will know to just come in.

And they do.

"Ace?" Jacques calls.

"In the kitchen," I call back over my shoulder. I turn down the burner on the stove. Jacques comes in, and the moment our eyes meet, my heart flutters. That weird connection is back, and it takes everything inside me to resist running to him and flinging myself into his arms.

His shoulders tense and his eyes narrow. He's fighting the same battle.

"What are you doing?"

"Making dinner. Or breakfast for you guys."

"It smells good." A beat passes between us before he moves closer. "How are you today? Does your head still hurt?"

"A little." I subconsciously reach up to the scab. "I'm mostly tired."

"You should stay in tonight," he says, instantly annoying me. Only because he's right.

"I can make my own decisions, thank you very much." I don't mean to snap, but there's something about him that gets under my skin. My insane attraction to him? I know he feels it, too. Why is it so easy for him to brush off?

"I don't doubt you're able to." His face softens. "I heard you last night."

I pick up a wooden spoon and stir the spaghetti sauce. If I had neighbors, they would have heard me, too. "Oh. Yeah…I…uh…"

"You're free to do as you wish, Ace," he says, almost bitterly. His eyes flash and he looks me up and down for a brief moment before looking away. Is that jealousy I'm sensing? "Though you should probably focus more on resting and taking care of yourself before you run off and have fun." His eyes drill into mine again, so intense I lean away.

Yes, that most definitely *is* jealousy. Is it terrible I like it? He'd only be jealous if he had feelings for me, just like the feelings I have for him. I shift my weight, uncomfortable. The others are fine with our arrangement...but what about Jacques? Because right now he's looking at me as if he wants to own me.

"Right, I, uh..." I'm floundering, feeling heat rush to my cheeks. "I, uh...I don't like being lonely," I blurt. God, how stupid did *that* sound?

Jacques's face softens. "I don't either," he says quietly, and takes a tentative step toward me. My heart is in my throat, and I'm back to fighting the urge to put my arms around him, to feel my heart beat against his and find out what his lips feel like against mine for real.

"I don't think it's stupid to question if you're doing the right or wrong thing," he says, taking the conversation in a totally different direction. I whirl back around to look at him. "I know you want to do the right thing. You and I...we're alike in that aspect. And sometimes the right thing doesn't seem like the best thing to do. Sometimes the right thing feels wrong."

"That's exactly how I feel right now." I swallow hard, eyes trailing down Jacques's muscular torso. "It's making me question everything. Before, I knew I was doing the right thing. It might take a while to get results, but I knew I was making the world a better place."

"And now?"

"Now I'm not sure. I mean, yeah, I get it. I'm *trying* to get rid of the vampires. But it doesn't feel like enough. I'm not giving my full attention to my job, and I feel really shitty about it." I haven't fully confessed it to myself yet. "I don't know." I shake my head and turn back to the sauce.

Jacques moves with such grace for someone his size. The energy around him is overwhelming, but not in a bad way. It surrounds me, fills me, makes me have to fight even harder to keep myself from turning and throwing my arms around his neck.

"Isn't that what life is about?" His voice is low. "Doing the right thing...making the world a bit more livable, if not for yourself, then for others. I gave up my life in order to serve others and I still questioned if I did the right thing joining the Templars."

"I thought you believed in their mission?"

"I did, but I was naive when I joined and thought everyone else did, too."

"Oh, right. They kind of turned into money-grubbers, right?"

"Yes. I actually understand that saying." His serious face lights up for a second.

"Thanks, I needed to hear that." I reach for his hand. My fingers graze his skin and he flips his hand over, lacing his fingers through mine. My heart skips a beat and suddenly the dream comes to life, playing out before me in a flash and it's like I remember everything.

The way his lips taste. The smooth feel of his hard cock in my hand. His gruff voice whispering something in my ear in a language I don't know. But most of all, the painful longing in my heart.

Jacques yanks his hand back. This time I know for certain he saw it too. Stepping away, he looks at the ground, chest rapidly rising and falling as he sucks in air.

"I'll tell the others you're making dinner."

"Wait."

He turns, wings swooping past me and creating a draft strong enough to nearly blow out the fire on the stove.

"Yes?"

I rush forward, stopping inches from him. Slowly, I run my eyes up and down his body, taking in every inch of muscle and every scar. He's been through a lot, and I want to know everything about this cursed man.

He bends his head down, forehead resting against mine. I put my palms on his chest, taking solace in his heart beating beneath my fingertips. I drag my hands down to his hips and slide them back under his wings.

After a moment of hesitation, Jacques does the same to me, holding me tight against him. I can't explain it and I know it doesn't make sense. Nothing about this should feel familiar, yet it does. Being in Jacques's embrace is like coming home after a long vacation. It's warm and safe and familiar, and I don't want to leave. Because if I do, there's no promise I'll come back.

I tip my head up, brushing my lips against his. A hard rush of desire goes through me, making me wet at just the thought of Jacques being naked and on top of me. I bring my hips against his, needing to feel more of him. He hasn't even touched me yet and I'm turned on.

Jacques cups my face in both his hands, leaning back just enough to study my features.

"You're beautiful, Acelina."

Beautiful. Not hot, or sexy. I part my lips, ready to say something back, when Jacques suddenly jerks away.

"What's wrong?"

"I can't, Ace." He lowers his gaze, face pained. My heart is in my throat. I don't handle rejection well, and I know it stems from my childhood of being passed around by family until my aunt finally took me in.

"Why?" My voice comes out in a harsh whisper, and I'm trying to remind myself that I don't have a deep connection with Jacques. Not really. But what I feel is so real.

"Your soup is going to boil over."

"It's sauce, not soup."

"Whatever it is, it's bubbling up."

Exhaling, I turn back to the stove and stick the wooden spoon back in the pan. The floor creaks behind me as Jacques leaves. I turn off the burner and go to the fridge, grabbing a bottle of wine. I struggle getting the cork out.

"Need help?" Hasan's deep voice rumbles through the kitchen. Relief floods through me just at the sight of him.

"I think so. The cork is breaking off."

Hasan takes the bottle from me and gives the corkscrew one good twist. "Wine?" he asks, sniffing the bottle.

"Yeah. It's sweet red and I actually have no idea if that was even a thing back in your time. I'm not really a fan of the way alcohol tastes, but I could use a glass right about now."

The wine glasses in the cabinet are dusty. I quickly wash five and pour wine into two glasses and offer one to Hasan. He takes a drink and makes a funny face.

"Don't like it?" I ask with a laugh. I welcome a mouthful of sweet liquid down my throat.

"It's very sweet." He takes another drink. "I wasn't expecting that. But I do like it."

I take another drink, looking at Hasan with the smile still on my face. He's at least six and a half feet tall, with large, onyx wings. He's a seasoned warrior, with the scars and tattoos to prove it, and yet here he is, standing in the kitchen of my family-owned mansion sipping sweet red wine with me.

And it feels like the most natural thing in the world.

Hasan stays with me while I finish dinner and helps me set the table. We don't talk about vampires or magic. Instead we talk about the modern world. I brought my computer today and plan to turn on a movie for the guys later. I refill my glass with wine and close my eyes, mentally calling out to the guys to test out this summoning thing.

It works.

Thomas and Gilbert come in first. They were outside exercising, needing to literally stretch their wings, and both are glistening with sweat, looking like they stepped right off a photoshoot for *GQ* magazine. Well, if *GQ* featured gargoyles, that is.

"Smells good again, Ace." Thomas comes up behind me and slips his arm around my waist, leaning over my shoulder to look at the spaghetti on the stovetop.

"Thanks," I say back. "Hopefully it's good. I don't cook too often." Though truth be told, I didn't make any of this. All I did was heat it up, and if this house had a microwave, I would have used that instead.

The timer goes off to take the garlic bread from the oven, and when I bend over to get it, Thomas purposely rubs against my ass. It's playful, makes me laugh, and for some strange reason, makes this whole thing seem almost normal, like I'm a regular chick cooking dinner for her boyfriend.

Only there are four of them.

And we're nowhere near regular.

"What's the plan for tonight?" Gilbert asks, helping me carry the food to the table. He sits across from me and next to his brother. They look so much alike, but when they're side by side like this, I can see just how different they are. Thomas's hair is a little darker and Gilbert's has more of a wave to it. They have the same sky-blue eyes and full, pink lips.

"I'm not sure," I admit, hesitating before I start to serve myself. Hasan is at my side, wings folded tightly behind him so he fits on the chair. Jacques hasn't joined us yet, and when I think about it, my heart hurts. It's not my pain I'm feeling but his. He's close by on the porch, pacing back and forth. "I dug deeper into this whole thing and it's bigger than I thought."

My chest tightens at the thought of it, and instead of reaching for the serving spoon, I go for my wine instead. "I thought the bar was the headquarters for it all, but there are cases of people going missing or being found dead from blood loss way before the club was even open."

"Of course there would be." Gilbert raises an eyebrow, not sure why I'm surprised. "Vampires have been around since our time."

His words, simple as they are, hit me. "I know. But thinking about them being well established in the area makes everything harder. Are they organized, like the mafia? Is it even possible to put an end to this? I find and kill the vampire who made those baby vamps. And then what? Another will just do the same. Or maybe they're in the system and have paid people off. They could be so assimilated into society and no one will believe me when I try to blow the cover off the vampire gangs." The panic inside me rises, forcing my words out faster and faster. I bring my wine to my lips again, and no one speaks.

Then the floor creaks again and we all look up to see Jacques entering the dining room.

"When you catch a bad guy, you're not ending crime in the city," he says, eyes spearing into mine. "And yet you feel like you did the right thing by ridding the streets of one more sinner." He takes a seat at the head of the table. "Vampires are pests. You will not rid the world of them. We couldn't back then, and we won't now. But if you stop just one, you're doing the right thing and making the world a little safer."

I set the wine down and nod. I know Jacques is right. I just wish I could get on board with it.

"Gilbert is right." Jacques reaches for a slice of garlic bread. "Vampires have been around for centuries. They've probably killed hundreds in your village, and those innocent lives lost will never see justice. It's not right or fair, but it's something you have to accept. Yes, more vampires can move in on the territory, but I imagine it's the same with the crime you fight in today's times."

I nod and put spaghetti noodles on my plate. "That is true."

"You said the attacks have been going on for a while," Hasan starts, and digs into his food as well. "Have there been others with bone missing?"

I shake my head. "No, but there are a handful of unsolved cases where the victims were found drained of blood. Some had puncture wounds—like from fangs—and the others were drained with IVs. It's been assumed the blood was sold on the black market, which is an illegal venue, so to speak, to sell things like bodies, babies, and weapons."

Thomas raises his eyebrows. "Some things never change. Humanity at its finest, even after a thousand years."

"Money can get you pretty much anything," I say. "Even more so now. But does that mean something to you?" I look at Hasan.

"Times have changed, but I'm sure vampires still like to stay hidden. New vampires—baby vamps, as you call them—are always a risk."

"Risk?" I ask, and take a bite of food.

"Newly turned vampires are insatiable," Jacques explains. "Controlling the hunger is something they learn with age, and going through the transformation requires a certain level of energy."

I chew my food, considering his words. "So, you think there's a new vamp in town, trying to stake out a claim."

Jacques smiles. "Yes."

Leaning back in my chair, I take another sip of wine. "The new alpha is turning people, and the new vampires are the ones responsible for the murders I'm trying to solve." I shake my head. "Saying it out loud gives me a headache. But to get to the root of this, I need to find the sire and kill him. Then things will go relatively back to normal."

"Precisely." Jacques picks up the glass of wine in front of his plate and takes a small sip, pulling the same face Hasan did. I turn away to keep from laughing. "Like you said, vampires have been here for years, and I'm sure other monsters have been, as well. But the savage killings are new, from the new threat. Kill him, and I know without a doubt, Ace, you'll be doing a great thing."

19

With the sun shining all day, the house had heated up on its own. With the heater running all day, plus five bodies in the house, it's become uncomfortably warm. I turn down the thermostat and unzip my hooded sweatshirt. Thomas and Gilbert are supposedly cleaning the kitchen, Jacques is outside keeping watch, and Hasan is somewhere in the house.

Yawning, I go to the large floor-to-ceiling windows in the living room and look into the dark yard. The back porch lights don't illuminate much around the house, limiting what I can see.

"Ace?" Hasan's voice rings out from the balcony upstairs.

"I'm down here." I catch his reflection in the window. Instead of going down the stairs, he jumps over the balcony, spreading his wings and gracefully gliding down.

"Show-off," I say with a smile.

He smiles back. "Being cursed..." He trails off and shakes his head. "Having the ability to fly almost makes up for it."

"Almost."

"Yes. Almost."

"I'll try to break it."

"I know." He stops behind me and brushes my hair over my shoulder. His hands go to my hips, and I step back until I'm up against him. I rest my head on his firm chest and my eyes fall shut.

"You're staying in tonight, aren't you?"

"Probably. I'm kind of out of plans right now."

"That's for the best tonight."

I spin in his arms. "How is it for the best?"

"You're exhausted, Ace. You can't go after vampires on a whim again. You have no stakes and no holy water. Your head injury is one blow away from becoming serious and I can tell you're sore when you walk."

"But the new moon—"

"Isn't happening tonight." He picks me up and I know there's no point to protesting, not that I want to anyway. Hasan is double my size, if not more. With a smirk, he crouches down, holds me tight, and jumps, taking flight. In just seconds, we land on the upstairs balcony.

"Whoa." My arms are still fastened around his neck. "That was incredible."

"Like I said, it almost makes up for the curse." He sets me down and takes my hand, leading me into the bedroom. "You need to take care of yourself, Ace. I'm serious."

"Yeah," I agree, knowing that going into the bedroom with Hasan isn't going to be restful. And I'm okay with that.

"I don't understand the way you dress." Hasan runs a hand through his hair, messing it up even more in a way that looks incredibly sexy on him. "What you were wearing at the bar is very different from what you are wearing now." He sits on the foot of the bed, eyeballing me.

"Yeah, I can see how that'd be confusing." I look down at the yoga pants, tank top, and zip-up hoodie I have on now. "This is comfortable, and what I tend to wear when I'm at home alone. Which is always, since I live alone." I wear this when I go out, too. Well, *if* I go out. "Anyone can dress however they want now. Well, here they can. Other countries still have dress codes."

He nods, brows coming together. "And you choose to wear that?"

I cross my arms. "It's not that bad. I might look slightly homeless, but at least I'm comfortable."

"I liked what you had on yesterday better."

I laugh. "At least you're honest." I fiddle with the zipper of my hoodie. "It did feel kind of nice to dress up a bit," I admit. "I don't very often."

"You should. The tighter fit looks good on you."

"Is that your way of saying you wish I'd put on a dress and a corset?"

He shakes his head. "Corsets take too long to take off."

"I can imagine."

"Come here, Ace."

I cross the room, going right onto Hasan's lap. He's hardness and muscle beneath me, and I feel so small and delicate against his large frame. I wrap my arms around his neck and he places his bear-like palm on the small of my back.

"I never believed much in marriage or two people being made for each other," he starts, voice soft. "That's part of why I joined the Templars. But if I had met you back then, it would have made me think twice."

My breath hitches and my heart lurches. I look into his eyes, trying to convey how much his words mean to me. I'm not good with stuff like this, even though I feel more for him than ever before right now.

"At least we met now," I whisper and he goes to kiss me. "Your vows," I breathe, regretting bringing it up as soon as the words escape my mouth. But I care about him enough to not want him to regret anything in the morning.

"Fuck the vows," he growls. "I want you, Ace."

"I've been with Thomas," I blurt out. "And Gilbert." *Together.*

"I know." He grips my waist tighter. "Do you only want to be with them?"

"No. I want you all."

"And I want to please you. In every way."

I close my eyes and lean back, pressing my pelvis into his. My legs are already spread wide just straddling him like this. I can only imagine what it will feel like to have this mountain of a man on top of me. In me. Fucking me.

Though something tells me I won't have to imagine it.

So much has happened in the last few days. Stress. Fear. A bit of self-loathing for having to lie. Life-altering information. I'll never be the same. But dammit, I can feel good for at least a little bit.

Hasan pushes my hoodie down my arms. It drops onto the floor behind us. Slowly, he drags his hands up my spine, not stopping until they're in my hair, pulling my head to the side. He tenderly kisses my neck, then brings his head down, burying it in my breasts for a minute before grabbing the hem of my tank top and pulling it over my head. Hasan licks his lips, looking at me as if he's a very hungry man and I'm an all-you-can-eat buffet.

He slips his fingers inside the cups of my bra, going right for my nipples. "I don't know what this thing is, but I think I like it."

"It's called a bra," I breathe. "You'll like it better off." I reach behind me and unhook the bra, smiling coyly as I slide the straps down my arms. He cups my breasts in his hands, lowering his head between them. I grind against him, feeling his cock harden against my core. With a lusty groan, he takes one of my breasts in his mouth, flicking my nipple with his tongue.

I continue to grind my hips against him, getting turned on from his hardness rubbing me through my pants. Moaning, I run my hands down Hasan's sides and tug at his waistband.

"Take your pants off," I whisper.

Hasan stands with me in his arms, spins around, and tosses me on the bed. Keeping his eyes on mine, he pulls the tie on his pants and lets them drop, fully knowing the shock value his huge cock is going to have on me. I swallow hard when I see it.

Oh. My. God.

"I don't know how that thing is going to fit inside me."

"I've made it work in the past." He smirks as he takes his cock in his hand. "I'm reasonably certain I can figure it out again."

I lick my lips as I watch him jerk himself. I never thought anything could make his large hands look small, and the sight turns me on, making my pussy throb and my entire body quiver with anticipation.

He comes back to the bed and I grab his hand and do my best to tug him forward. He humors me and falls onto the mattress. I move down, part his legs, and cup my hand around his balls and take him in my mouth. Hasan lets out a grunt, winding me up even more knowing how hot he is from this.

Hasan's hand lands on my head, fingers curling through my hair. I look up at him, so hot I can't stand it. I plunge my hand inside my panties, rubbing myself. Only minutes later we're both teetering on the edge of coming, but he doesn't get to.

I fall to the side, reaching for Hasan's hand. Not needing any more guidance from me, he picks up where I left off, stroking me until the sheets dampen beneath me as I come. Hasan sits up, large wings over me, and takes the rest of my clothes off. He climbs between my legs, carefully positioning his cock between my legs.

I bend my legs around him, spread as wide as they can go, and cry out as he enters me. He thrusts in hard, then pulls out until only the tip of his cock remains inside me, then slowly pushes it back in.

He does it again.

And again.

And again, until my body is aching to feel him inside me, stroking my inner walls in just the right way.

"Hasan," I pant, slitting my eyes open to look up at him.

He turns his head down, dark eyes wild. Keeping his eyes on mine, he pushes his cock inside me. My mouth falls open in a moan.

He groans and rocks his hips, hitting my G-spot in just the right way. "Say it again," he demands.

I open my mouth, but the only thing escaping my lips right now is a moan.

He pulls back. "Say my name, Ace." His voice is rough, filled with primal need.

"Hasan," I gasp, and he grabs my ankle, lifting it up. He thrusts in deep again, and holy fuck, his cock is so big it fills every single inch of me. Raising my leg into the air, he speeds up his movements. Reaching around with his free hand, he rubs my clit.

My head falls to the side and I fold the pillow over my face to stifle another loud moan as I come. The muscles in my thighs tighten and I grab the sheets, pressing my fingers into the mattress. Hasan's breathing becomes ragged and he pushes in deep as he finishes.

Heart racing, I'm vaguely aware of Hasan moving me up in the bed and tucking me under the covers. My eyes flutter shut as I surrender to some much-needed sleep.

———

I WAKE AROUND three AM needing to use the bathroom. I'm alone in bed, and the bedroom door is shut. Shivering the moment I pull back the covers, I grab my PJ shirt and panties, get out of bed, and pad to the bathroom. After I pee, I go to the top of the stairs, following the sound of Gilbert and Thomas talking. Knowing they're downstairs makes me feel safe, and for a brief moment I consider going down to see what they're up to.

Then I remember I have to get up in three hours, and get my ass back in bed. I'm sinking onto the mattress when something catches my eye outside the window. Out of habit, I reach for my gun, which I stashed in the nightstand.

And then I feel him.

"Jacques?" I call softly, and go to the window. He's sitting on the roof of the porch and the pained expression is back on his face. I twist the locks and push up the glass. "What are you doing up here?"

He turns, eyes softening when he sees me. "I'm making sure the vampires who got a taste for your blood haven't discovered where you are yet."

"Oh, thanks. Are you cold?"

He shakes his head, looking unsure. "No."

I fold my arms over my chest. "Want to come in and sit with me?"

"No." He turns his head away, scanning the horizon.

"Uh, okay then. I'm going to go back to bed then."

He nods but doesn't say anything. I shut the window and hurry back to the warmth of the bed. I pull the blankets up to my chin, telling myself Jacques's standoffish behavior doesn't bother me.

I slip back into sleep and my dreams take me to Jacques. He's human again, and we're back in the little cabin. Something about this dream feels weird, like I know I'm dreaming this time. Jacques is reading to me, smiling as he looks down at the book. He's speaking in a language I don't know, yet we both find what he's reading humorous. I stand from the chair I was relaxing in, moving to stir whatever I'm cooking over an open fire.

The same sense of total contentment washes over me. Bright sunlight shines through the windows, and Jacques puts the book down. He takes my hand and leads me through the open door. We walk through the field to the edge of a cliff overlooking the ocean.

He moves behind me, arms wrapping around my waist, and we just stand there together, watching the waves rolling in and out. Everything around us is perfect. Peaceful. Calm and quiet. I close my eyes and spin in his arms, bringing his hands to my belly.

My lips curve into a grin as I tell Jacques I'm pregnant. Jacques smiles, lifts me up, spinning me and kissing me at the same time. I smile back at him, but the moment my feet hit the ground, the ocean turns red. Black clouds stretch over the sun and the air turns cold.

Jacques is standing at the edge of the cliff, face sullen and hands bloody. I try to go to him but I can't move. It's like I'm not there, not in a body at least, and I'm being forced to watch a film play out in front of me. I can't talk, can't call out to him.

The horizon starts to fade away and my ears ring. Blood starts to drip down Jacques's face. His eyes fall shut to keep the blood from getting in them. An invisible knife slashes across his chest and red stains his white shirt. The air around us starts to buzz, and it's like everything is closing in on itself all at once.

Something pops, and the world goes black. Everything hurts and I can't move my arms. I blink, trying to get the blood out of my eyes, and realize I'm tied to a chair. Across the room, someone lights a candle, and soft, yellow light flickers around us, illuminating the pretty face of a woman.

A woman holding a knife in one hand and a spell book in the other. I'm seeing the world through her eyes, reading the thoughts in her head.

She is Braeya. The woman from the dreams. The one Jacques loves.

And she's a witch.

Horror fills me as I realize she's been casting spells on Jacques, making him see and feel things that aren't real. The love he felt both for her and from her...the freedom of living together at the edge of the world...the baby. None of it was real.

It was only a spell.

20

I stretch my arms over my head, eyeing the clock. I have half an hour until I can leave work, and, assuming there are no occult-like murders, I get the weekend off. Thank. Fucking. God. It's been a long day filled with briefings, meetings, and going over evidence. Nothing stacks up, and everyone is frustrated and confused. They're looking for a killer who doesn't exist. The baby vamps are dead and gone, but it's only a matter of time before more rise from the ground and begin a new reign of terror.

I straighten up my desk, pull my notebook from my locked drawer and stuff it into my bag, and shut down my computer. Just a few more minutes. I need to go to my apartment, take another load of belongings over to the estate, and try to hunt down my landlord and ask for my money back. Then I'll have to figure out moving, and it's ironic, as I have four very strong friends who can't be seen by anyone other than me.

I've lived a simple life over the last few years, but I've still managed to acquire my fair share of stuff. My furniture will be the hardest to move, which makes me lean toward selling everything but my bed. The estate has plenty of furniture in it already.

I miss the guys, and I want to talk to Jacques, though I'm not really sure what to say. Everything in the dreams felt so real—especially the sex. I saw every inch of him, and it wasn't some fabrication. I really saw him, scars and all.

I saw him laugh. I saw him smile. I felt how much he's capable of loving someone, and how he'd do anything for the person who holds his heart. Only, none of it was real.

The love, the perfect life, the baby…it was all mind games.

There's a commotion at the front of the station, and I get up to see what's going on. Two officers are trying to subdue Oliver McMillan, one of our "frequent flyers." He bounces from homeless shelter to homeless shelter, then sometimes lives with his daughter until he gets too paranoid to stay there anymore. I know he's been committed more than once, but due to lack of insurance and the fact he's not a danger to anyone, he's always let out to roam the streets again.

He's a crazy older man who thinks the government is watching him and has more conspiracy theories than anyone. It's rather sad, really.

"I need to talk to the person in charge," he repeats, ignoring the officers. "I need to tell the boss about the vampires!"

"There are no vampires. Please, Mr. McMillan," a young female cop says. She has compassion in her eyes, and I hope it stays. It's easy for the compassion to turn into frustration and annoyance. "There is no such thing as vampires. The boss is busy."

"Hey," I say, and hurry to the front desk. "What's going on?"

The female officer—Ella Cooper—turns to me, shaking her head. "He's been in here all week wanting to talk about vampires. We've very nicely asked him to go home each time." She gives her attention back to Mr. McMillan, trying to appeal to what little logic he has left.

"Vampires?" I echo, and Mr. McMillan stops struggling.

"Yes," he says, sounding exasperated. "They're killing everyone. We're all in danger, but no one will listen."

"I'll listen," I say, and Ella's shoulders relax with relief. "Let's go talk about this. Are you hungry?" I ask him. He eyes me suspiciously for a moment, and then nods. I motion for him to follow me, and we go outside and down the street to a cafe.

"You gonna tell me I'm crazy?" he asks when we slide into a booth.

"No." I grab the menus from the side of the table and hand one to him. "Order whatever you want. It's on me."

He licks his lips at the thought of food but doesn't look at the menu. Not yet. He's still trying to figure me out.

"Why are you doing this?"

"I believe you," I say softly, knowing the next few moments are critical. Mr. McMillan suffers from paranoia, and, while just minutes ago he was wanting to warn the public about vampires, he'll shut down if he doesn't trust me.

He narrows his eyes. "Why?"

I turn my head up, eyes meeting his, and look at him as just a person, not a cop. "I've seen things, things that can't be explained."

He continues to study me for another moment, then opens his menu. "You can stop the vampires?"

"I can try." The waitress comes over to take our drink orders. I wait until she's out of earshot to continue. "But I need your help. Can you tell me why you think there are vampires—"

"I don't think! I know!" He brings his fist down on the table, getting attention from a couple at the table next to us.

"Sorry," I say, and offer a smile. "I know you know. I mean, can you tell me *how* you found out about the vampires."

"Yeah, okay…I can do that." He shifts his weight, looking around nervously. "The sun is out. We're safe as long as we stay by the window."

I nod, reminding myself to have extra patience with this man. "The vampires are sleeping."

He looks at the menu for a minute, closes it, and leans back, waiting for his coffee. Once it comes and we put in our order for food, he starts talking.

"I've been staying at Christian Haven. You know of it?"

"I do." It's a homeless shelter offered by a church.

"About a week or so ago, a new guy showed up. Said he'd been on the streets, but I didn't buy it. He looked too...too put-together. Wasn't ever hungry. And he smelled funny."

"Like sulfur?"

"Yeah. Exactly like sulfur." He takes a drink of coffee. "He told us his name was Ben. He was quiet at first, but I knew something was wrong with him. He'd show up at night, turn down food, and walk around talking to the other guys. Then he told us about a place we could go to make a little cash but wouldn't give any details."

"Did you find out what he was referring to?"

"Of course I did. Two guys went. Came back with a hundred bucks each. Way more than *a little cash* if you ask me. So more guys went, but not all came back with cash. Everything was very hush-hush...until one of the guys who went the first time never came back. And before you ask—yes, I found out what happened. He became severely anemic and died. Did some more digging and found out more."

He stops, adds sugar to his coffee, and takes another drink. Anxious to hear more, I drum my fingers on the table.

"Turns out, the guys were getting paid to donate blood. Off the record. After hours."

"Where?"

"The HealthLife Center."

Holy shit. The HealthLife Center is a free clinic...and just down the street from Delirium.

21

I roll out my yoga mat and stretch my arms over my head. Sore from getting roughed up the last few days, my muscles are stiff and tight. Not working out for several days in a row has left me feeling a little lazy, too, and now's not the time to get out of practice.

I put my earbuds in, crank up my music, and start with a warm-up. I move into a sun salutation, focusing on my breathing and nothing else. With my eyes closed and the music pumping in my ears, I don't hear the front door open and close. The floor vibrates and my eyes fly open.

Through my legs, I see Thomas and Gilbert in the threshold of the living room, admiring my ass. I stand up and pull the earbuds out. I smile when I see them, realizing just how much I missed being around the guys during the day.

"Don't stop because of us," Thomas says with a smirk.

"We'll gladly keep watch," Gilbert agrees.

Bringing my arms over my head in a stretch, I cross the room and stop in front of Thomas. He looks as human as ever. There is no gray at all left in his skin. The claws have retracted back on his hands, and even the fangs aren't as obvious. The same goes for Gilbert, worlds different than the first night they woke up.

"Morning," I say with a smile, hugging them both. "I'm guessing you're hungry?"

Thomas smiles. "You know me well."

"I have a casserole in the oven. Hopefully it's good. You know I'm not much of a cook." I look past them and see Hasan and Jacques on the porch, looking out over the yard. Jacques says something, body tensing, and takes off, wings spread in flight.

I'll never get used to the sight of him soaring into the air.

"You've said that," Gilbert starts. "Do you have servants who cook for you?"

"No," I reply with a laugh. "Nowadays, you just go pick up your food from restaurants. I wish I could take you with me someday."

"Someday," Thomas echoes.

We go into the kitchen and the twins set the table while I check on dinner, though I'm not sure exactly what I'm checking on. I followed the recipe and still have five minutes left on the timer before I'm supposed to take it out.

Hasan comes in right as I'm putting bowls of salad on the table, stopping behind me. He wraps his arms around my middle, and

I put the last bowl down and twist in his embrace, hooking my arms around his neck. He kisses my cheek, beard rough on my skin. Shivers go down my spine, and I have to stand on my tippy toes to even come close to kissing him back.

"Do you need help?" he asks, breaking away from me.

I smile at his thoughtfulness, and the emptiness inside me fills even more. "Uh, you could fill glasses with water."

He nods and goes to the cabinet for the glasses. I take a moment, watching the guys help get the table ready for dinner, and realize how much I've wanted this for years and years. I've wanted it so much it turned into a dull ache in my chest, one I was starting to lose hope on ever obtaining.

A family.

Albeit a weird, dysfunctional family with four members here more or less against their will. I never thought I'd trust these guys, but it's there and it's growing. And I like them.

"I think I had a dream last night," Thomas tells me.

"You dreamed?" Gilbert asks his brother. "I haven't had a dream in a thousand fucking years. The last dream I remember was before the curse. It was about a dark-haired whore from the brothel outside of town."

I roll my eyes. "You can't call women 'whores' anymore, you know. Even if they sell themselves for sex. It's considered an offensive insult now."

"What do you call them, then?"

"Well, it's illegal, but they're called prostitutes."

Thomas makes a face. "That's a weird word."

"I guess. And there's only a few brothels in the country that operate legally."

"Interesting." Thomas shrugs. "I always thought they were crude."

"Not crude enough to stop going," Gilbert mutters under his breath.

I laugh. "Times have changed, right?" I look at Thomas. "What was your dream about?"

He flashes me a cocky grin and wiggles his eyebrows. "You."

Hasan puts another glass of water on the table. His hands are so big they dwarf the glass. "I think I had a dream, too. I don't remember people, only feelings."

"That's a good sign, right?" I ask. "Becoming more and more human would make it easier to break the curse. You all look much more human than the first night you woke up."

"We don't dream." Jacques's voice is sharp behind us, startling me just a bit. I quickly turn around, finding him a few feet back in the darkened hall connecting the kitchen to the dining room. His wings block out any light behind him. Still, I notice the bits of gray coloring left on his skin, mottled and blotchy. That pained look is back on his face, and it hurts my heart. I want to go to him, put my lips against his, and feel my heart beat in tempo with his heart.

But I don't. Instead, I turn the timer off with a few minutes to spare and pull the casserole from the oven. No one speaks as we fill our plates and sit around the table.

"You didn't get very much," Hasan says to me, eyeballing the small portion of food on my plate.

"I already had dinner," I tell him. "With a crazy homeless man who had great info on the vampires." Everyone stares at me. "I'll explain," I say, and recap everything Mr. McMillan told me.

"All signs point to the bar. And I did some more digging. The free clinic opened half a year after the bar. And they get a large donation every quarter from the people who own said bar."

I look up, a smile on my face. I always feel a rush when I get a break in a case. I've been chasing this lead for days and finally got through to something.

"You're right," Thomas agrees. "It's too big of a coincidence to be just that."

"There are pretty strict regulations when it comes to donating blood," I tell the guys, who thought the concept was weird. "I mean, you'll always run into people who don't follow protocol, but if a lot of blood went missing, it would be noticed. People would be fired and it'd get looked into. From what I've heard, it seems like the vampires really don't want to be found, especially if they've been here for hundreds of years."

I get up and go to my bag, pulling out a folder full of files. "I had an officer pull all unsolved cases with blood loss as the cause of death. I filtered through them to the ones that could be vampires, and most of these victims are homeless."

"People no one will look for or even notice if they go missing," Jacques finishes.

"Right," I say, excitement building. I'm getting closer and closer to cracking this thing.

"What is your plan?" Hasan asks carefully. He wasn't fond of my last plan so much, so he followed me to the bar.

"Tomorrow—during the day, of course—I'm going to check out the free clinic. You know, just poke around as a regular person, not as a cop, and see if I get a feel for anything. This clinic provides free healthcare to a lot of people, so I need to be careful in how I handle things. I don't want it to get shut down if it doesn't have to be."

"And if it does?" Gilbert asks.

"Then I'll shut it down. I can't imagine the whole thing is just a ruse, though. Or maybe I don't want it to be. It's open from nine AM to four PM. Even in the winter, those are daylight hours with human employees."

"And then what?" Hasan asks.

I shake my head. "I'm not sure, to be honest. I'm not going back to look for vampires at night again, I can tell you that much. Not until I've figured out how to do that thing again." I hold up my hand, imagining it on fire. "But I did pick up some nice-sized sticks from the yard and brought several knives for whittling wooden stakes later."

"I'll help you," Hasan says with a smile. "It's been a while since I've sharpened any weapons."

"It's getting late." Jacques tears his eyes away from the TV for the first time in at least half an episode. I was able to hook my laptop up to the old TV in the living room and stream Netflix, and the guys are enthralled. We're currently working our way through *The Office*, which I find hilarious no matter how many times I watch it. A lot of the humor is lost with the guys not understanding the references.

"I don't have to go to work in the morning, so I can sleep in. Which is exactly what I plan to do," I say, carefully dragging my knife down along the stick in my hands. I'm on my last wooden stake, thank God. I've gotten several splinters already. I run the knife down the stake again, then test the point. It's sharp. Very sharp.

I brush wood shavings off my lap and get up to put the stake with the others. Between Hasan, Jacques, and myself, we've made nearly a dozen stakes. Since the wood I used was from fallen branches in the yard, some turned out better and stronger than others, which is why we thought it would be a good idea to make several.

"I'll get holy water tomorrow," I start, and sit back on the couch next to Jacques. His wings go in toward his body a bit when I draw near in a subconscious movement he's been doing all night. I've tested it a few times to make sure. I get close, he tenses.

I hate that it bothers me.

"And then what, just pour it over the stakes?" I look at the pile of wood on the coffee table.

Without answering me, Jacques gets up. I look over at Hasan, hoping he knows what's up with his friend, but he's too busy watching Dwight on the screen to notice. I sweep shavings into a pile with my hand, making a mental note to bring my vacuum over from home tomorrow. The whole house needs to be cleaned.

A minute later, Jacques returns with a metal mixing bowl. He puts the stakes in it, sharp tips down, and sets it back on the coffee table.

"Fill this as close to halfway as you can. As long as the pointy ends are blessed, it should be enough. You're not going to stab the entire stake through their hearts."

"Oh, right. That makes sense. I only need a couple of inches to stab and kill. God, that's weird to say."

Jacques's face softens and he sits on the couch again, holding his wings open more than normal in an attempt to keep me away. "Are you all right with this, Ace?"

"Yeah. Well, as much as I can be. I've fired at bad guys, shot one before, too. Not fatally, though. I solve crimes. I help people. I'm not a…a…"

"Killer," he finishes for me, and I nod. "It's not the same thing. The vampires are already dead, you know that. Their human life, their soul, ended the day they were turned. You're doing them justice by vanquishing the devils inside them. Would you want that walking around in your body?"

"Fuck no." I grab the end of my braid and twist it around my fingers. "I didn't think about it like that. Thanks. Again. You're good at inspirational speeches."

He gives me the smallest smile and relaxes a bit, leaning back on the couch. Thomas and Gilbert come inside to get something to eat but stop dead in their tracks when they see the TV on. With the guys insisting someone needs to keep watch for vampires outside, Jacques quickly offers to go out and trade places with the twins. Anything to get away from me.

I show them where things are in the kitchen so they can make sandwiches and leave them to it while I go upstairs to change into my PJs and brush my teeth. When I get back down, Thomas, Gilbert, and Hasan are all eating turkey sandwiches while watching TV. I quickly make one more and take it outside for Jacques.

"Jac?" I call softly when I get onto the front porch. The chill is finally starting to leave the air and the feel of spring is setting into the earth. "Are you out here?" I stop at the edge of the porch and look out into the dark yard. I'm barefoot and while it has warmed up, the cobblestone path will be cold underfoot.

Something rustles ahead, and I cannot tell what it is from up here. The porch lights are too harsh and it's too dark. I can't see shit. I set the plate on the wide stone railing and step off the porch.

"What are you doing, Ace?" Jacques asks from above. He gracefully glides down from the roof, landing a foot from me.

"I heard something."

"Where?" He's immediately on the defensive.

"In the brush near the street."

"Stay here." He takes off to check it out. I watch, irritated to just stand here. That's not me. But I'm barefoot and it's cold and I'm fairly certain whatever I heard was a wild animal. I don't get a bad feeling about it, and while I'm the first—*was* the first, I should say—to call bullshit on any sort of psychic powers, I've always had good police intuition.

"It was a small gray creature with black stripes on its tail," Jacques says when he returns.

"Raccoon," I say. "They're all over the place. Cute, but pesky little things."

He nods. "You heard that from inside the house?"

"No." I motion to the sandwich. "I brought you something to eat before I go to bed."

"Oh. Thanks." He holds my gaze and the longing for him is back in my heart, though this time I'm questioning if it's from the dream or not. I know what I felt in the dream isn't real. My attraction to him is and has been since the first time I laid eyes on him. "You're doing a good job, Ace," he adds as I turn to go back inside. I pause, biting my lip.

"I actually feel like it now. Well, kind of. Assuming this new lead will turn into anything."

Jacques picks up the sandwich and sits on the cement railing, large wings hanging down behind him. "You're used to things going your way."

"Not in life. But in my job, sort of. I'm used to being able to figure things out. You know," I say, and lean on the railing next to him, "I used to debunk cases people thought had to do with anything supernatural. I've always found the person responsible."

Jacques turns to me, hearing the words I didn't say. "And now you're wondering if you put away the wrong people."

I didn't want to admit it to myself. I didn't even let myself think about it. Hearing it out loud brings about a bit of panic and regret...but also relief.

"Yes."

"Were the people you arrested bad people?"

"Always."

"Then don't feel bad." Jacques takes a bite out of his sandwich. The breeze picks up, blowing my hair around my face. I close my eyes and tip my head to the wind, letting out my breath and letting go of the guilt.

"You're beautiful, Ace," he says softly. "Beautiful and smart. You'll figure everything out."

"I wish I had your confidence in myself," I only half joke. "Or at least a guidebook—oh my God."

"What's wrong?"

"Nothing. Nothing at all. I can't believe I forgot."

"Forgot what?"

"The guidebook. Maybe. Or maybe not. I'm not sure what it is because it's written in Latin." I look at Jacques, not needing to ask it out loud for him to know my question.

"Yes, I can read Latin. What are you talking about?"

"A book I found in this weird box in the basement that stabbed me and needed my blood to open."

Jacques's face turns serious. "And you didn't think to tell me?"

I pull my shoulders back. "I don't have to tell you anything. And it was a few days ago, before I was sure if I could trust you."

"Show me this book."

"I'll get it. Hang on." I hurry in and retrieve the book. I grab my shoes and a blanket on my way out, wrapping it around my shoulders. Jacques takes the book, eyes wide as he looks it over.

"It's a grimoire."

I WAKE up around ten-thirty in the morning, and it was glorious to sleep in. I stayed up until almost dawn, sitting on the porch with Jacques as he translated the book. Though it was chilly at first, there was something peaceful about sitting outside in the dark with him. Worried I was going to get cold, he tucked his wing around me much like the very first night.

I drifted off with my head on his shoulder, waking when he wrapped his arms around me and carried me inside and up into bed, where I quickly fell back asleep. Clouds mute the morning sun now, and the air is humid like it's about to rain. Another lovely spring day.

I take my time getting out of bed, and then enjoy a long, hot shower. Well, not too long, since the water heater in this house sucks. Add a new one to my long list of updates this place needs.

Jacques left the grimoire and his notes on the kitchen table. I brew a pot of coffee while I read through them, admiring his incredible penmanship all over again. He was directly translating it onto paper but was explaining things to me in a way which made sense, and some of the notes don't. Not every word translated, so what I'm reading is patchy.

But this thing is without a doubt a spell book. Jacques thinks it's old, a few hundred years at least, and has been recopied from a previous version according to the notes written in the beginning of the book.

It's been in my family for centuries.

I run my fingers over the smooth leather, finding it hard to wrap my head around. My maternal family has been such a mystery my whole life, and now I'm finding out we have this secret and pretty badass history.

"Did you know, Mom?" I whisper and look up. The idea of Heaven is another thing I can't wrap my head around, yet I tip my head to the sky whenever I think about my parents. It went against everything I worked for, but thinking they were up there gave me a bit of peace.

After my coffee, I get ready for the day and head to the health clinic. Misty rain starts to fall when I park, and I pull my leather jacket tighter around me to try and stay dry. Going out of my way, I cross the street and walk by Delirium to try and look inside.

The windows in the front are tinted, and I can't see shit. Same goes for the door. Everything is shut tight, not letting a speck of sunlight filter in. I stand under the awning, holding my phone and acting like I'm texting as I look around. This place is so clean it's telling.

I cross the street again, go down a few storefronts, and enter the free clinic. A few people are in the lobby, and a young, smiling nurse sits behind the front desk. At first glance, this place is totally normal. I hesitate, putting on the front of nerves, and take everything in before I go to the desk.

"Hi," the young nurse says with the same broad smile. "How can I help you today?"

"My friend told me I could donate blood," I start, tugging on the sleeves of my hoodie. It's one of my favorites because it's oversized and so comfortable. Tiffany says I look like a homeless drug dealer when I wear it, and that could work in my favor right now. "For cash."

The nurse's smile doesn't falter. "We do have blood drives a few times a month, but there's no payout for it. The blood is donated by volunteers. If you've used needles recently we cannot accept it, though."

Yep. The drug dealer hoodie is working. "Oh, not a problem for me. When's the next blood drive?"

She flips open a planner and runs her finger down the dates. I peer over the desk, seeing only notes for regular appointments and events, nothing obvious like "secret vampire blood pick-up," but hey, a girl can dream, right?

"Two weeks from today. Would you like to set up an appointment time?"

"No, I'm not even sure what I have going on tomorrow, let alone two weeks from now."

The nurse laughs. "I'm the same way. We do take walk-ins if you still want to donate, but know sometimes you could wait a bit to get a spot without an appointment."

"Thanks. Do you have a bathroom I can use?"

"Yeah, it's right down the hall. You'll see the sign as soon as you turn the corner."

I smile. "Thanks."

There are a few exam rooms along the hall, and a locked door at the end that I'm guessing leads to the small lab and the nurses' station. Two of the exam room doors are shut and I hurry down the hall, going right past the bathroom to the door at the end. It's locked. Of course. The lights are off in the exam room next to me, which is odd only because every other room is lit up. Stealing a glance behind me at the front of the clinic, I step inside.

The room smells of bleach, which always strikes me as someone trying to cover something up, but this *is* a medical clinic. Someone could have puked all over this place before I walked in. Nevertheless, I go into detective mode, going over the room as quickly and thoroughly as possible, and find little drops of blood on the tile floor next to the exam bed. Maybe this room was used last night for a vampire blood drive.

Positive I found anything and everything out of place, I go back out into the hall and almost run into a man coming into the hall from the locked door. He stops short, nostrils flaring.

"Sorry," I say, and pull my hood up. He's wearing scrubs and has a stethoscope around his neck. His nametag says he's Shawn Welsh and a registered nurse. The hair on the back of my neck prickles and everything inside of me is telling me to run.

"Do you have an appointment?" he asks, voice raspy. He takes a step closer, looking at me so hard it's uncomfortable. If I was wearing anything that remotely showed my figure, I'd think he was checking me out.

"No, I was looking for the bathroom."

"It's right there," he says, and extends his hand to point. He leans in and inhales, eyes twitching. His cologne is so strong it chokes me.

"Yeah, I see that now. Thanks."

"Great." He forces a thin, closed-lip smile and breezes past me to the exam room next to us, knocking on the door before entering. The smell of his cologne lingers in the air, but so does something else.

The smell of sulfur.

22

I pour the holy water in the bowl, arranging the stakes so they get saturated. It's early afternoon, hours from sunset, and I'm more anxious than ever for the guys to wake up. There's no way the nurse at the clinic was a vampire. It's the middle of the day. There are other reasons someone can smell like sulfur. Old tap water can, for example. Maybe he washed his clothes in it?

Or maybe he's not a vampire but spends a lot of time with them.

I roll my eyes at myself. He looked at me funny…he smelled like sulfur…and, most of all, I got a bad feeling around him. But it can't be possible. Vampires sleep during the day, just like my gargoyles.

"Right, guys?" I ask, looking through the living room in their direction. I grab the grimoire and Jacques's notes and sit at the kitchen table. The book doesn't seem to be written in any order, with supernatural information and spells mixed in together.

Jacques's theory was the original sorcerer wrote things as he or she learned them, and the book had been copied in the same order.

The first spell Jacques translated is for protection during birth. It's intricate and complicated, making me thankful I'll have modern medicine to rely on as well if I ever have children. The next few pages are filled with notes from the original author, written casually almost like a diary, summing up a spell performed during the spring equinox. He'd gotten halfway through translating a full moon blessing spell before he had to retire to the roof for sunrise.

I close my eyes, going with my gut, and open to a random page. Like everything else, it's written in Latin, but this one has a crude painting of a person. The color has faded over the years, and the ink is smeared, but there's no denying the person is holding up a hand engulfed in flames. I scan the page and the word "ignis" jumps out at me. It's not a direct translation, but Jac told me it means fire.

With a surge of excitement, I get up and get my phone, using Google to translate as much of the text as I can. I have to fill in the blanks in more than a few spots, and some of the words don't even come up in the Latin-to-English dictionary.

"Well, I don't have crystals, sage, or whatever this is," I say out loud to myself, tapping my pen on the notebook. I'm not entirely sure what to do, either, but I think the spell is calling to boil the herbs in a cauldron, add the crystal, and then hold it for extra power? Or maybe you drink it like tea?

Not wanting to accidentally turn anyone into a frog, I close the book and go upstairs to change into my workout clothes. After warming up and stretching, I put in my earbuds and take off down the gravel road. I haven't been past the estate, and those kids I caught creeping said they lived nearby. It'd be nice to know who's around me, though I'm not getting neighborly enough to say hi, introduce myself, and invite them over for pie.

I make it a good mile down the road before the trees on either side begin to clear, and a neatly manicured lawn butts up to the rural road. A small white ranch-style house sits behind perfectly trimmed rosebushes, and an elderly woman reading a book waves to me from a rocking chair on the covered porch.

The house next to it is just as nice. It's a little bigger, with a basketball hoop in the driveway and chalk drawings on the sidewalk. There are five houses total in this little stretch, all nice and neat, and they don't look to be over ten years old. I turn up my music and push through another half mile before coming to any more houses. It's interesting how the estate stayed so isolated for years and years. There's no way it's by chance.

Hot and sweaty, I slow to a walk, stretching my arms over my head. I turn around and keep walking until my breathing steadies out, then stop to stretch my legs. A car comes down the road, going way too fast at first. It slows down to only five miles over the speed limit when the driver sees me, and I pick up my pace to a jog, raising my hand in a friendly wave to thank the asshole for not running me over.

I turn to get a view of the plates, not expecting to see brake lights. The black Toyota already passed me. Why is it stopping now? As a cop, I've seen enough to make me view everyone as guilty until proven innocent. As a woman jogging alone on a rural road, my feelings are amplified tenfold.

I turn down my music but leave the earbuds in, turning to take another look at the car and to commit the plate to memory. The tinted passenger side window rolls down halfway and I get a glimpse of a blonde woman in the seat. She's wearing a floppy hat and big sunglasses, looking classically beautiful.

But something about her makes me want to pick up my pace. I hold steady in my jog, my eyes darting along the road, looking for anything I can use as a weapon. Gravel crunches and the car takes off, tires spinning in its haste to get away. Inhaling a lungful of humid air, I push forward, getting more and more eager to get back to the estate.

I don't get ominous feelings. I believe in intuition in certain, specific situations, but don't think anyone can "feel" a universal warning.

But that's exactly what I'm feeling right now. Something bad is coming. And I'm not at all prepared.

Loose stone crunches under my feet and my body itches to break into a sprint, not stopping until I'm in the house with my gun on my hip and a wooden stake in my hand. Though it's not fear that's making me run. It's the overwhelming need to get ready for a battle, because, for some strange-as-fuck reason, I know it's coming. *Calm your tits, Ace,* I tell myself. There's no way to know that, and of course something bad will happen. Even before the gargoyles and vampires, bad things happening were a part of life. Hell, I'd be out of a job if bad things *didn't* happen.

I wipe sweat off my brow, slowing for a few paces when I get to the little collection of houses that look like they were taken right off Wisteria Lane. The garage door opens to the house with the basketball hoop, and Jared, the kid with the camera, steps outside, holding keys. An older man I guess to be his father is behind him, and Jared freezes when he sees me, face going white. I smile and raise my hand in a friendly wave, overdoing the neighbor shit this time just to see the panic rise on Jared's face.

His father's eyes widen and he waves back, quickly walking to the end of the driveway. I slow to a walk, welcoming the misty rain that's starting to fall.

"Sorry to interrupt your run," he says. For an older man, he's not bad-looking. Not at all. "But I thought you came from the old brick mansion up the road."

"I did," I say, brushing loose strands of hair away from my sweaty face.

"We thought we saw lights on the other night. It shocked me, that's all." He smiles and his eyes lighten. "I'm Richard, by the way. And this is my son Jared."

"Hi, Jared," I say sweetly. "And I'm Acelina, but everyone calls me Ace."

"Nice to meet you, Ace. Did you move in? I didn't think the house was move-in ready?"

"It's not quite. I'm working on it."

"I've admired that house for years. The architecture on it is stunning. Do you know the history behind it?"

"Dad," Jared scoffs.

"Sorry." Richard laughs. "I'm a history professor at Drexel and I find anything local particularly intriguing."

"Oh, neat. I don't know much. I inherited the house recently."

A car coming down the road gets all our attention. It's the black sedan again. It speeds past us. The windows are tinted darker than what's legal, giving me a reason to have it pulled over.

"That's the car I told you about, Dad," Jared says. "It's been up and down the road three times in the last hour."

"Really?" I ask. "You're sure it's the same car?" The hair on the back of my neck isn't prickling or anything…nope. Not at all.

"I think it is," Richard agrees. "It's gone by too fast each time to see the license number."

"Have you seen it before?" I ask.

"No. There aren't too many houses out here, and it's faster to get to the neighborhood down the road if you come from 500 South, not from our road, so something like this sticks out," Richard answers. "I thought maybe they were looking for land for sale—we get that a lot. People want a piece of the pie out here. But three, now four, times in an hour is unsettling."

"It is," I agree. "Have you seen anything else out of the ordinary?"

Richard shakes his head. "I hope this doesn't scare you off. We're normally peaceful around here and everyone in this little neighborhood feels quite safe. That's why we moved out here. The wife and I wanted a safer environment for the children."

"Right. Safety is important, so if you see it again, I need you to call me," I start, looking at his house. There's a security camera above the porch and near the garage. "I'm a cop."

Richard's eyes flick over my body. I get that reaction a lot, actually. I'm tall and slender, athletic but not buff. My physical strength gets questioned every time I tell someone what I do for a living.

He smiles. "It's nice having an officer of the law on our road." He pulls his phone out of his pocket. "What division are you in? I have a buddy who's on the force."

"Homicide. I'm a detective," I say, and give him my number. Jared crosses his arms, looking uncomfortable. The kid believes in gargoyles. I bet he believes in vampires, too, and I don't want him going out looking for something that will rip him to shreds.

"Don't go outside alone at night," I say, eyes going right to Jared. "We've had a lot of calls lately about cars driving by houses with children after dark. Better safe than sorry, right? Best to stay inside and lock the doors."

"I agree with you there. We're headed out to pick up dinner and I think it'll be a quiet night in for us."

"Yay," Jared says sarcastically, and rolls his eyes again.

"Be careful," I direct to him. "And it was nice meeting you."

"You, too. And if you ever need help with the house, I'm more than willing to lend a hand." Richard smiles. "The time when your house was built is my area of expertise and I'd jump on any opportunity to help preserve the history of a structure so magnificent."

"Thanks," I tell him, and take a few steps back. Keeping my music off and my vigilance high, I start to my house again, running harder and faster than I should, and am out of breath and hotter than before by the time my feet hit the cobblestone path leading to the front door. Not wanting to get achy muscles from stopping too suddenly, I walk around the house and look at the yard.

The misty rain brings on fog, and with sunset quickly approaching, mutes the evening light. There's a shed behind the house. It's newer, put in by the last occupant of the house, according to the records I got at the bank. The dilapidated pile of splintering wood and shingles was the original barn to this place, and it looks like it's been in a rotting heap for years. The chicken coop isn't in bad shape, not that I'd ever have anything to do with it. I like to eat chicken, and I can't eat an animal I've had in a little house in the backyard.

I roll my neck and stretch. My back is tight from stress, and I put one foot up on the step going to the back porch to try and stretch it out. It takes a while to get the knot to loosen enough to not be painful, and it'll be good as new with a back rub. I subconsciously smile and feel a tingle between my legs when I think of the last massage I got.

"Is it sunset yet?" I ask, looking up at the roof. From this angle, I can only see the tips of Hasan's wings. I walk backwards, keeping my eyes on my gargoyle, until I can see his face, twisted into something monstrous and set in stone.

Bending over to touch my toes in a final stretch before going inside to shower, I feel eyes on me. I snap up and turn around, suddenly unnerved. Taking a deep breath, I walk around to the front of the house. The fog is rolling in, getting thicker and thicker and harder to see through as the sun sinks lower in the sky.

"Hey, guys," I say to Thomas and Gilbert, rounding the house and coming up to the front porch. I pull my key from the pocket on the back of my sports bra and stick it in the deadbolt.

And then I notice the scratches on the door frame and know right away what they're from. Someone tried to break into the house.

23

I hurry inside, shutting and locking the door behind me. I flick on the foyer lights and hurry through the house to get my gun and a wooden stake. I leave the others soaking in the holy water. My heart beats rapidly in my chest, both from the run and from adrenaline.

Handling this like any other case, I do a quick check of the house, starting with the front. It's too large to comb through perfectly. Someone could easily be in here, moving from room to room without me ever seeing them.

The front door was locked when I came home, just how I'd left it. The windows are locked and the other exterior doors downstairs are shut and locked, as well. I go up the rear stairs and head into the master bedroom first. The windows over the porch might not be locked, and my heart beats a little faster the closer I get.

The last I remember was opening them to talk to Jacques. I cannot for the life of me recall locking them again. I push back the lace curtain. Thank God. I locked them. I check the rest of the house, turning on lights and feeling way too exposed.

Not every room has curtains, and with the lights on, it's easy to see in. And whoever is watching me is outside. I can feel it. I go back into the bedroom, the only room with curtains, and sit on the foot of the bed. I need a plan, but having no idea what I'm up against is a bit of a hindrance.

I carefully press the tip of the wooden stake against my finger to test the sharpness. My skin prickles, and I'm getting more and more anxious for nightfall. I want to kill these motherfuckers and end this once and for all. I go to the window, looking at the sky.

Then my phone rings, and the *Star Wars* theme song echoes through the large house. Having left my phone downstairs in the living room, it's a wonder I can hear it up here. I hurry down the stairs and pick it up, seeing whoever is calling is from work.

"Detective Bisset," I answer.

"Hi, Detective. It's Jane Simons. I ran the name you gave me through the system."

"Great, thanks, did you find anything."

"Yes, and it doesn't all add up, which is why I'm calling you instead of leaving the report on your desk."

My heart speeds up. "Go on."

"The HealthLife Clinic has Shawn Walsh on their employee records, and it looks like he started working six months ago. They were compliant with giving info and everything there went smoothly. But when I checked on the status of his nursing license, I found an issue. The only registered nurse in the state with the name of Shawn Walsh is a forty-three-year-old African-American."

Shit. He's using a fake name. I go over what to do with Jane for a few minutes before hanging up. Everything is coming together now. The sulfur-smelling nurse who has a fake name and just happens to work at a health clinic that pays homeless people for their blood.

Right down the street from a club that offers a vampire-sex service, so to speak.

They're connected somehow and I'm going to start chipping away until I get to the bottom of it. This new sire made a big mistake setting up shop here.

I open Facebook to do a social media search on the guy. He didn't look any older than twenty-five, making him an ideal candidate to have at least one social media profile. I find nothing. There are a handful of profiles belonging to guys named Shawn Walsh, and not one of them looks like the guy I saw today.

Before I can try Instagram, something thumps on the porch, and the wood creaks from someone walking across it. I trade my phone for the wooden stake and edge toward the window. The sun sets in forty-seven minutes. It's too early for the guys to be up, but whatever is out there is heavy and doesn't know about the creaky planks underfoot near the living room window.

The guys—even if they did wake up early—wouldn't walk over there. They have no reason to look in the window, and they know about the weak and rotting wood close to the house. Sheer ivory curtains hang on the windows in the living room, preventing anyone from looking in and getting a clear view of me, but allowing them to make out shapes and shadows.

They know I'm here and they know I'm alone.

Tightening my grip on the stake, I shut off the light and see a shadow cross the porch. My heart jumps and I race to the front door, moving as quietly as possible. I'm light on my feet and make it to the door with almost no noise. The feeling of being watched intensifies, and I know without a doubt there will be someone—some*thing*—on the porch.

With a surge of adrenaline, I ready the stake in my hand, shoot back the deadbolt, and throw open the door.

There is no one on the porch. I jump out, madly looking around, and silently shut the door behind me. A band of thick fog rolls through the yard, momentarily encasing me in white. The air is humid, chilly yet thick to breathe in. I take in everything around me.

The unnatural stillness in the air.

The lack of birds chirping.

And the lingering smell of sulfur in the air.

The sound of a car moving down the road echoes through the fog. Yeah, people do drive up and down the road to get to their houses, but I'm not taking any chances. With a quick glance at Thomas and Gilbert, I slip from the porch, keeping the stake slightly raised at my side.

It's not sunset yet. Vampires can't be lurking. But my spider-sense is tingling and a weird part of me wants them to be here. I want to look the sire in the eyes when I shove the stake through his nonbeating heart. I want to tell him the names of everyone he's killed and let him know this is their revenge.

They don't have a voice anymore, but I do. And I will shout it loud until every last vampire I can get my hands on is dead and gone.

Silently, I move down the cobblestone path. Trees block the road from direct sight, hiding the house from anyone driving by. It was done to hide the gargoyles, I'm sure, keeping this house as private as possible with the new developments going up around it. The car is getting closer and closer, going slowly in the fog.

I can still feel eyes on me, and I desperately want to know where it's coming from. I pause at the end of the cobblestone path, breathing in the fresh scent of earth around me. No matter where I turn, it feels like someone is behind me. Suddenly, the air becomes electric and static crackles at my fingertips.

I hold up my hand, heat spreading through my palm. It's hot. Hot enough to burn me. The heat registers but doesn't hurt. It's the strangest sensation and I cannot explain it. I look at my hand, willing it to ignite again.

The car drives past and I step into the driveway, looking around the trees. Squinting, I can make out taillights down the road, and it looks like a truck, not a car. I let out a breath and go back to the house, coming to a dead stop when I get to the porch.

The door is open.

I know for fucking sure I had closed it.

24

I freeze, staring at the front door. It's cracked open not even an inch. There's no way someone got in. I was only yards from the house. The porch creaks. I would have heard it, wouldn't I?

Fuck. I might not have.

Closing my hand into a fist, I channel energy down to it, and the heat comes back, but it's not enough to start the fire. Heart in my throat, I put one foot on the first stone step to the porch, eyes on the house. Thomas and Gilbert are on either side of me, but they're frozen, cast in stone, and won't wake up until the sun sinks below the horizon.

I swallow hard and go up another step, then move onto the porch, careful where I put my feet. The boards closest to the house creak the most. Stopping a few feet away from the door, I nudge it open with my foot and step aside, back against the house. I steal a glance behind me, playing all angles of an attack.

Distract me with the open door.

Grab me from behind.

No one rushes forward from inside the house.

No one comes up behind me.

I wait another beat and rub my thumb over my fingers as if it'll strike some sort of magical match and ignite the fire. Something sparks at my fingertips and I jerk my head down to look at it.

Someone runs through the house, footsteps reverberating through the large, two-story foyer. I look back up and see a shadow of a man move across the balcony. I push the door open and run in.

"Hey!" I shout, and race to the stairs, eyes madly darting around. Where the hell did he go? Dammit. This house is too fucking big. I stop on the landing upstairs. I don't know this house well enough yet. Some floorboards creak. Some don't. A few of the rooms are interconnected, making it easy to slip inside one and move down the hall, emerging from a completely different room altogether. I turn away from the master bedroom and take a few steps down the hall.

Most of the doors up here are closed, making the hall dark. The light is fading fast outside, and the fog wraps the house in a dim and eerie blanket of muted gray. I blink rapidly, trying to get my eyes to adjust to the dark.

If whoever is here came in to rob me, they're going to be sorely disappointed. I pull my gun from my holster and stick the wooden stake in it instead. It's not the steadiest, but it'll do. For now.

Flicking off the safety, I raise my weapon and advance down the hall. The familiar feel of my M9 in my hand gives me a bit of confidence. I'm an officer of the law and I'm going to catch and arrest the person who broke into my house.

Because that's what they are. A person.

It's not night yet. It can't be vampires.

The floor creaks behind me and I feel hot breath on the back of my neck. I whirl around, ready to pull the trigger.

But no one is there.

My heart lurches, beating faster and faster. That bad feeling comes back, and all ten of my fingertips buzz with electricity. Footsteps, heavy and deliberate, echo through the house. Someone is running down the back stairs.

I jolt forward, moving down the curved front stairs, and race into the kitchen. The back door is wide open and fog moves into the house. Not wasting time, I run out. If I move fast enough, I can catch the fucker.

Leaping from the porch, I land hard on the soggy ground, sending a shock to my ankles and making the dull ache in my previously twisted ankle come back. Ignoring the pain, I keep going, narrowing my eyes to try and see in this fucking fog. Something moves behind the shed. I go to it, moving to the other side to head them off.

Holding my breath, I keep the gun steady in my hand and inch around. The smell of sulfur lingers in the air, clinging to the thickness of the fog. I wrinkle my nose and get hit with a sudden memory of finding my parents lifeless on the kitchen floor.

I blink it away. I don't let myself think about that day, especially not now.

Mud sticks to my shoes as I move, and I lower my gaze to look for footprints. The grass is overgrown around the shed and is pushed down from someone walking. Taking a deep breath, I jump out, ready to confront whoever is on the other side.

There's no one there. My heart is racing and the feeling of being watched weighs down on me so heavily it's oppressive. And then someone jumps down from the roof of the shed. I move out of the way at the last second, but not without tripping over a tangle of dandelions. The wooden stake falls from the holster.

Scrambling back, I kick the guy hard in the shin. He stumbles, but hardly reacts to the pain. I crawl back on my elbows and raise my gun.

"Freeze or I'll shoot," I threaten, and move back more. The guy takes his time advancing, as if he already knows I'm fucked.

But he doesn't know me. I plant my hand on the ground, wait for him to take another step, then sweep my legs out, knocking his out from underneath him. He goes down hard and I get up, pointing the gun at his face.

"Who are you?" I demand. "What are you doing here?"

"I think you know the answer to that already, love," he says, voice velvety smooth with a faint accent.

"Enlighten me and maybe we'll go easy on your sentencing."

"You think you're going to live past tonight? Cute." He starts to sit up and I push the gun into his face. He tips his head up to mine and inhales deeply. "They were right. You do smell delicious. I'm not supposed to touch you, but I might have to taste your sweet cunt—and your magical blood—before she gets here."

He laughs at my shock, eyes going to mine. What's left of the sunlight reflects off the surface of his pupils, dimly glowing red. My shoulders tense and it feels like someone dumped a bucket of ice water over my head.

No.

No fucking way.

He's a vampire. My gun isn't going to do a damn thing and the stake...the stake is somewhere behind me. *Son of a bitch.*

Then it hits me. My gargoyles sleep until sunset because they have to. Vampires don't. They only sleep to avoid the sun.

And with the clouds and the fog, it's as good as night.

25

I only have seconds to act. The vampire in front of me laughs again and pushes up onto his feet. Something scuttles behind me.

When she gets here...

More are coming. The last time I faced two vampires I nearly died. This time I have the wooden stakes. I have a way to kill them.

Assuming they don't kill me first.

My eyes drop to the ground, looking for the stake. It's three feet in front of me, and the vampire is four. Pushing away all fear, I lunge for it, diving onto the ground. I grab it and roll back onto my feet in seconds. I whirl around, raising the stake, and slash it through the air.

The vampire, who hasn't taken me seriously since the moment he laid eyes on me, lazily ducks away. The sharp point of the stake catches him in the center of his chest, hitting him in the sternum. His skin breaks open, sizzling from the holy water, but his bone is too hard and the tip of the stake breaks off.

He cries out, clawing at his chest. My eyes widen, watching his skin bubble and burn, reacting to the holy water the same way the vampire's face did when I touched him with magic.

"You bitch!" he cries, and fangs slide down from his gums, covering his teeth. The stake won't kill him anymore, but it can still maim. And that's exactly what I'll do.

I slash it through the air, and the broken tip scrapes down his chest over the open wound. His eyes start to glow brighter in his rage and I realize that it must take an older vampire with more control to appear human. Like the one at the free clinic I asked a rookie cop to look into. I hope to God she doesn't decide to go over and question him.

The vampire in front of me lashes out, grabbing the stake from my hands. He tries to rip it from my grip. My gun is still in my other hand. I let the stake go, causing the vamp to stumble back. Then I hit him over the head with the gun before pressing the barrel into the open wound on his chest. My finger hovers over the trigger.

Shooting him won't kill him. Shooting him will only cause me to lose a bullet, an unaccounted-for bullet, and the shot will ring out for miles. Instead, I press the gun into his flesh and bring it down, tearing his skin further before shoving him back into the shed.

I whirl around and see someone quickly approaching from the other side of the house. I need to get in and get another stake. Now.

Breaking into a sprint, I jump up the porch steps, slam the door shut, and twist the lock into place. But the front door is still open and unlocked.

"Fuck," I mutter to myself, sucking in my breath. My body is alive with adrenaline, nerves on end and muscles twitching, ready for a fight. Slowly letting my breath out, I move as quickly and quietly through the house as I can to go into the two-story living room.

The bowl with the stakes is still on the coffee table, thank the fucking stars. I grab another, flick the water off, and grab an empty water glass one of the guys left on the hearth, stashing my gun behind the pile of firewood. The gun can't hurt the vampires, but if one of them got hold of it, they could end me. Easily. And killing me barehanded is already too easy for them.

I stick the cup in the bowl, filling it with a few inches of water before racing to the front door. I pour a bit of the water on the doorknob, then shut and lock the door. I swallow hard, mind racing.

One vampire I can handle. Two, I think I have pretty good odds. Three…yeah…as much as I like to think I can take care of myself in any situation, I need to be realistic if I want to survive.

Holy water hurts them, stakes can kill them, and the magic I don't know how to control causes their skin to crack and burn with just the slightest touch. I close my eyes and let out a breath, remembering the way it felt to have the flames around my fingers.

"Come on," I whisper, envisioning the flames. The heater kicks on, making me jump and almost drop the glass. I need to get it together. Focus. Figure out how the hell to do magic again.

The floor creaks above me. Dammit. I knew they were in the house. I slip through the living room and into the kitchen, mind whirling. Being trapped inside with the vampires is just as bad as being outside in the fog with them. In or out, I need to find them and kill them.

There's no running, and no one is going to save me this time. The sun won't set for another half an hour at least, and thirty minutes is more than enough for the vampires to tear me apart.

I edge toward the rear staircase, holding my breath, and listen. Whoever is upstairs is going through drawers, looking for something. I don't know what they—oh shit. I was too distracted to notice it was missing. There's only one thing in this house the vampires would want.

The spell book.

It was right there on the kitchen table and now it's gone. More terror floods through me now than when the vampire at the bar had his teeth on my neck. I hardly know anything about my family and I just got the biggest link to our past before it was stolen from me.

Anger fills me. I grind my teeth and squeeze the stake in my hands. My fingertips feel hot again, and the next thing I know, the water in the glass is boiling. With wide eyes, I look at it. Everything logical says my hand should be burning too. My skin should be bubbling and blistering right now, but I feel no pain at all.

The person upstairs moves through the hall and starts to come down the rear stairs. I take a step back and wait. Halfway down, he stops and sniffs the air. The fuckers can smell me.

"She's in—" he starts to shout but cuts off when I rush forward and throw the glass of boiling holy water in his face. His skin sizzles, melting off and falling in gooey puddles on the wooden steps. He reaches for me and stumbles down the stairs. I move over him, kick him hard in the dick, and bring the stake down on his chest.

He bares his fangs at me, eyes glowing a deep red. My fingertips hum with energy, but I can't get the fire to ignite.

"Tell me where the book is," I demand, digging the stake into his flesh. "Tell me or I'll kill you."

He pulls his lips back in a sneer, skin still bubbling. "Whatever you do to me will be merciful compared to what *she* has planned."

Whoever she is sounds terrifying.

"What does she want?" I push the stake down harder.

"You."

The front door rattles and someone curses, which only means one thing: another vampire is trying to get in and touched the holy-water-covered doorknob.

"I'm sorry," I tell the vampire, looking right into his eyes. I'm not sorry for what I'm about to do. I'm sorry his life was taken and he was turned into this monster. With one hard push, I plunge the wooden stake into his heart. He lets out a scream and his head flops back, eyes going black.

Blood pools inside his mouth, dripping to the floor. The area around the stab wound starts to bubble up, just like his skin when I threw the holy water on him. His whole body begins to react next, and, in just seconds, he's nothing but a puddle of goo.

"Fuck," I say, covering my nose from the sulfur smell that's a hundred times stronger now. Blinking rapidly, I tear my eyes away from the dead vampire, not letting myself fret over how the fuck I'm going to clean this mess up. Someone kicks the front door. Hard. Harder.

"Hey!" I shout, going through the living room to grab another stake. The tip on this one has been dulled, and now that it's covered in vampire mush, I can't be sure it has the same power. Holy water drips from the new stake. The vampire on the porch kicks the door again. "That door is original to the house. Have some fucking manners!"

I shoot back the deadbolt and throw open the door, planning on stabbing the vampire in the chest the first chance I get. But there's not one vampire.

There are three.

Three menacing, red-eyed vampires. All have their fangs out, and all three are dark-haired men, just like the others. It's too late to go back now. The door's been opened, literally, and the closest one charges at me. I go to stab him and another grabs my arm. I counter by spinning my body into his and elbowing him hard in the ribs. The forward motion of my arm continues and the pointy end of the stake hits the vampire right in the throat.

Blood sprays everywhere, and the vampire screams in pain, hands flying to his neck. Steam rises from his flesh, burning from coming in contact with the holy water. The vamp that grabbed me shoves me back into the wall hard enough to knock the wind out of me.

The third vamp comes in, pushing his bleeding friend to the side. The bleeding vamp is choking on his own blood and gasping for air. Vampires survive on blood and blood alone. If they lose enough, will they die too?

I don't have time to find out.

Desperately, I suck in air and push off the wall, slashing the stake at the third vamp. He catches my arm and twists. I cry out in pain and the stake clatters to the ground. Still holding my wrist, he knees me in the stomach and throws me on the floor. I skid back, sliding on the hardwood.

The other picks up the stake and snaps it in half.

"Oops," he says, throwing both pieces at me.

The vampire I stabbed in the neck has stopped moving. He's already dead...can he bleed to death?

One of the vampires crouches down over me and grabs both my wrists. He's stronger than me. Hell, he's stronger than any human man. I try to fight him off and I can't.

"You're a feisty thing, aren't you?" He brings his face to mine, smelling my hair. Then he runs his tongue along my ear, down my neck, and over my lips. "And you taste as good as you smell."

"Go to hell." I thrash against him, refusing to give up.

"I've been to hell, sweetheart. And came out a god."

"Get the fuck over yourself," I spit, feeling the fire in my fingertips. I twist my hands and dig my nails into the flesh on top of his hands.

He turns to the vampire behind him. "Hold her down. I wanna taste."

"We're not supposed to," the other says through gritted fangs.

"Just one won't hurt. She's a malefica." He licks his lips, salivating at the thought. With a sneer, he turns back to me. "I haven't tasted a witch in half a century. I thought you all died out. What a lucky day for me."

With no hesitation, he opens his mouth and brings his teeth down onto my neck. His fangs sink in, slicing open my flesh. He bites down hard, and my skin crunches under his teeth as it tears open. Pain radiates down my neck and I scream.

He moves on top of me, pinning me down with his body weight, and sucks at my neck for a second before taking his mouth off to lick the drips. Then he brings it back and sucks hard, pulling my blood out.

"Get off me!" I shout, doing everything I can to fight him, but he's too strong.

He takes another mouthful of blood and turns to the vampire behind him. "There are other juicy veins. I'll even let you take my favorite."

"If I get my mouth that close to her pussy, there's no way I'm stopping at just drinking blood. Move over."

"No," I cry when the other vamp closes in. "Get off me!" Suddenly, fire encases my hand and lights up the room. It takes both vamps off guard, giving me the half-second I need to yank one hand free from the grasp of the one holding me.

I go to press my hand into the face of the one who bit me, but he stops me, grabbing my wrist again. Though this time, he gets burned.

"What the fuck?" He recoils, cradling his hand, which looks like he just stuck it in a roaring fire—and held it there for several seconds. Scrambling up, I bring my left hand to my neck, holding it over the bite wound, and keep my right up in front of me. Neither vampire moves.

I can feel the energy leaving my body. Magic is as draining as the rapid loss of blood. I can't hold onto this fire much longer. My heart races and the faster it beats the more blood drips from my wound.

"Fucking witches," the other vampire sneers, and lunges for me. I hold my hand out and get him in the chest. His shirt catches fire and he madly flails at his chest to put it out. A handprint sears through the fabric and onto his skin. He looks down at it, then back at me, seething.

I back-step. I need to get into the living room and grab another wooden stake. Hell, I'll throw the bowl of holy water at them if I have to. Stars spot my vision. *Shit.* My hand shakes, giving me a warning the flames are about to go out.

Turning, I sprint past the sitting room and into the living room, hoping to lose the vampires in the house if they were to follow me. I grab two wooden stakes and whirl around, expecting them to jump at me from behind.

But they don't, and the house is silent. I'm panting, and when I bring my hand away from my neck, I see just how badly I'm bleeding. People are full of a startling amount of blood, and you can lose quite a bit before it becomes life-threatening.

The back door opens and slams shut, and the sound of heavy footfalls echoes through the kitchen. Shit. There are more of them. The magical fire has gone out now and my fingers prickle like my hand has fallen asleep. I plunge my hands in the holy water and splash more on my neck. It burns in the open wound. Not having time for pain, I inch out of the living room.

One lifeless vampire is left in the foyer. The front door has been shut but not locked. The other two are still in the house. They wouldn't have shut the door if they'd gone out. Voices echo through the house. I turn my head to listen, picking up on three new male voices.

That makes five vampires. *Don't panic. Don't panic. Don't panic.* I'll get out of this. Somehow.

With a stake in each hand, I silently move up the stairs to use the balcony as a vantage point. There might be two injured vampires upstairs. There are for sure three uninjured vampires in the kitchen. I'll take my chances upstairs.

Pausing on the landing, I hear the others.

"Fucking witch. Look at what that cunt did."

They're all downstairs. All five.

Five.

I slip into the master bedroom and shut the door as quietly as possible. I lean against it, tears filling my eyes. Exhaustion is hitting me hard. I shouldn't have used magic, but what other choice did I have?

"Hello, Acelina."

The voice in the dark makes me jump. I grip the stakes tighter in my hand, heart racing. The pretty blonde woman I saw in the car earlier saunters out of the shadows. She's still wearing the hat but has lost the glasses. Her tight black dress hugs every curve of her body perfectly, and she carries herself with grace in her five-inch heels.

There's no denying her beauty. One look at her is enough to make you fall in love with her or want to be her. Big, baby-blue eyes are perfectly lined in black, and her red lipstick is perfect. I'd hate her even if she wasn't a vampire.

She closes a book, setting it on the dresser. It's the grimoire. Relief washes over me. It's here in the house. It hasn't been lost forever.

"You're the sire," I say, straightening my back.

"Weren't expecting a woman?" She clicks her tongue. "Such a shame, Ace. You seem like such a progressive female, with you being one of the few in your line of work and all."

"It makes sense now. You obviously have a fetish for guys with brown hair."

"I do," she says with a smile. Unlike the others, only two of her fangs show, making her look a lot like a sexy TV vampire.

I hate her even more.

"Though I don't think it's fair for you to judge. It seems you have quite the fetish of your own." She inhales, eyes fluttering closed. "Mhhh," she breathes, as if she just smelled freshly baked cookies. "It smells like sex in here. Two—no, three different men? A girl after my own heart. Too bad I have to rip yours right out of your chest."

"You can try," I retort.

She makes a face. "Actually, I'd rather not. I just got my nails done." She looks at her long, pointed nails. They're painted black and have clusters of jewels on each one. "Oh, boys! She's up here!"

"You're making them do your dirty work?"

She shrugs. "That's why they're here, darling."

"So you're like the female Charles Manson of the vampire world."

Her full lips curve into a smile. "I like that. Maybe I'll use it as a catch phrase."

"Catch phrases won't work when you're dead."

"Too bad for you, then." She yawns, acting bored, and moves to the mirror to check her hair.

"I saw you. During the day."

She lets out a high-pitched and girly laugh. "Don't trust everything you read on the internet." She shakes her head. "You really are dumb, aren't you?"

"But sunlight…" I blink. It doesn't matter. All that matters is killing this bitch.

With a sigh, she turns back to me. "I might as well tell you. You're going to be dead soon and dying with this knowledge in your little brain will be like salt on the wound." Her lips curve into a smile. "We learn to tolerate sunlight in small doses. Not direct light, but cloudy days like today are as good as twilight for us older vamps. Remember that as I drain the life out of you. Everyone you hold dear…everyone you care about…they're not safe at night or on days like today. Which seems to be most days around here."

I swallow hard. "So the nurse at the free clinic is a vampire," I think out loud. This is bad. Really fucking bad.

She laughs again. "That idiot? No. Well, not yet. He doesn't fuck well enough for me to want him around forever." She turns back to the mirror. "I suppose he has time to learn. And I *am* a good teacher."

I look her up and down, weighing my options. Jacques told me the older a vampire is, the more powerful they are. And not just physically. Some have abilities and can kill you without even touching you. This woman has sired an army and has her back turned. She knows I'm not a threat, not in the state I'm in.

Keeping the stakes out in front of me, I circle around the room, going to the window. It's my only way out. I can't fight five vampires, but I might be able to get out and get away long enough to figure out how to recharge my magical batteries.

And we're closing in on sunset.

Never in my life have I admitted to needing someone. I've appreciated help. I've allowed them to ease the burden of something I'm more than capable of doing alone. But right now, I know in my heart I need them.

And they need me.

I reach behind me, feeling for the lock. I flip it and slide the window open. I'm halfway out when the bedroom door opens. My eyes widen in terror and I bring my arm back, chucking one of the stakes at the first vampire to enter the room. It hits him in the arm, tearing open his flesh. He yells and clamps his hand over the wound.

"What are you waiting for!" Vampire Barbie shouts to the others. "Kill her!"

I back up and topple out the window. My head throbs, and more blood drips down my neck. Clambering away, I look through the fog and see the outline of Jacques's wings.

He's still frozen in stone.

I get up onto my feet and hold the stake out in front of me. I'm fighting with myself not to get dizzy from blood loss. A vampire comes through the window, his tall frame rising in the fog. I recognize him as the one I burned back at the bar. His wounds haven't healed.

"I've been waiting a long time for this," he says with a sneer.

"A long time? It's been days, buddy. You're immortal. You need a better sense of time."

He throws his head back, laughing. I keep walking backwards, away from him. *Come on, guys. Wake up.* Another vampire comes out onto the roof. And another. And another, until they're all standing there, watching me. My heart is beating so fast it hurts. I'm cornered. I squeeze my eyes shut, screaming at Jacques to wake up. I feel something pass through me, and suddenly I can't breathe. Everything has been taken from me, and it's all I can do to stay on my feet.

"I'm disappointed, Ace," Vampire Barbie says. The others part way for her, looking at her as if she's a goddess. "As soon as we got your scent, we knew it was you who killed my babies. And the magic you pulled at the club...bravo. And this is how it ends? It's so anticlimactic."

Little pebbles crumble from the roof onto the sidewalk below. My eyes flutter as I fight to stay conscious. I shuffle back. "Just wait," I mumble, and my vision fades and I fall back, disappearing into the fog below.

26

"Ace."

Jacques's strong arms wrap around me. I feebly lift my head and force my eyes open. His large wings are outstretched and we're soaring into the air. I black out, not waking until he lands somewhere away from the house.

"Ace," he repeats. "Can you hear me?"

"Yeah." I try to lift my arms and fail. "The vampires..."

"It'll take them a minute to catch up," he says, and repositions me in his arms, ready to take flight again if need be. "They bit you."

"No shit, Sherlock," I mumble, opening my eyes and looking up at Jacques's handsome face. Is that a slight smile I see on his full lips? "I used magic again. That's why I'm...so...tired." My eyes fall shut.

"You woke me up before sunset."

His words are enough of a jolt to open my eyes again. So that's what that feeling was. It took everything inside of me to break through the stone. "Maybe I can break the curse then."

"I'm not worried about that now. I need to get you somewhere safe, Ace."

"No. I have to stop her."

"Her?"

"The sire is a woman. There are six vampires at the house."

"I saw, somehow. It's like you showed me and I just knew." Then he tenses and we both are thinking the same thing. The guys are going to wake up and have no idea. They'll be ambushed.

"We have to get back," I say.

Jacques nods. "You stay here. I'll go."

I shake my head. There's no way I'm letting him go alone. "I started this fight. I need to finish it. Besides," I start, "if they come back, I won't be able to fight them off on my own."

He brushes my hair back and looks at the wound on my neck. Able to see in the dark, he can tell just how bad it is. "Right. Take a minute, Ace. Catch your breath."

I didn't even realize I was panting. I close my eyes for a second and inhale deeply, feeling an ache in my side when I do. I'm going to be so fucking sore in the morning. Jacques puts both of his large hands on my shoulders and looks into my eyes, trying to get a read on me.

Gently, he swipes blood off my face and picks me back up, cradling me in his arms. I hook my arms around his neck. No matter how hard I try, I can't ignore how right it feels to be in his arms.

I rest my head on his shoulder for a brief minute as he takes flight and moves across the yard. We land soundlessly on the pitch of the roof. He doesn't let me go. Carefully, he moves along the pitched roofline, looking down into the yard. The vampires are nowhere to be seen, but we both know they are still around here somewhere.

The sun should be setting any minute now. He turns, wings whooshing behind him, and looks down at the front of the house. I almost don't hear it, the crackling of stone. It's quiet at first, and I hold tight to Jacques as I peer down at the porch below. Thomas and Gilbert break free first, which makes sense to me now, with the way the sun sets. Hasan is the last to be cast into the night.

Jacques snaps his fingers, and the twins turn at the sound. Along with night vision, the guys have impressive hearing. They leap onto the roof.

"What the fuck, Ace?" Thomas says when he sees me.

"Vampires," I croak out, and Jacques shakes his head, signaling for them to shut the hell up. He points to Hasan. Gilbert nods and takes off, running and jumping off the roof. He returns a few seconds later with Hasan. His face mirrors the same horror as the others at the sight of me, making me wonder just how awful I look.

tightens his hold on me and takes flight. More aware of going on around me, I risk getting hit with my fear of heights and look around. It's incredible to be soaring through the air.

He lands in the yard again, behind the shed and in a tangle of weeds near a cluster of trees. We're not far enough from the house to be safe from vampires, but if we go any farther, we risk being seen.

"How many?" Hasan asks as soon as we land.

"Six," I tell him. "I think I killed two."

"You think?" Thomas asks.

"I got one with the stake and he turned into goo. I slashed the other in the throat with the stake and he bled out. I think. Can vampires bleed to death?"

"Not so much to death, but they can be drained of their blood and left in a state of suspended animation for an infinite amount of time," Jacques tells us.

The info seems to be a shock to everyone, not just me this time.

"How the hell do you know all this stuff?" Gilbert says, shaking his head, and eyes Jacques curiously.

"You're getting off point," Hasan counters.

"Right." Gilbert narrows his eyes and smiles. "Let's go kill these motherfuckers."

"Let's strategize," Jacques says.

"No time." Hasan lifts his head, eyes narrowing to try and see through the fog. "They're here."

My heart skips a beat and I try to push out of Jacques's embrace, which only makes him hold me tighter.

"No, Ace," he whispers, mouth against my ear. "You could get hurt."

"I know." I tip my head up and meet his eyes. Little lines of worry form around his beautiful dark eyes. Hesitantly, he lets me go, hands lingering on my waist as if we're the lovers from our dreams, forced to say our final goodbye.

My skin prickles and the smell of sulfur fills the air. Hasan lunges forward, colliding with a vampire whose eyes go wide with shock at the sight of him. Hasan's hand wraps around the vampire's neck and he lifts him off the ground. The vampire's feet dangle and he kicks at Hasan.

Thomas and Gilbert rush forward, disappearing into the fog. Jacques turns, spreading his large wings. His dark eyes dance, looking dangerous. He turns, giving me a look that says *no one hurts you and gets away with it*, and catches another vampire, twisting its arm backwards, demanding it tell us where the sire is.

Another vampire soars through the air, landing on Hasan's back. I rush forward, stake raised, and sink it in beside the vampire's shoulder blade. He jerks back, hitting me across the face, and falls. The force of his body sends the stake in deeper, hitting his heart. He collapses in a puddle of disintegrated blood and bone.

The vampire in Hasan's hands looks like a rag doll, and in one swift movement, he twists his neck. I turn away, not wanting to see him rip another head off. It's not something you can unsee.

Hasan turns, standing in front of the vampire Jacques has in his grip. He squares his shoulders and opens his wings.

"Maybe he needs a little persuasion," he says, voice booming. He turns his head to me. "Still have that stake, Ace?"

"Fine," the vampire spits. Jacques twists his arm again and I hear bone pop and break. "She's long gone by now. Don't bother."

"Tell me her name," Jacques demands. Is it wrong to be getting turned on right now? Both Jacques and Hasan look so strong and powerful.

"My name"—a silky-smooth voice comes from behind me as slender hands wrap around my neck—"is Nariah."

She jerks my head to the side and slides her finger over the puncture wounds on my neck, making me flinch.

"Let her go." Jacques's voice rings out through the fog, deep and commanding.

"Yeah...that's a no from me. I had a good thing going on. Fresh blood from the clinic. Feeding off willing victims at the bar. And she had to go fuck everything up," Nariah says, bringing her finger to her mouth. "You do taste good, honey. I can see why these guys like you so much. But what I can't figure out is what the hell they are."

"Let her go," Jacques repeats, and releases the vampire he has in his grasp, turning him over to Hasan, then spreads his wings.

"Take another step and I'll rip out her jugular. We both know I can do it."

Jacques balls his fists but doesn't move. Nariah presses one of her fake, pointed nails into the bite and drags it down. I clamp my jaw shut, refusing to scream.

"Where are the others?" Nariah asks. "I know there were two more. Try anything, and she'll be dead before she hits the ground."

I look from Hasan to Jacques, trying to tell them it's okay. They both look so worried, and the pain on Jacques's face matches what I saw in the dream.

Only this time, it's real.

I'm not going to let this bitch get the best of me. I close my eyes and inhale, bringing in energy around me, and I hear a voice inside of me telling me what to do. I bend my elbow and hold up my right hand.

"Ignis," I say, and feel a rush go through me. It comes from my chest, cascading through my whole body and into my fingers. Fire surrounds my hand again. I curl my fingers into a fist, watching the flames move with me.

And then I hit Nariah in the face. She shrieks and moves away, long nails tearing the flesh on my chest. Her cheek is smoldering, but she's not catching on fire as easily as the others. She lets out a roar, eyes glowing a fiery red. I can't keep the fire going much longer.

Two large figures come from the sky, and Thomas and Gilbert each grab an arm. She thrashes, putting up a good fight for the two of them. I don't waste time. I rush forward with my hand out and press the fire into her chest. She screams in pain as the fire catches. She's not burning fast enough, and I feel like I'm going to pass out. I stumble back, vision blacking, but not before I see Hasan plunge a stake into the burning cavity of her chest.

"I got you, Ace," Jacques whispers, and his arms wrap around me once more.

"THIS MIGHT HURT," Jacques warns before he gingerly presses a warm, wet rag to my neck. I'm sitting on the couch and he's tending to my wounds. Thomas and Gilbert are outside, patrolling to make sure we got all the vampires. I had seen six when I left the house, and we killed them all. Better safe than sorry, of course. Hasan is also standing guard outside, keeping the same mentality.

Jacques carried me in the house and wrapped me in blankets, gently setting me down on the couch. I felt like a porcelain doll being wrapped in bubble wrap for shipping or something, but I didn't object. We went through a hell of a lot together tonight, and I'm so grateful for the guys.

Wincing, I rest my head against the couch. "Does it look like a hickey?"

"What's a hickey?" He leans in, moving hair off my neck.

"A mark left on your neck, or other parts of your body, from someone sucking on your skin in a sexual way."

"Oh. And no. It looks like a bite mark."

"Good, because that would be an awkward thing to explain at—fuck—work."

Jacques wipes more blood away. "I thought you liked your work."

"I do. This whole thing is a mess. Was a mess. I think. I hope." I sigh. "The sire and the new vampires are gone, we know that, but no one else does. We solved the case by killing a shit-ton of vampires, but at work, this is going to go unsolved."

"I'm sorry, Ace. Balancing two worlds isn't a burden you should have to carry."

"But I do."

"Yes, you do. I know you don't believe in fate, but I do, and I know you wouldn't have been chosen to fill this role if you weren't able to." He presses the cloth onto my neck, removing a chunk of dried blood. I don't have a first aid kit here, and the best we have is soap and water. If I wasn't so exhausted and still a little worried a vampire might burst through the door, I'd take a shower.

"Thank you, Jacq. Does it bother you if I call you Jacq? I never thought about it before. Us modern Americans like to shorten words whenever we can."

"No. I like Jacq. No one has ever called me that before."

"I'm glad to be the first." I look into his chocolate eyes, heart lurching. The same intense feelings for him rise to the surface. I don't try to push them away this time. I want to feel for him... and I want him to feel for me too. "So, the thing about vampires not being able to enter your home is bullshit, right?"

"No, it's true. They need an invitation."

"But they came in here."

Jacques's brows pinch together ever so slightly. "This isn't your home, Ace. Not in that sense. You call your apartment home. You've been staying here, but you don't live here."

"So where I *feel* at home is where my real home actually is? How does that work? And what if vampires aren't Christians? Does holy water still work on them? I have so many questions."

"I've noticed, and I don't really know how the magic works. I only know that it does."

He finishes cleaning the wounds and brings me a glass of water from the kitchen. He sits next to me on the couch and shyly wraps his arm around my shoulder. I scoot closer, eyelids heavy, and lean against him.

Jacques brings his head down and gently kisses my forehead. I close my eyes, relaxing against him, and fall asleep.

"Pizza?" Thomas asks the moment I walk through the door. "It smells like pizza."

"It is," I say, eager to sit down and hang out with the guys.. "I take it you're hungry?"

"Starving," he says, taking the pizza boxes from me and bringing them into the kitchen.

Jacques is at the table, working on translating the rest of the grimoire. He looks up, eyes meeting mine. My heart flutters and I smile. He closes the book and stands, stretching his arms above his head. And then he smiles, too.

The sun set about half an hour ago, and I'm just now getting home from work. I don't usually work on Sundays, but, after finding out about the nurse at the free clinic, I went to the office to do some research and then took an officer with me to question Shawn, and I'll just say he's having a bad day right now.

Talking to him turned into an arrest, after seeing several bags of blood out in the open in his house. When he was asked about it, he started ranting about vampires and how they are going to turn him into one if he keeps supplying them with fresh blood. He's currently in a holding cell, awaiting a psych eval before the case can even be considered for trial.

Everyone at the station thinks I solved the case and caught the crazy murderer.

Shawn—whose real name is Josh—might be crazy, and he's no doubt an accessory to murder, but he shouldn't be tried and punished for crimes he didn't commit. I'm conflicted yet again and keep reminding myself that, no matter what, this guy needs to be off the streets. He's unstable and is going to extremes to be made into a monster. If the vampires had followed through on their end of the bargain, he would have become a killer eventually. I stopped it before it happened. Yet I don't feel good about it.

I take my shoes and coat off, moving slowly. My body aches, and I had to wear a stupid scarf all day to hide the nasty bite mark on my neck.

"Do you guys want to watch a movie while we eat?" I ask, finding all four of them already digging into the pizza. I get a collective yes and we go into the living room. It takes a bit of finagling to get my computer onto the internet, and we flip through previews on Netflix until we find something we all agree on. I sit on the couch between Thomas and Gilbert and press play on a Batman movie.

Halfway through the movie, I start to get tired. I lean against Thomas, stretching my legs out over Gilbert's lap. Thomas hooks his arm around me, and Gilbert starts massaging my calves.

"Guys," I start, voice thick with sleep. I force myself up and look at each one of them. "I'm going to break this curse. I promise."

Jacques turns away from the movie just long enough to make eye contact for half a second. "I know. You're a powerful witch, Ace. You just need to learn how to use your magic."

"That's the tricky part. It might take me a while."

"That's okay," Thomas says, sliding his hand over my abdomen. "I'm okay with this."

His words bring a smile to my face, and I settle back onto his lap. For the first time, I'm not alone. For the first time, I have people around me I can count on.

I'm okay with it, too.

To be continued...

ABOUT THE AUTHORS

JADA STORM is the paranormal and fantasy romance pen name for NYT bestseller **JASMINE WALT,** who is obsessed with books, chocolate, and sharp objects. Somehow, those three things melded together in her head and transformed into a desire to write, usually fantastical stuff with a healthy dose of action and romance. Her characters are a little (okay, a lot) on the snarky side, and they swear, but they mean well. Even the villains sometimes. When Jasmine isn't chained to her keyboard, you can find her practicing her triangle choke on the jujitsu mat, spending time with her family, or binge-watching superhero shows on Netflix. You can connect with her on Instagram at @jasmine.walt, on Facebook, or at www.jasminewalt.com.

EMILY GOODWIN is the author of several contemporary and paranormal romance series, and writes the kind of books she loves to read. She's a sucker from bad boys, kickass females, lots of action and adventure, and always a happily ever afters. When she's not writing or spending time with her family, you can find Emma on the couch with a glass of wine and her latest Netflix addiction, or in the barn attempting to train her stubborn horse named Bob. Find out more at www.emilygoodwinbooks.com

ALSO BY JADA STORM

Her Dark Protectors

Coauthored with Emily Goodwin

Cursed by Night

Kissed by Night

Hidden by Night

Broken by Night

Dragon's Gift - The Trilogy:

Coauthored with May Sage

Dragon's Gift

Dragon's Blood

Dragon's Curse

The Legend of Tariel:

Kingdom of Storms

Den of Thieves

Printed in Great Britain
by Amazon